Fearless

Fearless

MARISSA HOWARD

For those who choose to fight fear instead of letting fear fight them.

1

ELSEWHERE

History: Entry 2

We've been in this world for three days.

Three breathtaking, terrifying days. And I don't know what's wrong.

I can feel it, burning inside me like the fire of the sun. It's eating at my insides. It's squeezing my veins, clawing at my skin like the way the spiked branches of the trees clawed the sky when we first came aboveground, first stepped through the Dome's door. It burns like touch. It's becoming me. And it's ~~terrifying~~ perfect.

Hope was once beautiful, promising. Hope betrayed me, and so did love.

They don't know. They think they're safe, that this world holds everything they're looking for. They think everything has changed. And they're right, in a way. One thing has changed: me.

2

HERE

I remember what it was like.

The cold, heavy air. The cracked walls as thick as a thousand stones pressed tightly against each other, back to back. Skin to skin. The gray walls, gray floor, gray ceiling, gray eyes, everywhere gray, gray, and more gray. The way the lights were strung up on the walls and flickering in and out, in and out, like they were choking.

I was choking.

This is your home now, they said with crooked fingers.

You'll be safe here, they said with glossy eyes, eyes that never moved.

It never seemed strange then—the way they moved, slow, like water mixed with mud. The way their eyes didn't blink, just stared, far off into one of the hundreds of curved gray walls behind me. The way their tight buns were cinched high on their heads and the bridges of their foreheads were pulled taut with each strand of hair. The way they never laughed, never cried. The way their mouths moved when they said the eleven words that everyone knew, the eleven words that became them:

What is done, is done for the good of us all.

But now, nothing was strange. Nothing, and everything.

. . .

I was running. Running through the wind and leaves and dew and green. Running from everything in the past, and to everything in the future. To everything that would come in this world—this world of blues and greens and purples and reds. This world with laughter and tears and winks and touch. This world with *love*.

The memories came to me like bursts of hot air, and I couldn't beat them, couldn't win. So I chased them.

Just love. Love like it's the air you breathe. His voice echoed my steps. His golden hair, almost as bright as his eyes, was in the sunlight, the air. Those eyes—like an ocean right before a storm breaks and the waves slow and the air is clear. Lander.

I shut mine.

We need to go back, Nash had said as he looked at me when I stepped out into the world, with the golden wildflower in my hands. I had glanced down, at the people. Our people. The laughter had come from Alese. Theodore had smiled back at her, beckoning to the people to follow him farther into the world. Most of them had shielded their eyes, squinting at the sun. I had nodded, knew what Nash meant.

Lander.

Gavin and Dalia had followed.

I had stopped when we saw him. His body, slumped down like he had given up. Like he had nothing more to work for. But he hadn't given up. He had given everything. I had looked away. I couldn't see him like that, eyes glazed over and gray. That wasn't Lander. That was never Lander.

I swallowed, but I kept running. Kept remembering.

It had taken us almost an hour to carry Lander's body up the stairs and past the thick gray door, into the world. This was his home—it had always been his home. We buried him between the trees, the yellow wildflower I had found in the doorstep placed carefully on top of the brown mound of earth.

The trees passed by quickly, and I kept running.

Everything is going to be okay now, Laney. Everything is going to be okay. Delma's words.

My steps quickened, my breathing was heavy. Everything was going to be okay. I blinked, passed a thick gray tree trunk on my right, and leapt over a tangled branch on the ground. Everything was going to be okay. It had to be. But it had been only a week. One week since we had discovered love again, since we had saved everyone from the gray underground bunker we had been living in since the world was destroyed. One week since we had opened the doors to the sun and sky and stars, and called them our home.

Crunch.

I turned my head slightly. That wasn't my footstep. I was alone out here in the trees.

Crunch.

I slowed my pace, looked behind me. The air pushed past my hair, tickling my ears. The sun melted into shadows on the ground where the leaves on the trees soaked in the light like a sponge. And then—a flash of black darted behind a bush to my left. *Black.* I froze. No one had black clothing. We all still wore gray.

I sucked in my breath and ran. I pushed faster, farther. My legs still weren't used to the fresh air, the endless paths. My lungs drew in breath like I had just surfaced from the ocean. I heard the footsteps quicken behind me, which sped up my pulse even more. I gasped for air. Ran past the grass and trunks and the yellow leaves that fell soundlessly from the sky to the ground. If the men with black eyes were still out here, still alive—I blinked quickly, terrified of the sudden realization.

Everything was NOT going to be okay.

I looked up, saw the familiar stubby tree with the roots that stuck up from the ground like a gnarled, brown chair. I was almost there. Just a little farther.

I felt a hand touch my arm just moments before I burst from the tree line, sending an electrifying pulse through my veins. I shrieked and whirled around, slamming my elbow into whatever flesh it could reach. The person behind me groaned, doubled back, and collapsed on the ground. I stopped, looked down, gasped for breath. That was too easy.

"Laney." Blond hair and brown eyes looked up at me, breathless. Relief rushed into my lungs.

Nash. It was just—

"Nash!" I stepped forward, didn't see any life-threatening injuries, then threw a yellow leaf at him that had gotten tangled in my hair. "Why were you chasing me? I thought you were—" I stopped, took in a breath, and put my hands on my knees.

"Thought I was who? Mr. Dabir?" Nash threw the leaf back at me playfully, in between deep breaths. "He's gone, Laney. We'll never see him again."

Nash was right, of course. We had waited four days for Mr. Dabir to come out of the Dome. He ran so deep into the maze of gray walls and pulsing lights that even Gavin, who had offered to look for him, hadn't found him after an entire hour. After we had carried out sheets and blankets and any supplies we could find, we had nailed big brown slabs we had cut from trees across the doors that afternoon. We had given him a chance, even though he had given Lander none. It was too late for him now. I hadn't even looked back.

Nash was still looking at me, a curious twinkle in his eyes. We were both breathing more slowly now, and I couldn't help but smile.

"What?"

He said nothing but reached his hand out toward me. "Help me up?"

His brown eyes suddenly turned innocent. It was amazing how fast Nash caught on to feelings. It seemed like everything a human could possibly express—sympathy, innocence, confidence, playfulness—Nash took on easily. He didn't just express it, he *became* it. It was second nature to him. Natural. It still didn't come easily to me.

I held my hand out to his, and he took it. Warmth rushed through me, and I had to pause for a moment. I was beginning to think that touch was something I would never get used to. Then I felt a sharp tug, and I was on the ground next to him.

"Rule number one in this new world, Laney: don't trust anyone."

I laughed and turned, settled my back against a tree trunk next to him. Nash scooted gently over to me, leaving less than an inch between us.

I still wasn't used to this world, this touch, and the overwhelming feeling of so many new things all at once. A new life, a new home, a new world. And he was okay with that. But there was something I had never felt before—a desire, a hunger for this blond-haired boy next to me with eyes like dusk. It terrified me and excited me at the same time. I hadn't told anyone—didn't know what it was. I was afraid.

Nash picked up a small branch on the ground with a single leaf still clinging to its end and drew two straight, tall lines in the dirt right next to me.

"Two LPs." He looked into my eyes and grinned, saying the acronym we all used for *love points*. "I'll be at one hundred soon."

"Two?" I thought back on our encounter.

"Yes, two." Nash held up his fingers as he counted. "I made you smile—one—and I made you laugh—two." He held up a smooth rock, so black it was almost green, and scratched the ninety-four that was scrawled across the top into ninety-six. Then he dropped it back into his pocket and smiled.

"I missed you, Laney." Nash's smile vanished and he turned, his face wide and open. "I feel like this is the first time we've been alone in—well, since we left the Dome."

I hesitated, didn't know what to say. It was true. We had been so busy looking for the best place to live and showing the people this world that we hadn't seen each other except in passing. Any time alone I had, I ran. It was a break from the crazy, my own little world. And I needed it.

I opened my mouth slowly. "I know."

Nash's face didn't move. He waited for more. Waited for "I miss you too" or "Let's leave these people and just live our own lives here in this world, so we'll never have to be apart." I gave him neither. I still didn't even fully know what the word *miss* meant, how it felt.

The trees in front of us moved suddenly, and Gavin pushed past them.

"There you guys are." He was breathing heavily. "I swear I checked this entire forest."

He leaned down, took off his shoe, and shook it. Two small gray rocks dropped to the ground. Then he straightened and looked at me. His eyes were bright.

"You guys are going to want to see this. Laney especially." He winked, looked between us once more, then disappeared again. The leaves fell back into place.

Nash looked at me once more, then stood and turned, craning his neck to see if he could catch a glimpse of what Gavin was talking about.

I stayed on the ground for a moment longer. His hair seemed to drink in flecks of the sun and winked every time he moved.

I looked at the trees, at their trembling leaves and the orange-red patterns the sun made on the grass. I breathed in deeply, the air fresh and round and perfect.

Everything was going to be okay. Everything was perfect.

3

ELSEWHERE

History: Entry 3

Perfect. They think this world is perfect.

If only they could see what it really is—the dead leaves and thirsty weeds, the air that is too hot or too cold or too wet, the way the animals cry out at night when they are starving or cornered or torn apart, limb by limb.

Limb by limb, piece by piece. This is how I will do it.

But should I? Feelings twist inside of me, and I can't make up my mind. I have to fight.

I have to do it.

I am an animal. I am hiding behind a bush or a tree or a large gray rock. I am waiting, watching. Days pass—seven, to be exact. I am still waiting. I have been watching her from the beginning. She is the smaller animal, unaware and giddy and stupid. She does not prepare, because there is nothing here to hide from.

This world is perfect.

I will attack. She will shriek. It will be too late.

It will always be too late.

HERE

It's amazing what color looks like when you've lived in gray all your life. Everything was gray—eyes, skin, walls, lights, the sky, the ground, clothes, water. Even some hair was gray— weaved tightly into buns with wrinkled fingers and coiled hands.

But now, only rocks are gray. Only the crest of a wave or a sliver of the moon or sometimes a star, when the night sky melts so deeply into itself that everything in the world seems to pause for just a moment. Some hair is still gray. But nothing else, and I mean nothing, has even a fleck of gray in it.

Some would say our world is now an inverse of itself, the very opposite of how we used to live and where we used to be. An inside-out world, where gray isn't life anymore. It's just a tiny piece.

When I stepped from the trees and into the clearing, I stopped. I always stop. The sight of people talking and grass swaying and everything *not-gray* is blinding, brilliant, like the sun. Like the color of Nash's hair.

And this was all new, a breath of fresh air after days under mud.

"Laney!" Theodore half walked, half ran to me when I pressed through the trees. Sweet, innocent Theodore. He was still limping, but with the help of Delma had healed nicely in a week. He was using a long stick he had found as support, and said more than once that "it was on the ground already. I didn't kill it, guys." He could never hurt anything.

His fire-red hair bobbed as he reached me.

"We've been looking for you. There's something...I need to...show..." He paused and pushed his hair back. I smiled. He was out of breath.

"What is it?"

Theodore stood, turned, and looked back at Nash and the others, who were farther into the clearing. His eyes followed the edge, past the grass and into the other side of the forest. Then he turned and looked at me again, his face glowing.

"You'll just have to wait and see. Come on!"

I laughed—I couldn't help it when I was with Theodore. "I'm right behind you."

Theodore took off again, a weave of reds and peaches and oranges. You almost couldn't tell he still wore gray clothes— the color of everything else radiated through him. And here, there was so much color.

A long field of blue-green grass sloped downward from the trees—so many trees—that bordered the field like a picture. And just beyond the bottom edge, hidden by bushes and branches and leaves, was water. Turquoise water as clear as the air. It was an imperfect circle, a little smaller than the pool of water we came across when we journeyed into the world what seems like so long ago. We had found this place after two days of looking, and Nash and I had decided that it was perfect. It had everything—a long stretch of empty land for Collaboration, water just a short walk away, and trees. So many trees. When she saw how sturdy they were higher up, in the branches, Alese had turned to me, her eyes shining. That night, together, we ripped cotton gray sheets from the Dome into ovals, and we tied them to the branches. We—all of us— slept in the trees.

People were scattered in the field like birds in the sky, sitting in circles or walking slowly along the blades, still mesmerized by the colors or the forest or the clouds. Eighty-eight. There were eighty-eight people in this clearing. Eight people were unaccounted for, including Mr. Dabir. We had watched everyone come out the Dome's door; everyone made it out except Mr. Dabir. We came to the conclusion that no one had taken a precise count in the Dome for a while—seven others had passed away from old age in the meantime. It was the only explanation. Though not all from old age. One of them was Adrian; I knew that for sure.

I caught up to Theodore, smiling at several people as I passed them by. Most of the eighty-eight still hadn't even talked yet, let alone smiled or laughed. They just sat or stood in the middle of the clearing and watched, their eyes a little less gray than they had been. But no one had gone back. They were giving it a chance, and that was all that mattered.

"Okay, I'm here. What is it?"

Theodore was standing at the edge of the field, his hands behind his back. Alese, Gavin, Dalia, and Nash were standing next to him.

"Oh, it's not here." Theodore looked at me with wide eyes. "It's through there."

I looked at Nash, expecting him to tell me something, but he just winked and looked back. "This was all Theodore, Laney. I forced it out of him a few minutes ago, but you'll just have to see for yourself."

Theodore rolled his eyes, his small smile turning into a grin. "I couldn't help it! He tricked me, Laney."

I laughed as Nash held up his hands in retreat, then stepped aside and beckoned his arms toward the trees.

I looked at Alese, at her sparkling brown eyes, and she beckoned with her chin.

"Okay. I'm trusting you."

I stepped up to the edge and pushed back some branches on a bush.

"Wait!" Theodore limped the last few steps to me. "Take this with you."

Theodore took his hand from behind his back, and in it he held a golden flower with round petals pointed at the tips, soft, like our blankets we had taken to the world above.

I sucked in my breath softly and stared at it for a moment, then looked at Theodore. His eyes were as green as the flower's leaves.

"I haven't seen flowers since—"

"I know." Theodore tipped the flower toward me. "Since we were in the world the first time, and we walked through that field of flowers." His face suddenly grew nervous, his eyes even rounder. "I figured you liked them now since you took one with you. And put one on Lander's grave. If you don't like them, I can take it back. I can—"

"Theodore." I took the flower from him and held it between two fingers, close to my heart. "I like it."

He grew silent, smiled a small smile, and stepped back next to Nash.

I took a breath and pushed through the bush. I knew this part of the forest. It was where I had chosen my tree, the one I slept in each night under the stars. Nash had insisted I choose first, and while most of the eighty-eight had claimed trees near the top and sides of the field, close to each other, I had chosen one at the bottom. It was quiet here, and from my sheet hanging in the trees I could see the water. During the day the water was a brilliant turquoise with yellow swirls from the sun, and at night, when the world turned from blue to purple to black, the water looked like a softened version of the sky. It made me feel something—it made me smile.

I twirled the flower in my fingers as I walked. A bird fluttered past me on my left, chirping four short notes before it leapt toward the water.

I passed a small bush with a square edge and a rounded tree trunk with weathered sides that made it look like it was melting into the stubbles of grass that surrounded it. Only a few more steps until my tree. I pushed a thick yellow-green tree branch out from in front of me, and my tree came into view. But it wasn't only my tree.

I stopped and stood completely still, like one of the trees.

A few feet before me was the familiar moss green and soft brown, but all around the trunk, encircling it completely, were waves of bobbing, brilliant yellow.

Flowers, sticking out of the ground like they had been there forever.

They were at least three feet thick on every side, and it made the greens and browns stand out like when I first saw the sun through the thick, gray door. Like today, my tree decided it wanted to be something more. Something beautiful.

I took a step back. Something bubbled up inside of me—happiness? Thankfulness? Surprise? I couldn't tell. But whatever it was, it was filling me up. Making me dizzy. But how? We hadn't seen flowers for miles in this area. Theodore must have searched for them and brought them here. Brought them here for me and planted them by my tree.

My heart was beating quickly. I didn't understand. I still didn't know why someone would go out of his way to help me. Take up his own time, and his energy, and a piece of his life. This must have taken hours.

I looked at it all one more time, at the rows of gold, at the memories of my childhood when I would spend all day in the wildflowers in front of my house, whirling and dreaming and staring at the sun.

Then I turned, Theodore's name on my lips. I was going to thank him. It would be the third time in my life that I said those words, but after what he did, I wouldn't hesitate to say them again.

I squeezed through two bushes and stepped around a tree. I still held the wildflower in my fingers, and I brushed it along a tree branch as I passed. A bush rustled to my left.

"Nash? If that's you again—"

A low, moaning sound split through the air, then stopped abruptly. I froze. The bush rustled again, but this time, the branches on the left side of the bush cracked, slowly, like the crunch of wood licked clean by a fire.

There was a moment of silence, of complete and utter stillness. Then a ball of coarse black-brown hair burst through the branches.

I didn't move. I didn't understand what was happening—what this was. The ball was running toward me, less than a dozen feet away. It was big—almost the size of Theodore. And its eyes were as black as the eyes of the men who had killed my mother—as black as Mr. Dabir's had been when he slit Lander's throat.

Reality rushed back at me like a flood. A sound bubbled up in my throat, and it took me a few seconds to realize I was screaming.

5

ELSEWHERE

History: Entry 4

Sometimes I like to pretend they know.

Like nothing is hidden anymore and everything is out there, for all of them to see.

Their eyes will be round, their mouths parted just slightly in shock or surprise or whatever they call it. Their hands will go to their faces, will finger the tips of their hair.

But why? they will say. *When?* they will ask. Stupid questions from mouths that shouldn't speak.

And I will laugh. And it will finally sound how laughter should sound.

And I will say, *Because* and *Always.*

It's too easy. She's too easy.

Soon they will see what's real. And they will never ask *why?* again.

6

HERE

When I was four, I saw black eyes for the very first time.

Up until then, I had only seen gray. Gray was the color that was everywhere, normal. Gray eyes meant everything was going to be okay.

I was at the edge of the field of wildflowers by my house, the side closest to the road. My mother had told me to stay away from the road more than once, but I saw a small blue-and-yellow-striped insect with wings like the petals of the flowers, floating on the breeze. It was moving slowly toward the road, and without realizing, I followed it. The colors were fascinating to me, so many variations of blues and yellows on two tiny wings. I pushed back bunches of flowers and held them briefly in my fingertips before letting them go, then watched them bob back into their proper place. But I never watched long enough to lose sight of the blue-and-yellow wings.

When the rows and rows of flowers ended, I stopped. A long brown path was stretched out in front of me, scattered with rocks and stones and dirt. I hesitated, then started to turn back. But before I did, I heard a deep rumble in the ground, and a few moments later, a car rushed past me. It was gray-black, with bright red marks slashed on the sides. Inside the car was a man, probably in his twenties, with a stubble of blond hair on his chin and a deep scar that curved from his chin to his eyebrow, like a moon.

The man's eyes met mine briefly. And when they did, he held up something in his hands. It was a prairie dog, a little ball of light brown fur with a pink nose and wide eyes. The man was holding the tip of a string that was tied around its neck. And then he smiled a wide, chilling smile with crooked teeth. It was then I realized that the prairie dog was dead, and the man's eyes were darker than I had ever seen. When he smiled, the sunlight reflected off them for a brief moment, and all I saw was black.

I ran from the car faster than I had ever run. I never told my mother. I didn't want her to know I had been by the road.

That moment—that small, sickening, terrifying moment— was happening again. It was happening right now.

I turned to run, just as fast as I had in the wildflowers, turned away from the black eyes and the ball of brown. I shut my eyes—my brain was pulsing in my fingertips.

"Laney?"

I stopped. Nash's voice. Or Gavin's, I couldn't tell.

I turned around quickly, braced for whatever was coming. Theodore stood in the trees. I looked behind him, beside me. The black eyes, the brown hair was gone.

Nash and Alese rushed through the bush, followed by Gavin. Nash stopped, looked around quickly, then back at me.

"What's wrong? What happened? We heard screaming."

I breathed in deeply, looked around again. My hands, my fingers, my legs were shaking. "There was something—brown hair—black eyes—" I gasped the words between breaths.

Nash closed the space between us. "Where? What was it?"

I pointed a trembling finger to the bush they had all just come from. Alese took slow steps up to it, then pulled a tuft of hair from one of the branches and held it up with wide eyes. "I think it was a bear."

Gavin took a step back. Theodore's eyes grew round, and his chin trembled. "What's a bear?"

Nash looked at me and I nodded, slowly. "Yes. It—it must have been."

It was silent for a moment.

Gavin's face became a straight line. "We can't tell them."

Alese looked away from the bush, dropped the piece of hair between her fingers. "What do you mean we can't tell them? If that was a bear, it's not safe here. Everyone has a right to know."

Gavin didn't move. "That was the first one we've seen. It could be the only one. It hasn't been a problem so far, so maybe Laney surprised it. If we tell them, everyone will panic." He took a deep breath. "They'll want to go back."

Back. To the Dome.

Nash was silent.

"That's lying, Gavin. What if someone gets hurt?" Alese twirled her hair between her fingers nervously.

"They won't. I'll take watch at night. Me and Dalia. At least for a few days, until we know it's safe."

Alese started to protest again.

Nash broke in softly. "Gavin's right. We can't tell them. They will go back."

Alese grew quiet. I looked between all of them, the picture of the deep black eyes still pulsing in my mind. Then Theodore stepped forward, slowly, his green eyes round with disbelief.

"I'm so sorry, Laney. I did this to you." He wiped his eyes with the hand that wasn't propped on the stick. "If I hadn't made you come here...You could've died." He looked up at me and there were tears in his eyes. Real tears.

"No, Theodore." The black disappeared for a second and the flowers rushed in, the golden petals surrounding my tree. "It was beautiful. I was coming to tell you—to say thank you."

His eyes widened at the words. And for a moment, he had nothing to say.

"So it's settled then." Gavin stepped forward and looked at all of us. "No one says a word."

Alese hesitated, the wind in the trees swirling around us and creating a chill in the air. Then she nodded. "As long as we keep watch. Keep them safe. But if that thing comes back, we're reevaluating."

Gavin nodded. Alese looked at us all once more, then stepped into the trees, back to the clearing. Gavin followed. Theodore's eyes were on me, but soon he turned too.

"Theodore."

He jumped when I said his name.

"Really. It was amazing."

The corner of his mouth turned up a little. I walked up to him to show I really meant it, and his smile curved.

"Hey, you have a twig in your hair." I almost laughed, but I was still shaken from what had just happened. He looked surprised, tried to brush it away. It was tangled in the red, and I pulled it gently and dropped it on the ground.

He smiled up at me once more and then followed Gavin and Alese through the green.

I started to follow too—I wanted to get out of this place as quickly as possible. It had made me feel fear again, something I hadn't felt since I was in the Dome. I felt sick. We lived in this world now so we wouldn't feel fear anymore. And yet there it was.

"Wait—Laney."

I stopped and turned, saw Nash standing with his arms crossed near the bush. His eyes were round with concern. "Are you okay?"

"His eyes were black." The words came out of me before I could stop them. I gulped down a breath.

Nash's eyebrows creased and he stepped closer. "When I heard you screaming—I hadn't heard screaming like that since I was a kid, when the world was destroyed."

I said nothing. Couldn't find the words.

"I was scared." Nash spoke softly now. "But it was a different kind of fear. I wasn't scared for my life." He paused, touched my arm, and heat flushed to my fingers. "I was scared for yours."

"I'm sorry." I think those were the words I was looking for—the words to say when you did something wrong, made someone worry. "I'll try to make sure you never feel that again."

"No, it's not that." Nash looked confused, like I had said the wrong thing. He didn't move his hand from my arm. "If anything happened to you…" He trailed off. He looked down, then up at me again.

The heat from his touch was blinding. I felt it on my skin, through my veins. I was suddenly hot—suffocating. I wanted out. I wanted out of this place. I pulled away. "We're going to be late."

Nash's arm still hovered in the air. "For what?"

I looked at him once more, and then at the sun, barely above the tree line in a blue-orange haze. We told time by the sun now, instead of with bells reverberating through the gray.

"Collaboration."

I pushed the fear from my mind, sidestepped one last tree, and walked into the clearing.

7

ELSEWHERE

History: Entry 5

I used to like Collaboration. Used to think it was useful—making laws and tying the world back together again. Well, what was left of the world.

But now I see it for what it really is—gray eyes and tight skin and blank minds coming together to do things that do not matter, to talk about things that should never be.

Things are always better left unsaid. Why tell someone something if it will cause them to think, to act, to do?

Hide it. Suppress it. Keep it locked behind clenched teeth and crooked lips. Then it belongs to no one but you. It's your starving prisoner, your precious treasure.

And you never know when you'll need it.

8

HERE

When the people surfaced above the Dome and into the world for the first time, their eyes were a mix of disbelief and fear.

It was the fear that I remember. This was new to so many—some of them had never seen anything but the Dome in their lifetimes—and I knew we had to keep some *normal* in their lives. Things they were familiar with. Gray was out. I wanted none of that anymore. Silence was also out. And then, Nash, Gavin, Dalia, Alese, Theodore, and I had decided on Collaboration. It was a regular part of life—always had been. And we could tweak it, just enough, to become a regular part of our new world.

Alese stood in the center of the field with a tangle of arms and legs and hair and faces surrounding her. But the tangle was wider than it should have been—people still weren't used to touch. There was about a foot in between each of the eighty-eight.

I sat in between Nash and Gavin in the front, and Dalia and Theodore were next to them. The people still wanted leadership, and since we knew the world best, they had all voted on it the second night. We were the new leaders or teachers, as they called it, and we sat cross-legged in the front of the pack every night. It felt strange to me.

"Hello, everyone!" Alese spoke, louder than normal so the eighty-seven circled around her could hear. Her face was flushed, but her smile was cheerful, as always. When it came to feelings, she welcomed them with open arms and felt them the fastest and the strongest. Her smiles were the widest and her laughs the loudest. And with her deep care and fierce love for people, she melted into the leadership role quickly and easily. She was the Mr. Dabir of our new world, but everything that he wasn't.

"Can everyone hear me?" She paused and the world was silent, so she went on.

"Like every night, we're going to start with love points. If anyone gained any new LPs today, will you please stand up?"

Love points. Created by Alese to encourage the people, not only to listen to her say what love is, but to *do* it. Anytime a person made someone smile or laugh, offered to help, touched another, or gave up some of their own time to better someone's life they gained a point. We all chose rocks from the shallow part of the water to keep track of our points, and scratched the numbers on the flat surface. Everyone carried their rocks with them.

Nash had ninety-six points, the third most, behind Alese. She didn't want to keep track at first, saying it was selfish because she created it, but when Theodore said it would be a good example for the people, she reluctantly agreed. Every time someone reaches one hundred points, or two hundred, or three hundred, they get a mark on their arm to show the world. Alese had three marks in a week. Three hundred points. Theodore had one mark—one hundred fifty-seven points. Gavin had seventy-six points, and Dalia had fifty-two. I had thirty-one, mostly by making Nash or Theodore smile. The most points after me was eighteen, I believed, from a boy about Nash's age with blond hair swept back like waves of grass and a smile that lit up his face. He stood often at Collaboration, and he was standing now.

Alese smiled at him as he did. I noticed he had ripped his sleeves so they stopped in rough edges at the tops of his shoulders.

"Branch. Good. Anyone else?"

Nash stood slowly next to me, along with Theodore and Gavin and two other people in the crowd I didn't recognize. One was a woman with tangled blond hair that reached to the middle of her back. The other was an older man with white hair. Delma stood last, her blue eyes full of laughter. She had taken on a role in the group too—the healer. And she was teaching people to write. It was something she remembered, and something she thought was important for our new world.

Alese nodded at all of them happily. "Let's cheer them on, shall we?"

The crowd was filled with a soft, somewhat-mechanical clapping sound. Alese had taught everyone to clap at the first Collaboration in our new world. She insisted it would get better with time.

"You'll get there, don't worry." She addressed everyone seated now. "After tonight, I think all of you might just gain another point."

There were some curious looks around me, and Alese grabbed on to the moment.

"Tonight, I'm going to teach you how to smile."

This was the secret—how we got Collaboration to work in this upside-down world. We used it to teach them how to love. They believed in it now, because of Lander. They just needed to learn how to do it.

"Easy." A voice came from the crowd. It was Branch. He stood quickly, faced the others, and opened his mouth in a wide, beautiful smile. "LP please." He held out his hand like it was something she gave him, and Alese tried not to laugh.

"To get an LP you have to make someone *else* smile, Branch. But you've got time, the night's not over." She winked and turned back to the people. Branch sat confidently, his arms behind him on the grass.

"Anyone can open their mouths wide and show their teeth," Alese went on, "but that's not it. The secret of smiling—truly smiling—is to think of something happy. It has to light up your eyes, your whole face. It has to make you feel like the world is yours, just for a moment. Like everything has stopped, and the sun is shining on you, and only you."

Alese paused. The eighty-seven were hanging on her every word.

"Right now, as I look around, I see wide eyes and hair—beautiful hair pulled down from buns—and unity and color, so much color. And that color isn't just in the world around me. It's in all of you. And that"—she took a step forward, making sure everyone could see— "that makes me smile."

Her mouth parted and her face glowed, her cheeks were swirls of reds and peaches. Her smile seemed to make the stars twinkling above her in the night sky even brighter. Even I was caught off guard for a second, lost in the curve on her face.

She embraced the silence for a moment.

"Let's break up into our groups now. I know you can do it. Just think of something good—something that makes you happy." Alese stepped from the front to stand next to all of us, and slowly, people stood. She looked at me.

"You guys ready?"

I nodded, and Gavin chuckled. "Let's see how this goes."

Nash, Gavin, Dalia, Theodore, Alese, and I went to our separate places in the clearing, and the rest of the eighty-eight dispersed among the six of us. We headed these groups each night, hoping smaller amounts of people would be less intimidating than standing out in a large crowd and doing something they had never done before.

My group had fourteen people in it tonight. I motioned for them to sit and noticed one of them immediately.

Arsen.

He was supposed to be in Alese's group.

"Alese sent me over," he said when he saw me looking, and held up his hands.

I said nothing and looked away, hoping I could just ignore him tonight.

After the initial count, Arsen had kept a safe distance the first few days after we stepped out from the Dome's door—always watching from some nearby hill or tree, alone. It wasn't until the third day in the world that he approached us. He had removed his sunglasses, and his eyes were a blue-gray, like water under a black sky. He said he believed now, because of Lander's death and the changes in the people. He apologized—*apologized*—and said he wanted to live with us, to learn with us. I was against it, but Alese couldn't bear to send him off. She said she would watch him, but I didn't trust him. I was amazed he hadn't caused a single problem in the five days he had been with us.

"Ready?" I looked around at my group—a small girl about my age with green-gray eyes was in front of me, a few older women were in the back, sprinkled with older men and a woman in her thirties or so, and then Branch. And Arsen, but I chose not to count him. Not after what he did to Theodore.

The girl in front of me nodded, but no one else moved. Branch looked away, bored. He had already proved himself.

"So one of the main things that we used to not be able to do but can do now is talk." I was fumbling for things to say. How would I get them to smile? "Tell stories. Stories about us, and our lives. We can share them with others now, not just keep them to ourselves. And a lot of times, these stories make us happy."

I fell silent, hoping someone would jump in. Branch shifted, looked forward.

"That sounds *wonderful*, Laney. Let's hear a story!" Sarcasm. How did he know what sarcasm was already?

I shot him a look and turned back to the group. The girl in front of me nodded with interest. I swallowed a sigh of frustration. This was not going well.

"Okay. Well, when we went aboveground a few weeks ago, we found this house." The girl's eyes widened. "And in the house was a small black box with leather that peeled at the sides. It looked ordinary enough. But this box—it sang." I thought back to the day when Theodore found it, the look of delight on his face, and the night when I watched the tiny figures twirl as Nash spun me around the room and touched his lips to mine.

I brought my mind back, looked around. No one was smiling, but the eyes of the girl in front of me were glazed over like she was dreaming of that very moment. Branch was looking at me, amused.

"I have a story." The woman in her thirties brought her gaze to mine abruptly, her eyes distant and her face a sunken, hollow white. She wasn't looking at me. She was looking through me.

"My name is Erika. I had a daughter once. Her hair was golden, like tufts of grass drying in the sun." The woman looked down and played with a few strands of grass in between her fingers. "One day, I walked outside, and she was by the stream next to our house, the water up to her ankles. She was singing, like your box, and sprinkling water onto her arms, her face, her hair. Singing was forbidden, you know." Erika looked back up at me, her eyes wide with alarm but blank, like the sky. "So I grabbed her by her shirt and pushed her under the water, and I didn't let go until she stopped. Until her hair moved like the waves, in one slow, silent motion."

Erika stopped. My throat tasted like bile, and I swallowed. Everyone was silent. Even Branch stared at her with wide eyes. The woman's eyes met mine again. Her mouth parted slowly, mechanically, and she smiled. *Smiled.*

I turned away quickly, tried to slow my beating heart. I thought of something to say—anything. My mind was a jumble of thoughts.

"Thank you, *Erika.*" A voice broke the silence. Arsen. "That wasn't creepy or anything."

Arsen stood, slowly, and turned to the group. "I think it's someone else's turn now." He cleared his throat. "When I was a boy, just a little innocent, brown-haired, blue-eyed boy, another little boy in my class used to say things to me. Secret things, things that weren't allowed. He called them *jokes*."

I was watching Arsen with narrowed eyes, though grateful that no one was looking at Erika anymore.

"These jokes were meant to make people happy—to make them smile or even, dare I say it, laugh." Arsen's voice was a tad too dramatic. But still, everyone was looking at him with genuine interest.

"I think I still remember a few of them—lucky you guys, I know. All right, here we go—" Arsen cleared his throat again loudly, making sure all the attention was on him.

"What do you call a fish with no eyes?" He paused for affect. "A fsh." No one moved. "Get it, because fish is spelled F-I-S-H?"

I was staring at him now, almost amused. He must have been spending time with Delma, learning to write.

"No? Okay, let's try another one. Why do bald men never use keys?" He paused again. "Because they've lost their locks."

A man in the back with a smooth, round head and white hair in wisps on the edges reached up slowly. His hand stopped, rested on his bald top. He looked at Arsen, then around him, then back at Arsen. Then, to my complete amazement, his lips cracked open into a smile.

"They lost their locks!" he exclaimed suddenly, and his smile opened wider.

Arsen looked at him with approval. "There we go. One more? Okay, let's see— Why are leaves always involved in risky business?" He looked at me, held my gaze, then looked back at the group. "Because they constantly have to go out on a limb."

The small girl in front of me looked up suddenly, surprised, and her mouth opened slowly. She looked delighted, like she finally understood this world. Branch smiled too. I was shocked. Three people. Arsen—*Arsen*—had made three people smile.

Alese clapped her hands from a few groups away, signaling the end of tonight's Collaboration.

"All right, everyone, good work! Sleep well!"

The group stood, the girl in front of me still smiling, and started walking to the trees.

I stood slowly, my eyes still on Arsen, who crossed his arms. "Three LPs please."

I rolled my eyes, but I couldn't hide my curiosity. "I didn't know you had any memories from before the world was destroyed. Let alone talked to other people."

Arsen shrugged. "Oh, I don't. I made that up."

I paused, surprised. "The jokes? You made those up?"

He started to turn but looked at me one more time before he did. "Those jokes were from the books. The books that I burned."

Before I could say anything else, he walked away to the opposite edge of the clearing, toward his tree.

9

ELSEWHERE

History: Entry 6

Tonight, when everyone else is sleeping, I'll slip away.

The night is like black eyes—both dark, silent, furious. Nothing can stop the night from coming, and nothing can stop me.

She was surprised today. It was almost funny—watching her fumble her words and think of "happy" things. Happy does not exist. I exist, and she exists, and they exist. That is what's real.

Someday, I'll tell him I surprised her. And he'll tell me surprise does not exist. He'll say I exist, and he exists. And that is what's real.

10

HERE

I'm six. I'm sitting in a classroom with short desks and cold chairs. Cold walls, cold air, cold skin—I wrap my arms around myself, the light fabric of my shirt and pants brushing against goose bumps. Gray wraps around me like paint.

I'm in the Dome.

"Very nice, Gavin. Keep it up. Mallory, try harder."

I look up. Mr. Dabir stands a few feet in front of me, peering down at the flat, gray-brown surface of the desks. Our desks. I look down. Small gray slabs of rock, chipped off from a wall in the Dome to resemble squares, are scattered across my desk. No, not just scattered. They're placed, perfectly, in horizontal and diagonal lines across the cold surface.

I remember now. We did this three times a week in the Dome. It was a version of our studies—to keep our minds sharp, so we wouldn't become one of them. One of the people with black eyes.

Mallory stands quickly, frustration barely visible on her face, and begins to walk to the back of the classroom to collect more pieces—more gray slabs gathered at the back in a box, taken from a wall at the farthest edges of the Dome. Not by us—no, never by us. Mr. Dabir collected them himself. He said none of us had reason to go that far, so no one would notice if a few chunks of the wall were missing.

As Mallory passes my desk, her foot slips. She trips, her arms stretched out in front of her to break her fall. And as she does, she bumps my desk—hard. The pattern tumbles off the slick surface and plops to the ground, one tile after another, sliding across the room and hitting walls and the stubby legs of chairs.

My pattern.

I had spent an hour creating it. It was the best. I knew it was. Patterns and sequences and putting things where they should be just clicks with me. And Mr. Dabir hadn't even seen it. Tears sting my eyes.

"Gather around, class." Mr. Dabir speaks and the others pause, then stand. Slowly, they form a circle around us. Mallory—half sitting, half lying on the ground with her arm propped up, cradling her elbow. And me, my hands on an empty desktop with an hour of work scattered behind me, on the floor.

Mr. Dabir looks from me to Mallory, and back again. "The first one to cry loses dinner."

My lip trembles. I look at Mallory, at her dark red hair pulled tightly in a bun, except for a single strand that must have pulled loose when she fell. She looks up at me, a strangled look in her eyes. Pain. She must be in pain.

Good.

I blink back my tears, mentally pull the redness out of my face. I allow a blankness—the hollow, empty comfort of gray—to fill my mind, and the frustration of losing my pattern eases. I'm not going to cry. I'm not supposed to feel anything, and tears are the worst of them all.

A single tear slips down Mallory's cheek, and she brushes it away with her hand quickly. But not quickly enough.

Mr. Dabir's eyes leave her for a moment, and when he looks at me, he nods with approval. Then his eyes fall on Mallory again.

"It's your second night in a row without dinner." He speaks the words slowly, like every second that passes is lead. "Class, let this be a lesson to you all. Crying is weakness.

Feeling is weakness." He looks at each one of us with eyes like thorns. "Today, Mallory is weak, and Laney is strong."

Mallory lets out a sob. Mr. Dabir looks at me one last time, at my frozen face and gray eyes. "Well done, Laney."

Then he waves the class to their seats and walks to the front again. Mallory is still lying on the ground, her arm in her lap and her head in her hands.

I look up, one last time. A boy with gray-brown eyes and blond hair stands in front of Mallory with wide eyes. Everyone walks back to their seats, but he hesitates. He stretches out a hand, then pulls it back quickly. What is he doing?

"Are you—" He coughs, and my head snaps up. Mallory's face reels up in shock. "Are you okay?"

He whispers the words, but it's loud enough for both of us to hear. I don't know what it means. I don't know why he would even think about—

"Nash. Go back to your seat, please."

The gray world explodes.

. . .

I sat up in a tangle of cotton sheets and frantically pulled my arms free. My fingers brushed something rough, and then something soft, like a petal. Wood. A leaf. A tree.

My tree.

I breathed in deeply, looked up. The night sky was dark, with only a few stars winking down at the ground. I was lying about thirty feet up, the branches surrounding me.

There was no more Dome. I was in the world now. This was my home. I hadn't thought about the Dome in a week, and now I remembered that day like it was yesterday. The pattern, Mr. Dabir, Mallory—and Nash. His wide eyes and reaching fingers.

I blinked. Nash. I wanted to see him. I couldn't be thinking about the Dome—not now, not while we were here. On day one, Alese had made a rule that no one could even speak of the Dome and our time there. It was in the past now, and memories of it would not help us move forward. It was like when we banned love from the world, but now, we banned the opposite of love. We banned thinking about a world where love did not exist.

I pressed my hands together, flexed my cold fingers. I reached for the branch by my head and I pulled myself up, forward. I climbed down, limb by limb, and dropped onto the ground softly, careful not to step on the flowers. If there was anything I knew, it was how to be silent.

I walked quickly in the dark, past empty trees blowing in the slight breeze that swept across the night. My tree was surrounded by empty trees, since everyone chose the sides or the top of the hill. Everyone except Nash. His was near the bottom corner of the field, a short four-minute walk from mine. He claimed he needed to be close to the people, but also close enough to collect water in buckets in the morning, and so he chose his spot.

I stopped. There it was, just around the bush to my left and a few steps into a small clearing. But my feet didn't move. I was suddenly very aware of the night—the slight rustling of leaves and insects chirping softly, like they were snoring.

I wasn't thinking right—I couldn't just go to Nash's tree in the middle of the night. He was sleeping, and I was supposed to be. What was I going to do—to say?

I turned around, started walking back. Stupid. This was stupid.

"Laney?"

I whirled around sharply. A tall shadow of a man stood under a tree to my left. Sharp chin, muscular build. Blond hair swept back like waves of grass.

Branch.

"What are you doing here?" I whispered the words softly, but furiously, so he would know he scared me.

He looked past me, at Nash's tree, then back at me again. His mouth opened slowly into a smile. "I could ask you the same thing."

My cheeks flushed red, and I hoped he couldn't see in the dark. "Nothing. I was just walking. Couldn't sleep."

Branch just looked at me, still smiling. "I could teach you, you know."

I looked back at him. "Teach me what?"

"How to smile easily, without trying so hard."

Tonight. He was thinking about tonight, at Collaboration.

"I know how to smile, thank you." I took a short, deep breath.

The air was silent, cold. Branch looked around him, and then back at Nash's tree. "You care about him, don't you?"

A jolt ran through my chest.

Branch smiled. "And it terrifies you."

I hesitated for just a brief moment, then crossed my arms. My chest was pounding. "And you're the love teacher, are you? What makes you think you know so much about love?"

Branch's eyes were locked on mine, but I met them. I didn't drop my gaze. I don't know what about this guy infuriated me. He reminded me of Arsen—except instead of defying love, he was stubbornly claiming to know it more than anyone. And even out here, in the dead of night, in the trees.

"Love is a dangerous and complicated thing, Laney." Though his mouth was pulled into a line, his eyes were bright, like the stars. "If you don't take control of it, it will take control of you."

The night grew suddenly quiet, the trees beside us like stones. Branch blinked.

"If you need any help, I'm here." He pushed the bush behind him back gently and turned. "Have a good night, Laney!"

I watched him walk away, my heart still pounding. His words tumbled through me like rocks. Without thinking, I stepped forward and around the bush. I peered up into the darkness, making sure we hadn't woken Nash. I wasn't sure how loud Branch had been.

The sheets hung above my head, perfectly pointed at the ends. They turned slightly in the breeze, back and forth, back and forth.

Nash wasn't even there.

11

ELSEWHERE

History: Entry 7

I imagined I saw him tonight.

His eyes were dark in the shadows around him, a deep gray that looked almost blue.

When he heard me, he turned, placed his palms on the cold ground, and looked up. He was dirty, and looked like he was covered in a thin layer of dust—like he was ancient, from a time before the Dome. From a time before love, even.

He said nothing for a while. I looked at him, and he at me. I placed a pail of water on the ground. He drank, but his eyes never left mine. And then I saw something in front of my feet. It was soft, painted in the dust and sand and rock with a finger. It was eight people, four with tiny dots for a bun and four with short hair. Their arms were stretched toward the sky, and their hands were touching.

I looked back at him. He bent slowly, his back stooping in the flickering light, and drew a single line through the hands, separating them. Slashing them through the middle, like a knife through the throat.

For a moment, I thought I'd see blood. I wanted to see blood. But it was just dirt.

He looked up at me again, motioned for me to bend toward his mouth. It almost made me sick, the way he crouched there like a tick festering into skin, never moving. But I needed him. And he needed me.

Two words slipped from his lips into the darkness. Two words that meant nothing to some, but meant everything to me.

"Teach them."

Oh, but if he only knew. I already was.

12

HERE

I woke to Theodore's excited footsteps, and then his voice.

"Laney, we're having Collaboration at lunch! We're having a family meal!"

A family meal? I rolled over and looked down, but he was already running to the next tree.

I swept my hair from my face and back behind my head, combing it with my fingers. When my feet hit the ground, I walked to the water.

The wobbly-looking circle seemed huge today, larger than it really was. Its wet turquoise ends melted into the yellow-blue sky, creating a sense that it was going on forever. I splashed some water on my face and listened to the birds, tilting my face to the warm sun.

This world was beautiful. I had a feeling I would never think otherwise.

Footsteps crunched the leaves behind me, and I heard the sound of a large pail dropping on the edge of the sand. I saw blond hair and brown eyes blurring into one on the surface of the water.

"You really love this place, don't you?"

I looked back, at Nash. "Yes." I was careful not to say the word *love*.

I pressed my hands to the ground and stood. I thought of last night for a brief moment, of what Branch had said, then pushed it to the back of my mind. Nash held a bucket in one hand, and I plucked the other one off the ground and dunked it in the water. He joined me. When my bucket was full, I grabbed it tightly with both hands and turned toward the clearing.

"Thirty-two."

I stopped. "What?"

Nash motioned to the bucket I was holding. "Thirty-two LPs. You'll be beating me before you know it."

I held back a smile.

The clearing was busy for the first time probably ever, besides the day we had all decided we would live here. Even then it was silent, with wide-eyed people turning slowly in circles, staring at the world. Now the eighty-eight were moving, and some were talking. I heard Alese's laughter ring above it all.

Gavin was near the middle, directing people holding thin cotton sheets, much like the ones we slept in. He smiled when he saw me.

"Dalia and I killed a deer last night while we were keeping watch. Alese wants to have a meal together—with everyone. To celebrate." He nodded toward the sheets. "I thought the extra sheets we had left over from *the Dome*"—he whispered those words— "would be perfect to put the food on. Like a table."

I smiled. Before we closed the Dome, we had managed to bring out enough food to last for months. No one had even seen an animal large enough to hunt yet—and since it was killing for survival, it was okay. Even in the Dome, we ate meat, for the first few months at least.

But here, everyone ate the food from the Dome, and everyone ate alone. We were allowed food three times a day, and Gavin was in charge of rationing it out. But when people received it in open hands, they always took it back to their trees or sat scattered in the clearing and ate in silence.

But today was going to be different. The smell of meat carried on the breeze from the top of the hill, and there was a glow in people's eyes that had never been there before. It was excitement—hope. They needed it.

Alese passed me with a sparkle in her eyes. "Just wait until you see what I have in store."

Theodore was next to her, and he laughed, then ran up the hill with his arms out at his sides. A few people he passed watched out of curiosity.

"Everyone pick a seat! I think Gavin did a fine job, don't you?" Alese winked at him, and he smiled proudly, glancing down at his work.

At least a dozen gray sheets were tied together tightly at the corners so they stretched across the clearing, almost reaching the other side. And on each of the centers Gavin had sprinkled a few pieces of long green grass to take eyes away from all the gray and give the "table" a spot of color. It was perfect.

The people swept slowly across the clearing with hopeful eyes, some in groups of two or three, but most alone, staring at what was before them. They each took a seat next to the sheets—short brown hair, pointed chins, angled elbows, long blond hair in waves, crooked fingers, straight shoulders—until the long gray rectangle with sprinkles of green was almost surrounded.

Each person was holding a flat rock, a little larger than the palm of their hands and different from the rock we used to number our LPs. These were our plates, washed clean with the water and dried in the sun. They set them on the sheets in front of them. I saw Nash place his bucket of water next to the blanket on the end and sit down. I did the same on the side I was standing on. Theodore was close to me, and I sat next to him quickly.

Alese stood near the middle of the table, beaming.

"Tonight's Collaboration was going to be about helping others. When you help someone else, you're giving a little bit of yourself—your energy, your time—to others." She paused for a second, looked at all of us. "So what better way to celebrate than to hold a competition, of sorts? Each of us is unique—we can all do different things. I know it's a little early, and the deer is still cooking." She was smiling, and she swept her eyes across the group. "The person to show us the most *unique* thing that they can do—to give a little piece of themselves to us, right now—gets to eat first."

I looked at Theodore. His eyes were on Alese, and he had a nervous smile on his face.

Someone stood suddenly—the woman from my group with the hollow eyes. The woman who had smiled for all the wrong reasons.

"Yes, Erika?"

Erika looked at Alese, her eyes wide, alarmed. "One hundred LPs."

Alese hesitated, unsure she had heard right. "What?"

"We don't care about eating first." Erika's voice was flat. "The winner gets one hundred LPs."

The air fell silent. The sun was diagonal in the sky, above the tops of the trees now, and sweat dotted my skin.

Alese looked around her, at the group, and no one argued. No one came to her defense either.

"All right. One hundred LPs." She tried to keep the smile on her face, and succeeded. I was surprised. She never gave away LPs more than when a person earned them, one by one. "Erika, would you like to go first?"

Erika closed her mouth, caught off guard for a moment. Then she nodded.

Slowly, she twisted her hair into four strands and then two coils, tying them at the ends so they hung down, like thorns on the sides of a stem.

"One of the main things that we used to not be able to do but can do now is talk." Erika spoke quietly, but looked at each of us, as if daring someone to interrupt. "Tell stories. Stories about us, and our lives. We can share them with others now, not just keep them to ourselves. And a lot of times, these stories make us happy."

I swallowed, a foul taste spreading in my mouth. Her words—weren't those my words?

Alese smiled at Erika, pleasantly surprised. "That's right. Good!" She nodded for her to go on.

Erika touched her hair for a moment, ran it over the splayed ends she had tied together. "I'm going to tell a story."

The other eighty-seven sitting around the sheets were silent, all eyes on Erika. I pressed my hand to the ground, resisting the urge to stand. No. Not again. Not the story about her daughter. Erika took in a breath, opened her mouth.

"When we went aboveground a few weeks ago, we found this house." She paused. A chill ran across my shoulders and down my back. "And in the house was a small black box with leather that peeled at the sides. It looked ordinary enough. But this box—it sang."

Erika stopped. Said nothing more and sat next to the sheet in front of her. Then she turned, slowly, and looked at me. Her eyes were dark, empty, and didn't blink. My story. Why had she said my story like it was hers?

Alese was still looking at Erika, confused. She knew Erika didn't go aboveground with us the first time. She must be wondering where she got this story, why she told it like it was her own.

"Okay." Alese hesitated. "Thank you, Erika."

Erika's eyes snapped from mine and stared forward, into nothing. I swallowed, glanced at Nash. He looked as confused as Alese.

"I've got something." A voice rose from the moment of unsettled silence. An older man with wrinkled hands and mint-blue eyes stood. I recognized him immediately.

Alfred Porter.

The first man in the Dome who had helped us, who had joined the circle in the fight for love.

Alfred walked to a large patch of dirt where it looked like grass had struggled to grow for years but never had luck. He stooped to the dirt, slowly, like he could break at any moment. He made a few long, slow strokes with his finger, then stood.

"Love. L-O-V-E. I just learned to spell it yesterday. I've been practicing." Alfred looked at Delma, who was sitting a few people to my left, and winked. She blushed, but then quickly regained her composure and smiled.

"That's wonderful, Alfred." Alese was beaming again, no sign of Erika's performance on her face.

The small girl from my group with green eyes and a splash of gray at the edges, like a storm, raised her hand slowly. Alese nodded.

"Go ahead, Brooke."

The girl slowly rose to her feet. The air was silent, the breeze that was once there now a slowly rising heat. She paused, titled her head to the trees, and listened. No one moved. And then, slowly, one leg and arm at a time, the girl began to move.

She wasn't walking or running, like normal movements we all did every day. Her arms swept around herself in soft, curved lines, like they became the breeze. Her feet joined in on the movement, slowly, until she was twirling, skating over the green tips of grass. She was the tiny plastic figurine in the black box we had found in this world what seems like so long ago. She was moving both with and apart from the world, a flower in the middle of the silent sky.

I looked around me, at the others. Alese's face was bright, like the sun. Gavin was watching with wide eyes. Nash seemed taken, in another world. And the others—I blinked—the others were smiling. Half of them, at least. Half of the eighty-eight were smiling.

Brooke stopped, spread the edge of her shirt out to the side, like a dress, and bent, just barely, toward us.

"Arsen taught me that. He's better than I am." She looked at him, and he at her. He was beaming, his eyes like the sky. Arsen? I couldn't have heard right.

Someone clapped, then another. Soon, the air was filled with a much less mechanical clapping sound than I had ever heard from the group.

And it was this moment that changed the entire demeanor of the group. It was this moment that flipped the day upside down.

Brooke sat down next to Arsen with a flourish, and three hands raised in the air. A tall man stood, clapped his heels together six times, and then sat, trying not to laugh. Dalia clapped a pattern on her lap with her hands, and then Gavin joined in, and there were a few chuckles around them. Nash stood and did something with his hands—a trick, where a piece of grass disappeared from his palms. A few people squealed, delighted. I smiled, wondering where he had learned it. Delma showed us a basket she had made, weaved from grass she had found between the trees. Six people stood and showed that they could smile, that they had been practicing.

On the fifth person who stood to smile, Branch caught my eye. Before I looked away, he winked. Then he stood, said he had made up a game while he was here, in the trees, and offered to teach people how to play. Seven people lifted from their seats and followed him to the edge of the clearing.

For the people remaining, Theodore stood. And then he sang, just like he had that day in the Dome at Collaboration, and the day the black box opened and sound tumbled out. Goose bumps pricked my skin, and the world erupted with clapping again. Theodore blushed, looking happier than I had ever seen him.

Alese's face was wide-open, laughing as someone ran to join in on Branch's game or clapping when someone else rose to his feet and presented to the world. A few people were still seated around the sheets, faces motionless and eyes drained. Erika was still staring forward, at no one. But more people than I had ever seen were up, away from their seats, out in the clearing. They were smiling, their eyes brighter than they ever had been. They were seeing what this world was, what it was to feel, and they were embracing it. They were grasping it with all they had.

I looked at Alese again. This celebration was exactly what we needed. It was perfect. And we hadn't even started eating yet.

"I want to go again." The words jolted the air, cloaked with coldness. Erika stood.

Alese stopped, her mouth turned down slightly. She looked around her and everyone had paused, eyes turned to Erika. Alese nodded slowly. She couldn't cut her down in front of everyone. It wouldn't look right.

Branch noticed the sudden silence from his corner of the clearing and gathered the group, who jogged over to us. The smiles on their faces were wide. A spot was open next to me—Theodore was a few seats away now. He had been teaching someone to sing. Branch took the spot but kept his eyes on Erika.

Erika nodded when she saw everyone was watching her. Then she brought one finger up, away from her clenched palm, and scraped the air, waving it toward her. She was motioning us to follow. Then she turned and walked slowly to the trees on the side of the clearing where Branch had been, watching the ground carefully before she took each step.

I looked at Alese, and she shrugged. After a moment of hesitation, she followed.

When Erika reached the edge of the clearing, she stepped into the trees. I was in the middle of the group. Nash was near the front, because he had been sitting closer to her.

The air was colder under the canopy of leaves, and I shivered. Branch was walking silently next to me.

"Close your eyes!" I heard Erika say the words loudly, and they sounded shrill at the edges. There was a pause, a murmuring from the front of the group. Then Erika: "Open!"

Someone shrieked.

"Get back, everyone get back!" Alese yelled the words, and they were higher pitched than usual. Something was wrong. I stopped suddenly, my legs like lead.

I heard Nash speaking, but couldn't make out the words, and then suddenly people started coming toward me, quickly, back the way we had come.

Away from Erika.

Branch started to move, then looked at me.

"Laney!" He stepped back and grabbed my hand, pulling me with him before I was trampled. A tingling heat rushed up my arm from his touch, but it was dulled by the looks on the faces that passed—confusion, alarm.

Fear.

"What happened?" The words rushed from my lips suddenly, and I breathed again.

Branch was pulling me quickly, back to the clearing, and a man passed by on my other side. He had brown hair that was graying at the edges and two eyebrows that were different sizes, splattered on his forehead like paint. He looked at me for less than a second as he passed.

"Someone's dead."

Branch didn't let go of my hand. I clung to it. I didn't let go until the trees opened up to the sky.

13

ELSEWHERE

History: Entry 8

Let me tell you a story.

Once, there was a boy who had one long eyebrow across his face and an arm like a tree limb, twisted at the ends.

One day, he followed a butterfly into the forest. It was blue with spots of yellow, like the sky. Soon, the boy realized he was lost, so he climbed a tree. At the top of the tree, he could see his way out.

He smiled.

He also saw the butterfly, just a few feet below him, and he reached for it. With his grasp no longer on the tree, he fell.

The butterfly was beautiful, and he was not.

The butterfly lived, and he did not.

14

HERE

The first hour of the first day we came up from the Dome, we took a count.

Everyone stood in two long lines, one in front of the other, stretching between both sides of the brown rock wall that was circled around us, almost like the Dome. Except instead of ceiling, there was sky.

Some fidgeted nervously, glancing back at the large gray door that was just a few dozen feet away. And those not looking at the world with wide gray eyes looked at each other.

People look different when you've seen them in one place all your life and they're suddenly somewhere else. Somewhere colorful, and open, and huge. They must have felt small next to this new world—in the Dome everything was lines and curves and enclosed spaces. And out here—well, out here was everything else.

"Wait! Let me go back!" someone had shouted, sprinting from his position in line toward the door. It was a boy, with red hair that looked spiked, like grass.

Nash was standing by the Dome's door, and he had stepped in front of it. But he was gentle.

"Trust me. Just trust me." He put his hand out slowly, steadying the boy. "This is better. Give it a week, and then"—Nash looked at me—"and then, if you still want to go back, you can."

The boy had slowly sunk to the ground, breathing deep and strained breaths. But he nodded.

"One week. Okay. One week."

He turned to me to see where Nash had looked, and I saw one long red eyebrow on his forehead, stretched from each end of his hairline to his nose, before he took his place in line again.

Eighty-eight. We had counted eighty-eight people that day dotted in lines between the brown walls, including me. We counted twice.

And now, today, when Alese lined up the living, she counted eighty-eight again.

Eli, that was the boy's name, the boy with red hair who Erika had led us to. He was behind a thick tree trunk, face turned to the sky and arms spread wide. One of his arms was sticking out of a bush splattered with thorns, and it was mangled, like a tree branch. He sat half propped on the bush, half lying on the ground. His eyes were snapped open, like he had seen something terrible before he died.

"But how are there still eighty-eight?" Nash's question jolted me from my thoughts—from the picture of the boy that was slowly staining my mind. There were still eighty-eight living people in this forest. With the boy gone, there should only be eighty-seven.

Alese looked around her, at the brown tree trunks and thin leaves, and hugged her arms against herself. She had told everyone to go back to the clearing, had counted quickly, and then asked Theodore to stay with them, to serve the deer. Nash, Gavin, Dalia, Alese, and I had stayed behind in the trees.

I slowly closed my hand and opened it, still feeling Branch's fingers on mine. He was back in the clearing now too, said he would try to start a game again, take their minds off what had just happened.

"Maybe we counted wrong?" Gavin's mouth was turned slightly with confusion. I noticed he held Dalia's hand in his.

"No. I counted three times that first day," Alese said. "Twice in line and then again while everyone was walking out. There were eighty-eight, including me."

"But he was a part of the eighty-eight," Nash said, referring to the boy.

The group grew silent. I was confused. "But there's no one in the world but us. Unless—" My voice broke off, and I stopped. Panic stabbed my chest, cold and real.

"Unless there is." Gavin looked up at me slowly. "Someone came into our group after we took a count that first day. Someone who doesn't belong."

The reality of what he just said hit me like a ton of bricks. I saw my mother suddenly, falling in the field of flowers as the man with black eyes lowered his gun, his lips curling into a grin. I tried to swallow, but my throat was dry.

They were dead. All of them. The men with black eyes were supposed to be dead.

The idea that someone was living with us each day— eating with us, attending Collaboration with us—and hadn't come up from the Dome with us? I sucked in a breath and pressed my hand against a tree, dizzy with fear.

But who were they? And why didn't they say anything?

"Do you think—?" Dalia spoke, her face white. "Do you think that extra person killed him?"

Alese opened her mouth, then closed it.

Nash shifted, shook his head. "He's been dead for a while. This wasn't recent. The smell, the rotting flesh—he's been here probably since soon after we arrived, and no one noticed."

"No one but Erika." Dalia's face turned hard, and she looked toward the clearing.

"Erika said she found him—her tree *is* right over there." Alese looked to the left, past some bushes. "I don't know if I believe her, but I also don't know if I think she's capable of murder. And she was with us before, in the Dome. I remember her."

"So how do we find the fake? I haven't noticed anyone with black eyes. Shouldn't they have black eyes?" Gavin let go of Dalia's hand and pressed his fingers to his temples, then ran them through his hair in frustration.

"I don't know." Alese looked at all of us, then at the ground. "I thought we were the only people left—I just, I don't know."

"We could ask them questions about the Dome," Gavin said. "We're assuming this person joined the group *after* we came out of the Dome. Since the person never lived there, they're not going to know anything about it."

"That might not work," Dalia sighed. "It's not that hard to think about what life in a huge gray Dome would be like. They could lie, pretend they lived there, and we would never know."

Alese looked gratefully at Gavin for the idea, then nodded at Dalia. "She's right."

Silence fell over us again. I heard a bird singing high up above me in the clouds, thought of the time we had all seen a bird for the first time in thirteen years. It must be nice to live in the sky, fly anywhere you want, never have to look down. You'd never have to experience the dirt, the rocks. Death.

The men with black eyes.

Nash looked at Alese. "The best we can do right now is make sure everyone is safe. It's getting late."

The sun had almost reached the other side of the sky, like it had gotten to the top and slipped down on the surface without meaning to. The celebration—the dancing, the singing, the laughing—had gone on longer than I thought. Nash was right—the afternoon was almost over. It would be dark soon.

"I'll stand watch tonight," Alese said. "Me and Theodore. If any of you see *anything*, come tell me. The people are in danger now. Whoever this person is, pretending to be one of us"—she swallowed, like the reality was too painful to bear—"they're probably dangerous."

Nash nodded.

A tree branch next to us was swept aside and Branch appeared. He looked around when he saw all of us, and his eyes stopped on me, then flitted to Alese.

"Sorry, I didn't mean to interrupt." He plucked a leaf out of his hair. "Everyone is asking questions, getting scared. I thought you might want to know."

Alese nodded, looked at us once more, then followed Branch to the clearing. Nash's eyes met mine, and he took my hand. I let him. We followed.

"Will everyone please sit down?" Alese was at the center of the clearing, and people rushed to her when she appeared. They all had wide eyes, like animals that were seconds from being attacked.

"Who was that?"

"Who killed him?"

"Someone's dead?"

Questions pushed through the air like raindrops. Alese held up her hands.

"We don't know anything; I would tell you if we did." The late afternoon air grew quiet and had a slight chill.

Someone stood. "Was it one of them? The people with black eyes?"

The group rustled to life again, and someone let out a cry.

"Please, we're going to figure it out. Let's all sleep in the clearing tonight. Gather your sheets and bring them back here. We'll have people posted, watching. You'll be safe."

Conversation filled the air—questions and fears and brows pushed together with worry.

"Everything will be okay!" Alese tried to speak over it all, but only a few people heard her.

One stood, and then another. Voices were getting louder, faces harder. Nash held my hand tightly, watching it all. Alese was losing them.

Fear was a dangerous thing—it had turned us into what we were in the Dome. And fear was as real in this clearing now as the trees and the grass and the sun.

Before I realized it, I stood. "A bear."

The people near me stopped talking, looked at me.

I raised my voice, louder, stronger. "It was probably a bear!"

This time almost everyone went silent. I saw Branch out of the corner of my eye, watching me with a curious look on his face. The blood drained from Alese's face, and she stood there, frozen. But she knew as much as I knew—they needed an explanation. Even if it might not be the real one.

"A bear charged me yesterday. Someone saved me, and it ran." I looked around me, at the wide eyes, and swallowed. "That was probably what killed him."

For a moment, no one said anything. Then someone spoke. "Why didn't we know?"

Alese looked from me to the person, slowly. "We didn't want to scare you." Her head dropped a little. "We should have told you. I'm sorry."

The grass swept in waves around us, pulling at the air. I still held Nash's hand, couldn't find the courage to let it go.

"So the clearing then." Another voice. Gray hair, blue eyes like the color of ice, but warm, like morning. Alfred. He nodded at Alese, showing her he understood. Around him, other people began to nod too.

"Ten minutes. Be back here." Alese looked at everyone, waiting until they stood and began walking to the trees before she sat down on the grass beneath her.

There was another person still seated near the end of the sheets and she rose, slowly. Her knotted hair looked wild under the shadow of the clouds that were slowly moving across the sky. Erika.

She stared straight ahead before she turned to Alese and smiled.

"One hundred LPs, please."

Then she walked away, in the direction of the body, to her tree.

15

ELSEWHERE

History: Entry 9

This world is perfect.

16

HERE

The clearing was almost empty in seconds.

Everyone scraped their plates on the grass—most were empty; despite the fear, hunger had still won—and then looked straight ahead, to the edges of the clearing. They walked as one, just like we had in the Dome, until they split at the last second—stepping behind this bush or that rock to their trees.

Eyes were still wide, but back to a glassy color rather than bright with fear. A bear wasn't as bad as a person. Bears didn't think, didn't plot, didn't hate. I knew that's what they were telling themselves.

The slight breeze picked up, and Gavin was struggling to fold the table sheets in the wind. Nash, Dalia, and Theodore had gone to their trees. Alese stood at the top of the clearing biting her lip, her eyes round. I walked up to Gavin, grabbed the other end, and helped him get the sheets into six plump, square piles. He looked at me gratefully.

"Laney..." He trailed off. His eyes were wide, but understanding. "They're going to find out, somehow."

I nodded, pushed my hair behind my back. "I know. But it buys us time."

I walked to my tree more slowly than I should have. I needed to think, but my head was pounding. How would we find the person who wasn't supposed to be here? As far as I knew, no one in the eighty-eight had black eyes. No one showed any signs of hate or destruction—well, besides the boy's death, if that were the same person.

I shook my head. If the person were sleeping in the clearing with us, we didn't have much time. At least they couldn't get away with anything in the middle of a field, with tangles of people all around.

When I rounded the square bush to my tree, I stopped. A leaf was stuck to the trunk, pinned by a small, pointed piece of wood. I stepped closer. On the leaf, someone had scraped words with their fingernail.

MEET ME.

Next to the words was a small, wobbly circle.

The water.

Someone wanted me to meet them by the water.

I grabbed the stick by the end and pulled, hard. Then I plucked the large dark green leaf from the wood before it fluttered to the ground. The leaf in one hand and the stick clutched in the other, I stepped out of the trees on the other side, where the water stretched before me like the curved floors of the Dome.

A bird chirped to my left. I looked around, but saw no one. Slowly, I knelt and touched the stick to the water. The bright blue rippled into greens and purples and yellows, grazed by the sun. I kept my eyes on the edge of the trees.

A bush moved slightly. I clutched the stick, held it up by my chest.

"Whoa, Laney. That's not the way to greet a friend."

I lowered the stick, my cheeks reddening slightly, and let out a breath. It was Nash.

My hands were still shaking, but I tried to get back to my normal. I needed it. "I didn't know you knew how to write." I held up the leaf.

"I'm learning. Delma is a very patient woman." Nash half smiled.

And the sight of him there almost made me forget.

I could see him perfectly in the light of the sun slowly sinking to the tops of the trees. He was about a hand's length taller than me, his shoulders and chest broad and hard, like the trees. His gray shirt and pants fit him well, and he still wore the gray shoes we were all issued in the Dome. His skin was starting to brown slightly at the edges, a contrast from the milky white we had all been from years of not seeing the sun. And his hair—that golden hair, like the flowers from my childhood—was pushed back at the front, showing off his striking brown eyes.

I realized I was staring, and looked away quickly to the water. "We shouldn't be here. Alese is going to worry. And if there's someone out there, someone dangerous..."

I swallowed, the reality filling my mind again.

Nash stepped down next to me onto the edge of the blue. "I know. We'll go back soon. I just—I needed a minute. Without all that craziness. And I promise, you're safe with me."

I looked at him, his eyes now focused on the swirling yellows and purples and greens. "Are you scared?"

He looked back at me. "Can we talk about something else? Just for now. Before we head back to the clearing."

He looked down again, and I could see it—he was worried. If it wasn't about the intruder, it was about the people—the eighty-eight we had taken from one world to the next, and now everything we'd done so far might all go back to the way it was. He cared about them. And now they were in danger. I felt my heart drop a little. And I tried to forget— *needed* to forget. Just for a moment.

"Remember that time when you and Arsen were about to get into it, and Theodore started the Word Competition instead?"

Nash looked at me, surprised. "That was all Arsen." There was a slight smile on his lips.

I breathed in, a little less shaky than a few seconds ago. "That always took our minds off things before. Even for a second."

Nash smiled, this time across his whole face. "Name the order of the people around the blanket-table today, from you to me. Go."

I hesitated, caught off guard. "Wait—"

"I said go. Unless you surrender already?"

Nash smiled playfully, the sun touching his light brown eyes. I almost smiled back.

"Never." Then: "Theodore."

"Dalia." Nash didn't hesitate.

"Gavin. Of course." I thought of the two of them, of the way they had grown to like each other, and how I could almost never find them apart.

"Brooke."

"Arsen."

"Branch." Nash said his name without flinching. Branch's face flashed into my mind for a brief moment, but I pushed it away.

"Alfred? No, Delma." I strained my mind, tried to think.

Nash silently counted five seconds on his hand, putting each finger down one at a time. Soon, his fist was empty.

"Laney, this just isn't your game."

I let out a small cry of frustration. "How do you always remember everything?"

Our fake-normal was almost starting to fool me. Nash made it easy to be around, to talk. He reminded me why I liked living in this world so much.

"You already lost this competition, like, five times. I'm starting to feel bad."

I smiled. We definitely hadn't played this five times.

Nash looked at me, then at the water. Then, without hesitation, he took a few steps back and sprinted to the circle of blue. He jumped in the air and landed in the water, drops raining onto the edge and soaking the bottom of my pants.

He came out smiling, sucked in a breath, and pushed his hair back. Water was streaming down his face, and I couldn't help it—he was so unpredictable, so *not-gray*—and I laughed.

"What are you doing?"

"Taking your punishment. The least you can do is say thank you." Nash just looked at me, his sopping shirt up around his shoulders, and the water spreading slowly in circles around him.

"And give you another LP? I don't think so."

Nash laughed. "Okay, okay. At least help me out?"

He walked closer to me, and I stepped to the edge of the bank, careful not to soak my shoes. I held out my hand, and he took it. And then I was under walls of blue, the sun swirling above me in a wet and runny haze. I pushed my head out of the water, gasping for air. Nash was next to me, grinning.

"Twice, Laney. Didn't I tell you not to trust anyone?"

I pushed my soaking hair behind my shoulders, felt my clothes floating around me, heavy. "You're right. I'll never trust my *friend* again."

Nash's smile stayed, but his eyes fell slightly. "Well, maybe not *never*."

I looked up at him. He was standing close to me, close enough to feel the edge of his shirt brush against my arms. Close enough to see the outline of his chest underneath the water—square, the muscles smooth and hard and soft, all at the same time.

His eyes were on mine. He took my hand slowly, reached for it under the water. His fingers brushed the tips of mine and then, carefully, touched the lines of my arm, the curve of my neck, and stopped on my chin.

The heat I had felt before, when he touched my hand by the trees, started rising inside me slowly, wonderfully, like water. The fear rose too, but I pushed it back, buried it. I felt Nash's other hand touch my back, press his palm to it, gently bring me closer. I realized I couldn't feel the water anymore. My heart was pounding in my chest.

Nash's eyes were serious but soft, like the eyes of the man and woman in the photograph we had found on our first journey in the world above—a memory, a dream.

Then he gently cupped my chin up toward him. And his lips were on mine.

The whole world seemed to stop, the sun in the sky and the grass on the edge of the sand and the water, all frozen like a photograph. I took a breath. And then it all rushed to life again, brighter and stronger and more colorful than I had ever seen it.

The warmth rushed through me like a flood, my arms and fingers and the tips of my toes tingling. I lifted my hand from the water and put it on the back of Nash's neck, pulled him closer. His lips were still pressed against mine, and his tongue slid playfully across my teeth.

I didn't know what this was—what this feeling was that made me want to abandon everything and think about nothing but him, but for the first time, it took control of every piece of my mind, and I didn't stop it. I wanted it, more than I had ever wanted anything.

My hand—the hand not on Nash's neck—moved to the tip of his shirt. I could feel it moving back and forth with the rhythm of the water. He moved closer to me, and my fingers brushed against his chest. I pressed my palm against it, running my hand over his stomach, back to his chest, up to his shoulders. I could see him close his eyes, take in a breath from my touch against his. No one had ever touched his chest before.

I balled up the edge of his shirt, by his arm, and pulled it over his head with one hand. I blinked. His bare chest, his soft, wet skin, pressed against my shirt, my arms, my neck.

My head was exploding, my body bursts of blues and greens and reds.

And then the world rushed back, and we were in the water, and the words Branch had spoken to me penetrated my mind.

If you don't take control of it, it will take control of you.

I breathed in sharply, took my hands off Nash's chest, pushed back. He was dripping. The last few rays of the sun highlighted his damp hair.

"I'm sorry."

Two words, and I pushed across the water to the edge, my clothes falling like weights as I climbed onto the shore.

"Laney, wait!" Nash said, the sound of the water splashing around him as he followed. "If I did something wrong—? If I took it too far—?"

But he didn't, that was the thing. It was all me. I let it control me—for a moment.

I wrung my shirt out, the bottoms of my pants, my hair. The sun was almost gone, and gray clouds were slowly pushing out the blue and filling the air. I felt a raindrop sting my cheek.

Nash was suddenly next to me. "I got you something."

What? I turned to him. He was standing on the edge, his feet still in the pool, water dripping from his hair and his clothes. His shirt was hanging from his hand, limp, and his bare chest glistened. His eyes were wide, and they searched mine. "Please don't leave yet."

Nash lifted his feet from the water and jogged over to a tree a dozen feet behind me to my right. He disappeared behind it for a second, then reappeared, holding something small and square and red in his hand.

"It's paper." He said the words as he walked back, stopping in front of me. "I found it when we went back into the Dome to get food that first day. Here—I want you to have it."

He held it out to me, pressed it in my fingers. The top felt slick, like wet grass. Some sort of cover. I turned it in my hands, flipped it open. Inside were dozens of pieces of paper held together by three round metal rings, stitched to the edge. I let out a long, slow breath.

"But how—?"

"I know, we didn't have paper in the Dome." Nash looked as impressed as I was surprised. "I found it in the prison room on the way back, the one with three cells." He looked down. "I stopped in there—Lander."

He trailed off, but I understood.

"You've caught back on to writing faster than anyone, Laney. Someone needs to write down what everything is— smiles, laughter, touch. Like one of the old history books before they were all destroyed. We need to keep record of it, just in case." He paused, and the events of the day came tumbling back to reality. "There's no better person to do that than you."

Nash stood there in front of me, with his hands down at his sides and his chest breathing in and out, slowly, beautifully—I forced myself to look at his face. His mouth was turned slightly, like he wanted to smile but something was keeping it from breaking free.

The paper felt cool in my hands, and I thought of the warmth that had spread through me just moments before. I thought of Nash, of this crazy thing called love that was unpredictable and raging and compelling and exhilarating and dangerous.

"Thank you."

I walked from the edge of the water and into the trees as the rain began to fall, slowly, like leaves from branches. And when I reached my tree, I found a black rock that smudged when I ran my fingers over the top of it, and opened the paper book to the first page. I pressed the rock against the surface, and I shielded the white from the rain as I wrote:

Love:

Like a storm. It starts silently, with the trees and air frozen, paused, broken.

And then the world takes a breath, and the first raindrop falls, and another, and another. Soon the air is full and the clouds are thick and the world is electric with lights and sounds and breaths.

And it doesn't stop. And you don't know whether you are dancing, or drowning.

17

ELSEWHERE

History: Entry 10

I don't like many things. But I do like storms.

They're wet, strong, determined, powerful—like me. They fill up the air when a person is least expecting it and rain down fury and confusion when the world was blue not even a moment ago.

No one likes storms.

And as of today, no one will like me.

A storm is coming. I can feel it. It's pulling at my insides, prickling my skin, trying to break free.

It's been one day since the last storm. One day.

Be patient.

I'm coming.

18

HERE

I remembered her. I was seven, she a few years older than me. And she thought she saw her mother.

We were walking through the hallway as one, like we always did. The gray walls echoed with every footstep, but since we were side by side, step-by-step, it was as if one very large person was walking alone. I remembered thinking that the first few years I lived in the Dome. Eventually, the sound became as common as the gray walls and tight buns and white skin, and I didn't notice it anymore.

She was walking a few rows ahead of me—black hair like charcoal, and small lips that pressed together when she was thinking.

I don't know what was different about that day, what changed from the day before that, and the day before that. But I know I heard her shriek, disturb the line for just a brief second. Only a few heads turned, and mine was one of them. Everyone else was too focused on the gray, the steps, the hallway—getting from one place to another was priority, and glassy eyes noticed nothing else.

A few steps later, my line passed her. Ms. Geena, one of the teachers, had pulled her from the hallway inside a classroom. And through the doorway, before the line forced me to move forward, I saw her pointing toward us, her eyes a little less gray.

"My mother! I saw her—"

And then Ms. Geena had slapped her, with a glove on her hand, so their skin didn't touch.

The next time I saw the girl, the hope was drained from her face, her eyes as gray as the shoes on our feet that had pounded the floor.

I'm not sure what the girl had seen—it was extremely unlikely her mother was in the Dome, since only a few from each town had made it out. But that day was the first time I had heard someone shriek from excitement rather than fear.

As I squeezed my shirt and pants one more time, placed the paper book inside the back of my shirt, and rounded the tree line, I saw her again. She was sitting near the bottom of the clearing, her sheet on her lap, and she was looking at me with piercing gray eyes like the moon. Her black hair was tied firmly in place on the top of her head, like it had been that day so many years ago.

I forced my eyes away and up to the center of the clearing. Almost everyone had gathered there already, sheets balled up next to them or over their laps or on the tops of their heads, to block the rain that was falling lightly. Many of them were staring at the sky with wide eyes, and I could hear Alese shouting over the wind that it was "just rain—little drops of water falling from the sky. It won't hurt you!"

Many of the eighty-eight had never seen a storm before, and those who did had forgotten. The Dome was as calm as its smooth walls of gray.

I saw some bushes move at the bottom of the field and Nash pushed himself out into the clearing. His shirt was back on, now a little wrinkled, and still soaked.

My cheeks grew hot.

I turned away quickly. I needed to find Branch. I needed his help.

The wind rushed past me in a single breath, flipping up the ends of sheets and swirling them in the air. My hair flapped wildly against my shoulders.

I looked around me, at the faces that dotted the grass, but I didn't see him. I met eyes with Gavin, and he waved me over.

"This isn't going to be good, I can tell!" He had to shout to be heard over the wind. "I know Alese wants everyone in the clearing so we can keep watch, but I think we're going to have to move to the trees for shelter."

His eyes were on the sky, and Dalia stood next to him, her hands on her hips.

I followed Gavin's gaze. The sky was now a murky gray with black pricking the edges. Thick, heavy clouds filled the air, and the rain was falling heavier by the minute. For a brief moment, I was grateful for the rain. No one was wondering why Nash and I were wet, because everyone was.

I looked back at Gavin. "I think you're right."

He nodded, then took off to where Alese was standing to tell her.

Dalia's eyes met mine, and she shook her head. "She's not going to like it."

There was a string of conversation between Gavin and Alese that I couldn't hear. Nash joined them as soon as he reached the center of the clearing, and I could tell he agreed with Gavin. If anyone had seen storms before, it was Nash. He knew how dangerous they could be. And deep down, Alese knew too. When we had made it back to the Dome on our first journey to the world above, a storm had almost killed us.

Finally, Alese slowly nodded her head. Her eyes, though, never left the other eighty-seven. If she had to stop blinking to keep them safe, she would.

Alese walked to a higher part of the hill and waved her hands, made sure all eyes were on her, then motioned to the trees behind us. A few people jumped to their feet and took off as soon as she put her arms down. They were scared.

Gavin ran back down to me and Dalia.

"We're going to the bank by the water. It's more open there than the trees." He took in a breath, watching the people move quickly, their sheets grasped tightly in their fingers. "Alese wants to make sure we don't lose sight of anyone."

I nodded, suddenly realizing I hadn't grabbed my sheet like everyone else. It was still hanging in my tree. There was no time now, though. I followed Gavin and Dalia as they jogged after the mass of wide-eyed people through the trees, to the water.

When I pushed through the branches, I saw dozens of people huddled against the tree trunks on the edge of the grass that slowly turned into sand. The glassy surface of the water wasn't calm anymore—the wind pulled at the tops of it and created waves sloshing against each other, like the way eyebrows crease together when someone is furious.

Alese pointed to a large tree with a trunk that could fit six people inside if it were hollow, and the people pushed toward it against the wind and rain. A few other trees, a little smaller than the first, were plopped in a large circle but pushed closer together than most trees were. It created a kind of wall—the rain still fell, but the wind wasn't as strong and the air wasn't as electric.

We all crammed into this space, many still careful not to touch, but an accidental shoulder bumping another shoulder or hand grazing a hand was impossible to avoid—it was much smaller than the clearing.

Alese put her hands up, and the murmuring from the few who had decided talking was for them slowly tapered off. I squeezed in next to Dalia, with Alese a few feet to my right.

"We'll wait it out in here." Alese pushed her long brown hair behind her back, brushed the water from her face. "Hopefully it won't last long."

Our half-circle shelter in the trees, like a large cupped hand, fell silent again. There was a boy around my age in front of me with blond hair that looked almost white, and he was staring at the sky with wide eyes. A girl to my left was whimpering. And when the first flash of light lit up the air with hot blues and yellows and a low rumbling sound groaned through the leaves, two people screamed.

"Alese!" A voice broke through the terrified silence. I tried to crane my neck toward the sound, but too many bodies blocked my view. "What's the next topic for Collaboration?"

Alese didn't answer right away, caught off guard by the question. She looked at the person who had spoken, then kept her eyes on the people as she answered.

"Touch."

A body shifted, opened up my view. Branch's face appeared. "Then teach us about touch. Right here."

I saw Branch's eyes sweep across the group of people, particularly on the people who had screamed, then stop on Alese again. He was trying to help them take their minds off the storm.

He nodded his head, encouraging her to speak.

"Okay." Alese wrung her hands together in front of her and gathered her thoughts quickly. "Touch is a piece of love that is like nothing else I've taught you."

A few eyes looked from the sky to Alese when she said those first words. It was working. She continued.

"Touch is— It's magical. One moment you're alone, and the next, you're not anymore. If someone touches your shoulder, it means they're there for you. You don't have to be scared. You don't have to be alone." She took a breath. "If someone touches your hand, holds it in theirs, it means they care for you. You're someone that they don't want to let go of."

More heads slowly turned to Alese. Their eyes focused on her as they began listening.

"And if someone touches your lips, well—" Her words fell away, and she smiled. "We used to be told touch was a bad thing, and it can be. But it can also be one of the best things out there, one of the greatest ways you can show someone you care about them."

I saw Branch smiling in the middle of the eighty-eight. Nash was next to him and his face was open, his eyes soft.

"So if you feel like holding someone's hand or putting a comforting hand on their shoulder, do it." Alese's voice was quiet now, and the wind seemed to slow even as she spoke. "But it *has* to be done out of love, and with the other person's consent. Anything else—well, anything else won't get you an LP."

I saw Dalia smile at that last sentence and squeeze Gavin's hand a little tighter. His head turned and he kissed her on the cheek.

"Anyone want to try it?" Alese's question caused the group to fall silent again.

Then a man raised his hand, looked around at the people closest to him—his eyes stopping on Erika—and planted a kiss on her lips.

She shrieked, stuttering backward, and bumped into others, who immediately recoiled from her touch.

"No, that's not what I meant—" Alese was losing them, and fast. Eyes filled up with caution, swept the room, and looked suspiciously at those next to them, daring them not to move a hand, or worse—lips.

Alese had stepped away from her spot, was moving quickly toward the man and Erika, when a sound stabbed the air and pushed past the wind.

"Hep…EE!"

I put a hand on Dalia's arm, strained my ears to hear. Someone—something—was wailing. And then, when the wind paused to take a breath and the sheet of rain pulled back, I heard it.

"Help me! Someone—help!"

A chill sliced across my back. He had gotten someone. The eighty-ninth imposter had gotten someone.

I looked over at Alese, and her face was white. She pushed past the tangle of bodies, everyone spilling out of the shelter behind her. When there was room to breathe, I took a deep breath and ran after everyone else.

The air bit my skin as we pushed out into the open again, the wind back at a full rage. I looked to the people beside me, standing on the sand with their sheets wrapped around their shoulders, shaking. Their eyes were on something. They were looking at the water.

Alese was yelling, her face full of alarm. I squinted through the rain. In the middle of the water, the waves were larger, the splashing longer and wider. And then I saw an arm. And hair. And wide green-gray eyes.

Brooke.

I blinked, and the water pulled her under again.

Alese was suddenly next to me, her brown eyes round. "I can't swim."

Branch appeared in front of the people, his view finally open. Without hesitation, he took off. He kicked off his shoes as he ran to the water, but before he reached the edge, I heard a splash on my other side. Someone else had gone in.

"Branch!" Alese yelled his name, but Branch had heard the splash too. He saw the other person swimming toward Brooke, and he still jumped in. Seconds ticked by, the air pulsing blue and gray and the water thrashing, covering Branch completely and then sinking, quickly, so I could see him again.

Branch reached Brooke seconds before the first person did, and they both pulled her to the edge together and lifted her onto the rocky ground.

The first person who had jumped was breathing hard, his hair a mess of matted brown. Arsen. It was Arsen who had saved her. Arsen, and Branch.

Brooke's body was sprawled on the ground, her eyes closed. She wasn't moving.

"We need help!" Alese ran to the girl and grabbed her shoulders, pulling her to higher ground. Another woman who was close pressed her fingers to Brooke's shoulder, and a man with black hair broke from the crowd, knelt, and pressed his hands to her stomach. I went to her head, sunk to my knees, and placed my hands on her soaking hair. Branch was next to me.

The rain was falling slowly now, separated, like stars in the sky. The air was quiet except for the wind that still picked up the leaves and dropped them down again repeatedly.

I felt Brooke's head move, and she took in a long, slow breath. Alese's face sank in relief.

"I'm okay, I'm okay." Brooke looked from Branch to Arsen, then all around her, at us. "Thank you."

Something tumbled out of me then: a sigh of relief. First the boy, and then Brooke almost drowning…It was too much.

Then as the rain made indents on the water in front of us, Brooke looked at Arsen once more, and her mouth opened into a wide grin.

I blinked.

She was on the verge of laughter. Laughter?

Slowly, she turned her head toward the soaking wet boy with dark hair beside her and nodded. "You were right, Arsen. It worked."

I took my hands off Brooke's head. I looked at Arsen, then back at Brooke. With one swipe, she pushed the water off her face, held up her finger, and pointed to everyone around her that had helped, everyone that was touching her.

"You, and you, and you, also you, and you—get an LP. Look—" She gestured to our hands. "You're touching me. And you helped save my life. I guess that's two LPs."

Then while we were watching, Alese's eyes wide-open in disbelief, Brooke stood quickly, painlessly, like she hadn't just almost drowned. And maybe she hadn't.

Arsen looked down at Alese. "It wasn't working, Alese. They were going to destroy each other." He gestured around us, at the people, most who were too busy staring back at the rain to notice what was happening. Arsen shrugged. "We wanted to help. And Brooke is a good swimmer. Now they can all see that touch can, in fact, be a good thing."

Branch stood slowly, anger rising in his face. I put my hand on his arm, and he stopped.

Arsen looked at me, at my hand on Branch, and smiled. "Look, Laney's getting the hang of it."

Then he took Brooke's hand in his and kissed it, and she looked back at us all with satisfied eyes. They walked together back to the clearing.

Alese stood, her face pained. "The storm's almost over. This was complete...chaos." She looked at the people, almost apologetic. "Let's head back to the clearing, take another count."

I took my hand off Branch and he turned to me, water still trickling down his face. "Why did you stop me?"

"It's Arsen." I took a breath, watched as the others stepped through the trees to the clearing. "He's not worth it."

Alese counted the group six times. Six. It wasn't long before the night wrapped around us like our sheets had in the rain.

There were eighty-seven.

The girl with charcoal hair, who had screamed for her mother in the Dome's hallway while we marched by in the gray, was gone, like the rain.

19

ELSEWHERE

History: Entry 11

It's funny how alike trees and people are.

They both have skin, arms, fingers. They're both tall, stuck in one place, hard on the outside and soft on the inside. And they both look strong, durable, invincible—but they're not. You can easily break them with the carve of a knife or the snap of a hand.

She was like that.

Gray eyes like the clouds—hard and strong and empty.

This was the reason I chose her—because her eyes were empty, searching, and she needed someone to fill them.

The storm was terrible and fierce and perfect. And the way she was standing—hands pressed against the tree trunk on the bank behind the others, watching the water with wide eyes—was perfect.

No one noticed. I knew they wouldn't. Gray eyes are always one step behind, one moment too late.

So I took this "tree"—coal-black hair and trembling branches and searching eyes—and I broke it. I snapped each branch, piece by piece.

And it was almost sad how easy it was to saw straight through, to her heart.

20

HERE

If grass were gray and peach and brown and blond, scuffed and twisted and lumpy, the clearing would be empty. And it almost looked like that as the sun touched the tips of the field the next morning—row after row of limbs and hair and gray sheets and closed eyes.

Most everyone had slept last night, even after the disappearance of the girl with charcoal hair—Blakely, I soon learned was her name. Alese and Gavin and a few others who knew the girl had been out all night, searching for her in the trees. They had returned about an hour earlier, downcast heads and puffy eyes, and lay down next to the rest of us.

I knew because I didn't sleep. Couldn't sleep. That water—first hot, wonderful, and uncontrollable soon turned treacherous with a near-drowning, or so it seemed, and the reason all of us didn't see Blakely get taken—had defined my day, taken over my mind, and made my thoughts run tirelessly.

Branch was lying a few people to my left, Nash a few people to my right. I was sandwiched between them, and suddenly I felt hot, like I needed to get some air.

I stood, careful not to step on the fingers and hair of the people around me. I touched the paper book in the back of my shirt, steadied it so it wouldn't fall out. I noticed it was still dry, and I breathed a silent sigh of relief.

With the sun still half down, making the world a puddle of shadows edged in gold, I made my way to the bottom of the group of people and sat down at the very edge of the clearing, so Alese or the others could still see me if they woke.

The wind was blowing softly now; the storm was long gone, like when you wake from a dream and it's fuzzy, the memories rounded and blurred. The leaves on the trees in front of me shuddered, waking with the rays of the sun. At their tips, stretched over the ground of rocks and grass, they touched—leaf to leaf, branch to branch. They were fingers reaching, clinging to each other. Like Nash and me.

I wrapped my arms around me and forced myself not to turn and look back at him.

Instead, I looked to the left across the grass and stopped on the last row of people, the row closest to the trees at the bottom of the clearing. Some of them I recognized. Red hair and clothes that were just a little too big—Theodore. Gray-tipped hair and a smiling, wrinkled face, even while he slept—Alfred. Delma was sleeping next to him. I wondered if Alfred considered her family now. He had used that word once, had remembered his family from the time before the Dome.

The person next to Delma was sitting cross-legged, staring at the trees before her. She was small, straight, but it was the way her hair pooled in shadow that made me look closer—the way her lips were pressed together gently, carefully.

I blinked. A jolt of surprise ran through me.

Blakely. It was Blakely.

The girl's eyes snapped from the trees suddenly, like she knew I was watching. They clicked on mine. Gray, like the storm clouds that filled the sky.

And then she smiled.

I pressed my hands on the grass beside me, pushed myself to my feet. My head was pounding and I felt dizzy as I started walking back to the group again, back to Alese, my eyes still on the girl. Her eyes had turned to the trees again.

I had made it a few feet when Nash stirred, opened his eyes, and saw me. His eyebrows creased when he saw the look on my face, and, quietly, he stepped over sleeping bodies as he hurried to my side.

"It's her." I whispered the words frantically, below my breath, but they came out louder than I had intended.

Nash blinked, still not completely awake. "Who?"

I motioned to her, to the girl who was sitting in the closest row to the front, right next to the others. Next to all of us. Had she ever been gone? No, she had to be. Alese had counted six times.

Nash saw her—his searching eyes stopped on her black hair, her pale skin. Her head turned toward us, quickly, like she had with me. Then her eyes fell away again, to the trees. Nash turned back to me, fully awake now.

Next to us, the group was slowly waking, the sun climbing out from the ground and into the sky. And Blakely just sat there, unmoving, her eyes on the brown trunks and green leaves.

Nash took my hand in his, squeezed it. "She looks okay. Maybe she just left for the night? Wanted to sleep somewhere else?" I could hear the hope in his voice. The warmth flooded my fingers, and then he let go. "I'll go tell Alese."

I nodded as he turned and made his way to the top of the hill. Everything that had happened between us the day before seemed far away, trivial. My feet were frozen, like a tree trunk sticking up from the ground, unable to move. And then, like a large gust of wind disturbing the branches, a sound filled the air.

"Blakely! It's you!"

I winced, turned my eyes quickly. Delma. Delma was awake, and she was right next to Blakely.

Delma sounded ecstatic. I didn't know what it was about this scene that made me uneasy. I wanted everyone to keep sleeping, to not notice Blakely, until we figured out *why*.

Why she was gone. And now, why she was back.

Everyone near the bottom of the clearing was awake now. Delma turned, knelt in front of the girl, and placed her hands on Blakely's shoulders.

Blakely didn't move—didn't flinch. From what I had heard about Blakely from the others, she was skittish. Nervous. She coiled back in defense every time someone even came near enough to *almost* touch her. This is what the people who knew her from the Dome had said last night, so we wouldn't frighten her if she were found somewhere alone in the trees.

But she just sat there, next to the others, her shoulders unmoving under the pressure of Delma's hands.

I heard Delma speaking to her.

"My goodness, are you okay? You look fine." Pause, as she looked her over. "Where were you last night, sweetheart? You gave us such a scare."

I stepped slowly down to the bottom of the clearing again, stood parallel to them, still a dozen feet away. Blakely said nothing, didn't turn, didn't move.

In a flurry, Alese was next to her, kneeling by Delma. Nash was still at the top of the clearing, talking to Gavin and Dalia and a few others who were all looking at us.

The world was awake now, worried eyes and stretching arms and frantic breaths all combined into one.

Branch was walking down to us and he looked at me as he passed—my feet frozen to the ground, standing apart from everyone else, staring.

He let out a breath. "Laney, what are you doing? Come on."

I took a deep breath, hesitated once more, and then followed him.

"Where have you been? Are you okay?" Alese's face was wide-open, a mixture of relief, confusion, and concern.

Blakely was still silent, her mouth parted slightly now, her eyes fixed forward.

"Blakely, we've been looking for you *all night*. Where were you?"

Silence. The group standing around her, now eleven or twelve curious people, shifted uncomfortably. For all they knew, she could have been taken by the bear. One of them walked away, up the field toward Nash and the others.

Alese looked back at Branch and Theodore and I, her eyes wide. She shook her head, unsure what to do.

Branch looked down at his sheet, the gray balled-up fabric held loosely in his hand. He looked at me and held it out, and I took it. He nodded once, as a quick thanks, and stepped next to Alese. She moved to the side, out of the way.

Branch knelt slowly, his knees on the dark green grass and his blond hair still rustled from the night before. He was directly in front of Blakely, and he stayed there for a moment, watching her. Slowly, he followed Blakely's gaze to the trees, and his face was bathed in sun for a moment. It was the first time I noticed that his eyes were golden, like his hair. Then Branch brought his eyes back to her again.

"Hey." His voice was soft, and I could barely hear it over the sound of the breeze swirling the leaves. "What are you looking at?"

Blakely sat still for a moment, her legs crossed and her arms resting gently on her knees. Then, like the bending of a branch in the wind, her head turned, looked up slowly. She met Branch's eyes.

"The trees."

The words came out slowly, smoothly, like butter. Her eyes left Branch and swept across all of us, sending a chill through me when they locked on mine for less than a second.

Branch nodded carefully, encouragingly. "Okay. Good. Is that where you were last night?" He followed her gaze again. "The trees?"

The air fell silent again. Branch didn't move. "Blakely?"

The girl's eyes widened, her head snapped forward when she heard her name. Her eyes locked on Branch and didn't look away. "Last night?"

"Yes, last night." Branch was speaking cautiously now, aware that her name had caused some sort of distress in the girl. She pressed her lips together, opened her mouth slowly.

"The girl. I was looking for the girl with you."

The breeze swept past us and I held Branch's sheet closer to me, my mouth dry. Branch took a slow, deep breath. He was completely still.

"*You're* the girl, Blakely. We were looking for you." He paused. "Don't you remember?"

Blakely's eyes glazed over and her mouth twitched slightly, as if she wanted to smile. "No." Her gaze drifted back to the trees. "Blakely's gone."

A bitter taste filled my mouth, slowly, like lead.

"Gone? What do you mean?" Branch's voice was edged with fear.

"Shh." The girl lifted her hands from her knees and placed them on Branch's shoulders. Touched his neck. His chin. "It's okay. I'm here."

She breathed deeply, simply, then opened her mouth slightly at the edges. Her lips formed a curious smile.

"You're like the trees."

21

ELSEWHERE

History: Entry 12

They're starting to get nervous.

People taken, snatched up by the wind, one by one. The others are wondering if they'll be next—I can see it in the way they stare at the trees, eyes white, like the skin under their nails.

But what they don't realize is this: they're exactly where I want them.

Fear is where I put them, and fear is where they'll stay.

22

HERE

I've only seen a man kill an animal once.

I was three, living in the world before the Dome with colors that were less bright and eyes that were still gray.

The day had been cloudy, with rain falling from the sky off and on, like the wind. I was sitting inside my house on a small white chair I had pulled next to the window, watching the storm swirl dust and wildflower leaves in the air.

And then I saw him—brown hair, tall, a leather face like he had been out in the sun too long on days unlike this. He was standing in the road behind the field of flowers, and I could see a bird lying in front of him, flapping one wing, trying to stand. The other wing was folded up and over the body awkwardly, like it was broken.

The man picked up the bird slowly with two hands. He looked at it for a moment, stroked its head, breathed in the raw smell of the rain. And then he snapped its neck. He slowly knelt and set it on the side of the road, then while I continued to watch, plucked a flower from the field and placed it on top of the small blue body.

The man turned just for a moment, and I remembered his eyes. They were smaller, gray-blue like the bird. And they were sad.

I didn't understand then, but I do now: that man believed he was helping the bird, saving it from a lifetime of pain and helplessness. That was the first time I had ever seen someone kill out of love. Lander was the second, though he died for love instead.

But today, love was nowhere to be seen.

After Blakely spoke to Branch, Alese pulled Nash, Gavin, Dalia, Theodore, and I to the side and declared that we needed to hold a Collaboration. After pausing for a moment, her eyes fell on Branch, who was a few feet away.

She brought him into the circle.

I could tell she trusted him now. First, Branch had saved Brooke. And now he was the only one who could get Blakely to speak. It was Alese's way of saying he was one of us now. I didn't know what to think.

After the plan was formed, I walked back to my tree to gather my sheet that was still hanging from the branches, probably soaked. But before I reached the square bush and rounded tree trunk with weathered curves, I stopped. A low tapping sound was coming from my right. There was something strange about it. It wasn't a bird; I was sure of it.

I knelt and grabbed a pointed stick from the ground, then followed the noise. And when I rounded a tree and almost pushed back the leaves on a bush, I saw her.

Blakely.

She was standing in the middle of the trees, holding a large squirrel in one hand and a stick in the other.

My heartbeat quickened and I knelt behind the bush. Blakely was humming—*humming.* It was a slow, low sound with long notes and sharp edges.

I looked around me in one sharp motion. Blakely was alone. Why would they leave her alone?

I heard a long scraping sound and saw Blakely by the tree, running her stick across it. The squirrel was squirming in her hand, trying to break free, but Blakely held it tightly, like she didn't even notice.

She tapped the stick a few times on the tree trunk, to the beat of her song, and then held it in front of her eyes. Her lips parted in a small, approving smile. Then she held the stick to the squirrel and slit its throat, slowly, stopping when she was halfway done. She dropped the stick.

The squirrel was making a sound now, crying out in pain and fear and confusion. I swallowed, the sound beating against my ears. I closed my eyes, wished I was somewhere else. Anywhere but here.

Another sound split the air, and my eyes snapped open. Blakely was laughing. And then, quickly, she reached around the squirrel's neck and snapped it with her fingers.

I sucked in my breath, ducked deeper into the bush, and her eyes went to the tree next to me.

Sweat trickled down my back.

The sun melted through the leaves and I could see her eyes. They were gray, focused, hardened in slits. And there was something else. Satisfaction? Satisfaction from what she had just done.

I heard a voice calling for her, and she turned, placed the dead squirrel on her shoulder, and smiled. "Coming, Branch!"

Her face changed suddenly—her eyes were wide, innocent, helpless. A girl who could never kill an animal out of pleasure.

She walked off toward the voice in the trees.

I let out a breath. Something was wrong with her. She didn't have black eyes, but—something was wrong. I didn't know what it was. But I still felt chills from what I had just seen.

I went back a different way, sloped up through the trees and went out through the side of the clearing, away from where Blakely had been. When I pushed through the branches, everyone was where they had been, scattered throughout the clearing. Blakely was at the bottom, next to Branch. Someone let out an excited cry.

"Look! Meat!"

As I watched, a small group of people began to crowd around Blakely. Besides the deer Gavin had killed, we never had meat. Animals were few and far between here, and even harder to catch.

Blakely was smiling proudly and holding the limp squirrel between two fingers up in the air. I walked down closer so I could hear.

"How did you catch it?" Someone from the group was staring at the squirrel with hungry eyes.

Blakely turned to Branch, whispered something in his ear. She would stare at people all morning, watch them like she had every right in the world. But she never spoke, not to anyone but Branch.

Branch turned to the others. "She said it was wounded, and she ended the pain. Well done, B."

I blinked. It wasn't wounded. I saw it alive and well, with wild eyes.

I watched, astonished, as a slow clapping sound filled the air—about eight people in the group were pressing their hands together and apart.

They were clapping. For Blakely. I felt a sting of relief when I saw that Branch wasn't clapping too. He was standing there, next to her, watching them. Then he turned to the girl with black hair like the night.

"What do you say we go clean that, prep it for dinner, together?"

Blakely's eyes lit up, and she looked delighted. She nodded quickly and then followed Branch through the trees, to the water.

A sour taste filled my mouth and I swallowed. Why was he talking to her? Better yet, why was he *helping* her?

Alese hurried down through the grass, to my side. "This is it! I told him to distract her so we could have Collaboration without her."

I looked at her, my feet still rooted to the ground. Well, at least he wasn't doing it on purpose.

"Come on, Laney! We don't have much time before they're back."

It only took a few minutes to gather the remaining people near the top of the clearing, the farthest away from the water we could be, so Blakely wouldn't hear. Alese stood at the very top of the hill, motioning the group to come closer to her. And they did—long legs and gray shoes scuffed the grass as they scooted toward her.

I found Nash, Gavin, Theodore, and Dalia at the front of the group and I sat next to them, between Theodore and Nash.

The air was cold today, and, for once, the heat of bodies surrounding me felt nice.

"Hi, everyone! Sorry to call this so last minute." Alese's face was flushed, and she sounded out of breath. She spoke more softly than she usually did. Her eyes flitted to the trees at the bottom of the clearing.

"I'm not going to teach you anything today. We need—" She paused, breathed. "We need to take a vote."

There was a slight murmuring sound among the people behind me.

Alese's eyes fell on the trees again. "And we need to do it fast."

The air was silent. Alese gathered her thoughts.

"You all know that Blakely was taken last night." She swallowed. "And a boy was killed." She brought her hands to her face, like she was in pain.

A man in his twenties with red, shaggy hair stood abruptly. "We don't know if B was taken. She said she doesn't remember."

B. Apparently that's what Blakely had asked people to call her now.

Alese looked at him. "She was taken. I counted the group multiple times, had people searching the field and trees and water. She wasn't here."

A few people in the audience looked around at the trees with wide eyes, like they had just realized the reality of what Alese had said.

Another person stood. "You said the boy was killed by a bear. Was that—was that not true?"

Alese's eyes went to him, and she looked back and forth between the two. "We don't know if it was a bear. We *think* it was a bear. It could have been anything."

Almost half the group sat up higher at that, raised their voices from whispers to soft words. A few people cried out, some whimpered in fear.

And Alese realized she had made a mistake.

A small woman with eyes shaped like almonds and thick gray hair like strands of rope stood quickly to her feet. "The people with black eyes are still alive! And—" She paused, looked around her with wide eyes at the clearing, the trees. "And they know where we live!"

The man with red hair spoke again above the frantic sounds of the group. "Some guy with black eyes is stalking our group? Hiding in the trees out there, just watching and waiting to snatch someone else..."

Theodore turned to me, whispered under his breath with wide eyes, "They don't know that he's one of us."

I shook my head quickly, the sounds of fear and anger making my head fill with dread.

"So let's move!" Another woman, with long fingers and tangled blond hair. "Let's find a new place, one where he can't find us."

The air grew silent, and then one by one, people began nodding their heads, agreeing quickly and frantically.

"Let's think rationally here!" Alese's voice pushed out over the others. "In the clearing, we have the upper hand. We can see if he takes anyone else. We have water, we have food—"

"Let's take a vote!" A voice rang above Alese's, and this time I couldn't tell who it was. Everyone looked at Alese. She said nothing at first, looked out over the worried and angry faces.

"Okay." She breathed in slowly. Her voice was softer now. "Okay."

She looked at us, her eyes stopping on Theodore and Gavin and Dalia and Nash and I for just a moment too long.

Then she looked back at the group. "All in favor of staying here, in the clearing, raise your hand."

I rose my hand quickly. Nash, Gavin, Theodore, and Dalia lifted their arms next to mine. I looked back at the crowd. Only five other people had their hands up. Delma, and Alfred, and a few others I didn't know. My heart sunk.

"Thank you." Alese's words sounded pained. "All in favor of finding a new place to live?"

The clearing filled with hands pointed to the bleak blue sky.

They didn't know. They didn't know that moving places wouldn't help—it would just make us even more vulnerable, and the person harder to catch. He would move with us, everywhere we went. He was among us.

I looked at Alese, and she blinked. I knew she wouldn't tell them the person lived with us in our group. It would make everyone stop trusting each other, cause blame and panic and complete chaos. It would be the end of us.

"That's majority." Her voice changed, and she was confident again. In control. The people might not want this place anymore, but they still needed a leader. She pressed her hands together.

"I'll send out a few people tomorrow morning to search for a new place to live. There's no sense in all of us going when we don't know which direction or how far. The rest of us will leave when the group returns."

A few people in the audience nodded, including the shaggy redhead. They were satisfied. But we couldn't leave. It was suicide. I looked at Alese again. She pressed her hands together.

"It's lunchtime. Let's eat."

A breeze blew past as the people began standing, one by one, and headed to wherever they kept their plates in between meals. When almost everyone had left, Alese stepped down next to Nash, Dalia, Gavin, Theodore, and I. Her eyes were wide, and I could tell she was trying hard to hold on to her confidence.

"Tomorrow, Laney will go. Laney and…" She hesitated, looked over our small group.

"Me." Theodore stepped forward. He didn't have his stick, but I could barely tell his leg had been hurt.

Alese shook her head. "Your leg, Theodore."

"It's fine." Theodore jumped up and down a little. "See? I want to help. I'll keep Laney safe."

A smile tugged at my face.

Nash stepped forward. "I'll go too."

"Nash, I need you here. To keep us safe. The people look to you, respect you. I can see it." Alese looked down at the bottom of the clearing, saw Blakely push out of the trees with a large slab of cleaned pink meat in her hand. A tall shadow with golden hair led the way, holding back the leaves as Blakely stepped through.

"Branch will go. I trust him."

Nash's eyes followed hers. He nodded.

"But, Alese, we can't move to a different place." I spoke for the first time. "You know as well as I do that it's the most dangerous thing we could do."

Alese looked at me, then at the others, one by one. "We're not moving. I'm sending you three out there tomorrow to make it look like we are—to make them happy. To buy time." Her eyes filled with sadness for a brief moment, like she didn't want to betray them. "When you return, you'll say nothing you found would be survivable for eighty-eight people. You'll say we need to stay."

I swallowed, and my throat hurt. I nodded.

Alese looked at the group of people that was beginning to gather in the middle of the clearing, looked at us once more, and nodded. Then she headed toward them, and the rest followed, except Theodore. He stayed back, stood next to me like he was frozen to the ground.

"It will be okay." He spoke the words softly, like I had to him so long ago, just before we stepped through the Dome's door. I nodded and tried to smile. He didn't know how much I needed to hear that.

"Hey—are you okay?" Theodore's eyes went behind me, and I turned. A girl about my age was sitting there, in the grass, like she had never left Collaboration. Her hair was almost white in the light of the sun.

Her eyes left the trees and turned to us. "I want him to take me next."

A breeze swept past us, and the hair on the back of my neck stood.

Theodore looked confused. "Who?"

The girl looked at us, her mouth a straight line, but her eyes large, longing for something. Her fingers clung to the ends of her too-long sleeves that hung off her arms.

"The man with black eyes. I want him to take me next."

I sucked in my breath. "Why would you ever—?"

"I want them to clap for me. Like they do for B."

23

ELSEWHERE

History: Entry 13

My mother told me a story once, late one night.

Shadows were leaking into the gray and the gray leaking into shadows, making them one and the same.

The night was dark, but not as dark as her eyes. Her lips parted slowly before she spoke, cracked open like they had been sealed shut for days and were just now finding a reason to be lips again.

Once upon a time, there was a man, a nobody in his group of people. He was small and simple and not very smart. One day, he was walking through a field and he was stung by a wasp. The sting caused him to have hallucinations, to do things he would not have done otherwise—to stand up and say things among the people, to have inventive and crazy ideas, to laugh loudly and dance in the streets and shout for people to join him.

And some of them did, because they were bored, and because they wanted something different. Then more people joined, and more.

And soon, they thought the man was brilliant. All because of the sting of a wasp.

And when the day passed and the sting faded and the man went back to being who he was—a shy, stupid nobody—no one noticed.

They were still singing in the streets and dancing in the rain.

24

HERE

That night, I had a dream that I woke in the house I used to share with my mother.

The window was open, the air cool and frosted from the small white flakes that had fallen the day before. I pulled the covers up to my chin, the darkness softened by the gray-white light of the moon.

The air was gray, thicker than it should be. I pressed my hands to the sides of my blanket and sat up. I sniffed.

A light coating of something pungent and raw coated my throat, and I coughed. Smoke. Which could only mean—

A small *boom* echoed through the air, followed by the sound of crunching metal, flames crackling outside my door.

My heart leapt in my chest. Fear. It was as real as I had been told it was.

I swung my feet over the side of the bed and tumbled to the door. The doorknob was hot, so I grabbed one of my coats that was lying on the floor, pushed the door open with the fabric.

The wall of gray and hot white slammed into me, and I stopped, shielded my eyes and my mouth. I walked through the smoke, down the hallway, and stopped at the top of the stairs, where the flames were too hot and the air too thick.

I looked down, past the roaring air, and I saw her.

My mother.

She was sitting with her legs crossed in the middle of the living room, her hair falling in soft waves around her head. Her eyes were fixed forward, her gaze soft. And her lips were curved in a smile.

"Mother!" I screamed the word, but she didn't hear. Didn't look at me.

The flames were at the top of the ceiling now, orange and white and purple. My mother's hair caught fire, then her red cotton dress.

But still she sat there, smiling.

Finally, her eyes turned to me. She opened her mouth to say something, to push one last sentence past her lips. I was trembling, craning my neck to hear.

And then she laughed, her voice bubbling up over the waves of orange.

And the house was an explosion of white.

The dream was still in my mind when I woke, was still as vivid as the colors of the trees and sun and sky when Alese gathered Branch, Theodore, and I to pack some food and extra sheets.

I placed the notebook Nash gave me in a pack when no one was looking. I didn't want to risk leaving it here, but I didn't want it next to my skin when I was sweating under the sun either. Our first journey in the world was tiring, vigorous. I had a feeling this would be no different.

Nash appeared from the trees when I was alone, gathering water in large enclosed cylinders we had found in the Dome when we went back for food. His eyes were fixed on me, and I couldn't tell what he was thinking.

"Be careful, okay? Keep an eye out at all times. You don't know what's out there."

I looked up from the water and my eyes met his. He was worried. I could see it in the corners of the sparkling brown.

I stood, the water containers as full as they were going to get. "It's just a few days. I'll be fine."

Nash nodded, but he didn't move. His arms were at his sides, the edges of his hair blowing softly in the wind. I could hear my heart beating, and my chest ached suddenly. This boy—I could feel more feelings for him in a day than I felt in the lifetime before the Dome. I set the water down at my feet. Then I reached over and took his hand in mine.

The warmth made my fingers tingle, and I let out a breath. Nash smiled. And that smile—the way his mouth curved slowly, crookedly, and the way he wove his fingers through mine more deeply, made my heart leap in my chest. And I leaned forward, quickly, and kissed him.

Nash's lips lingered on mine for a moment, and his other hand tightened around my waist. I melted into the kiss, his touch. The warmth exploded through me, and for a brief moment I thought of my dream from the night before—the white, the screaming flames.

Nash pulled away gently and looked at me. Our faces were so close, his nose almost touching mine.

"You'll get the rest of that kiss when you return." He smiled again, and his eyes were as bright as the sun.

I laughed. I felt the beating of my heart slow, felt the warmth fading slowly, thickly, like mud.

The bushes behind us suddenly rustled to life. Branch appeared.

"Laney, are you ready? It's time—"

He paused when he saw Nash, his arm around my waist, his fingers threaded through mine. I stepped away quickly, heat rising to my cheeks.

"Yes. Just—just a second."

Branch's eyes stayed on us for a moment longer, and then he nodded, looked back at the trees, and disappeared.

I reached down and picked up the water containers, balanced them in my hands.

"Be careful, Laney. Promise me." The intensity of Nash's gaze made panic rise in my chest.

I nodded.

Nash took a container from me and we walked back to the clearing together, in silence. We had almost pushed through the trees when I turned to him, the light of the sun making the edges of his eyes round and clear.

"Keep an eye on Blakely, okay? I don't trust her."

Nash looked back at me unphased. "Of course."

I breathed in before we pushed the last branch away. I could hear talking and moving on the other side.

"Okay, well…I'll see you."

Nash's lips opened in a small smile. "I'll see you."

The daylight filled my eyes and I had to blink to see the clearing. A few figures came into view—Theodore and Alese, standing in the middle of the grass with Gavin and Dalia. Branch holding backpacks a few feet away, talking to Delma. And Blakely, sitting at the bottom right corner of the clearing, far away from everyone else, staring at the trees.

"There she is!" Theodore's face brightened when he saw Nash and I. Alese smiled and looked away from the group that slowly gathered around her.

When I reached them, I set the water down next to me, bending the grass beneath it.

"Laney, that goes with Branch! In the backpacks." Theodore smiled and pointed to the tall boy with golden hair, who was laughing at something Delma had said. Branch turned, the smile still on his face, and stepped over to me, placing the water in each backpack with a *plunk*. His eyes met mine, and I looked away.

"You guys ready?" Alese tried to sound enthusiastic, but I could tell she wanted this to be over with—this journey to nowhere, for nothing, just to make the people happy.

Theodore nodded, his eyes bright. "Maybe we'll find another house!"

I smiled, the memory of wooden walls, chipped cups, and a tattered rug filling my mind.

Delma rounded the group and stopped next to me. "I snuck some cookies in the backpacks for you." She winked, her voice barely a whisper. "Have a safe trip, okay?"

I smiled and gave Delma a quick hug.

Branch hoisted one of the packs on his back, and Theodore grabbed the second. We were only taking two this time—it wasn't going to be a long trip.

Nash squeezed my hand one more time, then let go.

As Branch took the lead and Theodore and I fell in step behind him, through the grass and out of the clearing, the people began to clap. I looked back, once more, my eyes searching for Nash, but I caught Alese's instead. She mouthed, "Thank you" and "Stay safe," and I nodded. Someone yelled, "Don't get caught by the man with black eyes!" as we pushed into the trees.

We walked the first few minutes in silence, the air around us warm and wet from the dew on the trees. The sun was almost directly above us in the sky—it was already nearly midday.

A small brown bird suddenly flapped in front of Theodore and he jumped, then laughed.

Branch glanced back at him and smiled. "Gotta watch those birds—they'll get you if you're not paying attention."

Theodore grinned and stretched his arms out, brushed his fingers against tree trunks as he walked. "I know they won't hurt me." He stopped, so suddenly that I almost walked into his pack. "But that might."

Branch stopped too, and the air grew quiet around me except for the chirping of a lone bird. I looked around Theodore, to a small clearing of thickets and flowers next to us, and saw a large brown body in the middle of it. It looked like a deer but had long, thick spirals of brown coming from its forehead. I didn't move.

The animal was still for a moment, but reared back suddenly. I could see fear in its eyes. But for some reason, it didn't leave. And then I saw it: a long, twisting rope of green wrapped around the animal's foot. It was stuck.

And I couldn't believe our luck.

"Branch, we're not far. We can take it back to everyone, for food. This will feed them for at least a few days." I spoke softly so I wouldn't scare the animal even more and reached for the knife in Theodore's pack.

"No."

My hand stopped, my fingers nearly gripping the smooth wooden handle. I looked up. Branch was setting his pack on the ground slowly. He looked at my knife once, his eyes hard. Without knowing why, I lowered it.

Then, as I watched and the greens and yellows of the leaves swirled around us, Branch made his way to the animal, one step at a time. When he reached it, he put his hands out slowly. The animal pulled back, wide-eyed and breathing hard. Branch spoke softly.

"There, boy. You're going to be okay."

The animal's breathing slowed, and Branch had his moment. In one swift motion, he knelt and pulled the green rope from the animal's leg. The animal stepped back, the brown points pulsing in the air, and looked at Branch for a moment. Then it ran into the trees.

I said nothing, my eyes still on Branch as he walked back to his pack, picked it up again.

"You only kill if an animal is already dead." Branch looked up at me. "And by dead, I mean wounded to the point of no return."

"But the people—" The words tumbled from my lips, soft.

"The people have enough."

His eyes fell on the knife again, and his face darkened.

And that simple movement made me feel wrong for some reason, exposed. I slipped the knife back in my pack.

Theodore moved for the first time since he saw the animal. "What was that?" His eyes followed the direction the animal had run.

A smile pulled at the end of Branch's lips. "A moose. He was a big guy, one of the biggest I've seen."

Theodore grinned, his eyes still on Branch. "You remind me of someone."

Branch pulled the pack on his back and stopped, facing Theodore. The light melted through the leaves and lit up his eyes—gold, bright, like the sun when it first comes up in the morning, stretching its rays onto everything it sees.

"You wouldn't know him." Theodore shook his head slightly, shifted the weight on his back. "But you might have seen him. His name was Lander. He was the one Mr. Dabir killed."

Branch nodded slowly, like he remembered. The brightness of his eyes faded a little. He turned, his feet falling back on the path again. "And what was Lander like?"

Theodore smiled, started walking again. "He was...nice. He helped people, even when they had nothing to give him in return." The back of Theodore's red head bobbed up and down as he spoke, and his eyes fell on the clearing where the moose had been, one more time. "He was a lot like you."

25

ELSEWHERE

History: Entry 14

The funny thing about love is this: you have to choose it.

It doesn't fill you one day, suddenly, when you're least expecting it. It doesn't latch on to your skin like a leech, waiting to be pulled away and sucked off when it's not wanted.

It's there, alone, unmoving. Waiting for someone to pluck it up and take it with them. Waiting for someone to choose it.

But that's not the case with hate.

Hate is everywhere—in the shadows and the edges and the air. It's the darkness in the eyes and the sharpness of a smile and the wildness of a laugh. It's breaths and pricks and pinches and strokes. It's everything.

You don't choose hate.

Hate chooses you, with long fingers and open arms.

And when it does, there's room for nothing else.

26

HERE

No one could ever truly explain what the world looks like.

It's an endless photograph, a limitless book that never runs out of paper or white space or ink.

All eighty-eight of us could write for days, weeks, months, years, never stopping for anything except air and water, and there would still be white space to fill. There would still be corners of the world we haven't seen—crevices of trees, the line of a leaf, or the look in a moose's eyes when someone sets him free.

The world is boundless. I could see that just from walking a few hours, just from leaving our little piece of it and wandering into the rest.

The sun was slowly slipping through the air, as if held by a string. Branch still led the way, pushing back leaves for us as he walked and laughing when Theodore commented on the staggering height of a tree or asked why this squirrel looked fatter than that squirrel. Branch and Theodore were getting along well, like they had known each other much longer than just over a week.

Once, Theodore had asked where Branch was from and Branch had said the trees, much like these. Branch hadn't asked Theodore back. He knew Theodore looked too young to remember, and probably didn't want to bring up his forgotten childhood. I was grateful for that. Although I couldn't get the sight of him and Blakely out of my mind, which disgusted me—why would someone like Branch trust someone like her?—I was still determined to get his help. I just had to wait for the right moment to do it.

"Should we stop for the night?" I heard Branch's voice and saw the back of his head turn. "The sun will be down soon."

Theodore nodded. "It's not like we're in a hurry to get anywhere." He chuckled.

I followed Branch and Theodore into a small piece of open ground beneath the trees and set the water I had taken out of Theodore's pack an hour earlier on the grass and crumbled leaves. Theodore set his pack down, a thin cloud of dirt and dust rising when it touched the ground. He waved it away, unzipped his pack, and handed me a rolled-up sheet.

"I'm going to go get some wood. It will be colder tonight." Branch set his pack down, wiped his hands on his pants, and stood.

"I'll set up your sheet for you!" Theodore volunteered, and Branch nodded a thanks.

I stood too. "I'll come with you."

Branch had turned, headed into the trees, but he stopped. "I can get it, Laney."

"The more we have, the better. That way we'll have extra for tonight." I brushed my hands together, looked at Theodore. "Will you be okay for a little bit?"

He smiled, unzipped Branch's pack, and pinched his sheet with two fingers. "Of course."

I looked at Branch, then walked past him in the direction he had been going.

I walked for thirty seconds without turning around. I looked at the different trees—some thin, with brown trunks and red-tipped leaves, and some larger, with white-speckled branches that seemed to touch the sky.

"Laney, you're not even looking for sticks."

Branch had followed, just like I'd hoped. And now we were out of Theodore's earshot.

I whirled around. "I need your help."

Branch was kneeling down, picking up a small pointed branch that had fallen from a tree, and he stopped with his hand still poised in the air. "What?"

"Look, at first I was wondering why in the world you would even talk to Blakely, let alone be *friends* with her, but I don't really care about that anymore. It's your life. You can do what you want. I just need your help." The words were tumbling out of me, faster than I'd ever known I could speak. But this was serious—Nash and I were at stake.

Branch had straightened slowly, was looking at me with the corners of his mouth turned up slightly. "Laney, what are you talking about?"

I was going to avoid it completely, but he had asked. And the question came out of me before I realized I had opened my mouth.

"Why do you let Blakely follow you around all day? Don't you know you shouldn't trust her?"

Branch just stared at me, his hands clutching a few pieces of wood. "Of course I don't trust her. The only way to make sure she doesn't do anything—hurt anyone—is to keep her close."

The air slowly left my chest. So he wasn't as stupid as I had thought.

A breeze swept through the leaves and I felt goose bumps on my arms. Branch was right. It was going to be cold tonight. We had gone mostly uphill today, and if I remembered correctly from my first journey to the world above, the higher we went, the colder it got.

Branch leaned down again, started picking up more pieces of fallen trees. "You said you needed my help?" His voice had a small edge of amusement to it, and I didn't know why. It made my cheeks hot. The reason I had followed him into the trees came back to me.

"I can't—I can't control it." The words left my lips, and suddenly I felt small, like I was tearing off a piece of my heart and offering it up to a stranger.

Branch didn't stop picking up sticks, so I kept going.

"You know how you said love will either control you or you'll control it? Well, I want to control it." I swallowed, my throat dry. "Teach me how."

Branch's arms were almost full now. He didn't look at me, didn't take his eyes off the ground. He gave no indication that he had heard anything I had said.

"Branch—"

"I'm sorry, Laney." He looked at me, that familiar sparkle still in his eyes. It looked like he was trying not to smile. "I honestly feel a little bad."

I stood there in silence, surprised. "What? Why?"

He stopped for a moment, shrugged. "There's no way to control love—it's impossible."

When he saw my expression fall, his face softened. "But I *can* teach you what love is."

I didn't move. A sinking feeling filled my chest, followed by the aggravating prick of being lied to. "Why did you tell me you knew how to control it then? What was the point of that?"

Branch didn't move for a second. A bird landed in the tree behind him and chirped loudly. He smiled. "I was just trying to get your attention. Apparently, it worked." Then he turned suddenly, started picking up sticks again and placing them in his arms, this time whistling a tune similar to the bird.

I stood there, at a loss for words. Was he serious? I clenched my fists, and my head felt light. Embarrassment at going to him for help in the first place flushed my cheeks.

"The fire's not going to build itself, Laney. Are you going to help?"

I looked at him, at his full hands and angled face and bright eyes, searching for the perfect pieces of wood. The heat that I felt before built up slowly, until embarrassment turned to anger. I had been waiting *days* for his help, false hope and a waste of time. In that moment, more than anything, I needed to strip away some of his pride.

Before I knew what I was doing, I walked across the grass and leaves, stopped in front of Branch, and kissed him. I pulled away quickly, simply. Branch just stood there, speechless, surprise finally—*finally*—filling his eyes. I looked at him one more time.

"Controlled it."

Then I stepped past him, into the trees, toward Theodore.

Branch suddenly came to life. "Laney, are you serious? You can't just kiss someone!"

I kept walking. At least he was listening to me now, with a new knowledge that I was not someone to mess with.

"Laney, stop."

I whirled around. "You said love couldn't be controlled. Well, I just controlled it." I crossed my arms, and he stared at me in disbelief. Then, slowly, his lips spread open, the corners of his mouth curved up to his cheeks.

He started laughing.

"You think—you think that's love? Kissing someone you don't even know because you're angry?" He doubled over, his laughter filling the air.

The heat from my cheeks faded quickly, and I stood there in astonishment, watching him.

"Have you learned nothing from Alese?" Branch straightened slowly, his eyes still lit up from the moment.

I didn't move. "Of course. I have thirty-two LPs."

Branch looked amused. "LPs are nothing, Laney. Love—real love—is so different from that. It's not a competition."

I couldn't think of anything to say. I had no words for him right now.

Branch walked back a few steps, knelt, grabbed one more stick to add to his pile, and then hugged them all to his chest.

"Apparently, you still have a lot to learn—not about controlling love, but about love in general." Branch's eyes met mine once more before he walked away, and he shook his head in disbelief, the smile still on his lips.

I gathered as many sticks as I could before I headed back to Branch and Theodore. When I stepped past a tree and into the small stretch of empty ground, a fire was already going, spraying white flames into the air and a long line of gray smoke up into the tops of the trees.

Theodore was sitting next to Branch on a small tree stump, his legs stretched out in front of him and a small curved stick in his hand. He was pressing the tip of the stick into the dirt and dry leaves, swirling it up and down, back and forth.

"Look, Laney! Branch found me a stick that looks just like one of the old, forbidden pencils. Delma taught me to write half of my name—he just taught me the rest." Theodore gestured excitedly to the ground next to him, where *Theodore* was sprawled out in wide, swooping letters.

I bent and let the sticks fall from my arms to the ground in a small pile. I smiled quickly at Theodore and looked at Branch, but he was watching Theodore's hand.

After everything that had just happened, he still had time to think about Theodore, out there, in the trees. I shook my head in disbelief again.

It wasn't long before the night was on us like the air—blue under the moon, and cold. I wrapped my sheet tightly around me and rearranged the half-empty pack I had placed under my head as a pillow. I could feel the square, hard surface of the paper book under my head.

Theodore, Branch, and I were all sleeping a few feet away from each other. We had fallen asleep with the warmth of the fire on our faces, but now I woke in the cold.

I moved a few inches forward, scooted toward the last few coals that were purple-gray and barely burning. My arm brushed against Theodore's stick, and I turned. Under the small pricks of light from the stars, I could just see the outline of what he had been drawing next to his name.

It was three people—small circles for heads, sticks for arms and longer, wobbly circles for bodies. They were walking, their legs extended, and surrounding them were multiple long lines dotted widely at the tops—I could only guess that these were trees. And the three tiny people, scuffed in the dirt and tangled grass, had their arms outstretched: they were holding hands.

27

ELSEWHERE

History: Entry 15

I don't think about the days that came before. Can't think about them.

They're gone, not even a memory, because no piece of them remains. Just like love, when it was banished from the world and it left a trail of ash in its path.

This is what remains. Ash and smoke, broken pieces and charred edges. This is what exists.

I could still hear the screams in my mind, could still see the wide eyes and twisted faces, laughing wildly as they tore the leaves off trees, if I wanted to.

But I don't.

Seconds tick forward, not back, for a reason.

And every second that ticks forward is a second they see me as someone I'm not. My face is a mask, round and smooth and beautiful.

And it's so perfectly shaped, so carefully molded and formed, that even she doesn't notice.

Tick...Tick...Tick...

28

HERE

I woke suddenly, a sound in the trees jolting my head to my chest.

I blinked, the darkness settling around me. It was still sometime in the night, the sun not even a speck at the edge of the sky. I spread my hand on the ground and pushed, raising myself to a seated position. I shoved my sheet to the side, and it fell in a tangled heap. Branch was next to me, a stretch of dirt in between, his chest rising and falling slowly. Theodore was on his back, his mouth open and his arms sprawled out lifelessly next to him.

Snap.

There it was again.

I rose to my feet silently, my heart pounding in my chest. It could just be an animal. That's probably what it was—a squirrel nibbling on a branch or another moose, moving clumsily in the dark. Still, I grabbed a stick from the pile I had dropped and touched the end quickly, made sure it was sharp.

It's funny how living in a Dome for so many years, gray walls and thick air like the night, can make your eyes adjust more easily to the darkness in the world. I saw outlines of trunks and leaves hovering in the still air, wrapped in blue-gray, moments after I stood. I saw a small bunch of pointed grass next to my feet and a slightly worn-down, walkable path farther into the trees beyond that.

I stepped quickly, pushed some branches out of my way as I walked toward the sound. I held my arm chest-high, poised with the stick clenched tightly in my fingers.

Snap. Craaack.

I stopped. Looked back. Branch and Theodore were out of sight now, the trees around me a dark, wet shadow.

"Laney!"

The voice came from behind me, and I jumped. It was low, raspy, followed by coughs, like the person couldn't breathe. *The man with black eyes.* My heart was in my head now.

I stepped toward the sound slowly, my raised arm shaking. There was a bush. I sidestepped around it, the pointed branches stinging my arms. I should get Branch. I shouldn't be out here all alo—

My heart leapt in my chest. A person—a girl—was lying on the ground, facedown, with her arms stretched out in front of her and her hands open, scraping the dirt and grass. She lifted to her knees suddenly, her face still turned to the ground, and flung her arms out in front of her, catching the dirt with her nails. Then, slowly, painfully, she pulled herself forward.

With horror, I realized she had been moving, crawling across the ground like this. That was the sound I had heard.

"Laney."

Her voice was barely a whisper, like fingernails scraping a tree. I clung to the stick in my hand, knew I should run, but my feet were frozen.

Brown hair, long, tangled to the ground with dirt crusted at the edges. Gray pants, a gray shirt, like the ones we all wore in the Dome. I blinked. It was one of us. *She* was one of us.

Slowly, she lifted her shoulders, her neck, her head. Turned her head toward me, raised it just a few inches from the ground. And, in the black air, I could just make out the pointed chin, the round cheeks, the soft, brown eyes.

Alese. It was Alese. But how—?

"He came," her voice groaned, rising thickly from her lips. "He came for all of us. They all came."

"Alese, what—what are you talking about? What happened to you?" My voice was a squeak, not audible. I was frozen in time, my feet rooted to the ground. I touched the tree behind me.

"Laney—" Alese spread her fingers, planted her palm farther into the ground, but her arm was shaking. "Run."

Then her head fell to the ground again, her hair spreading out around her in a circle. My knees buckled underneath me, and I was on the ground in front of her. I reached out, lifted her head in my fingers.

What did she mean, *they?*

"Alese—" I swallowed, bile filling my throat. The gray had been too thick before, the darkness a shadow on her face. But now, under the thin pricks of light from the stars, her face was in full view.

Brown and yellow spots covered her cheeks, her eyelids. Her face was dotted in lumps, twisting her cheeks and distorting her chin, and it felt weak in my fingers, like the watery skin of an egg that would break with just the prick of a finger.

Bile filled my throat and I watched her eyes roll back into her head.

I screamed.

"Laney?"

A voice filled the air next to me—clear, deep. Branch.

My throat let out ragged breaths, my voice felt raw.

"Laney!"

His hand pressed against my shoulder, and my eyes snapped open.

The trees. The sky, yellowed at the edges with the light of the sun. My sheet, wrapped firmly around my legs and chest.

A dream? I breathed deeply, looked over at Branch, who was sitting next to me, his eyes wide.

"You were screaming."

I closed my eyes, then opened them again. Alese wasn't here—she was back in the clearing, taking care of all the people. She was okay. A dream. It was just a dream.

Branch was still looking at me, without a trace of amusement on his lips.

"I'm fine. It was—it was nothing." I choked out the words, then breathed in deeply again.

A few moments went by before Branch nodded, then looked at the sky. "The sun's up. We should get moving."

Theodore appeared suddenly, out of the trees. I hadn't even realized he wasn't here.

"Look what I found, guys." He was smiling, and his hands were cupped. He stretched them toward us. They were filled with small blue berries. "Breakfast."

Branch balled his sheet up, stuffed it in his pack, and grinned. He leaned over and plucked one out of Theodore's hands, popped it in his mouth. He closed his eyes, savoring the taste. "You're the best, Theodore."

Branch lifted his hand, and Theodore poured the berries into one hand and slapped it with the other.

"That's a high five, Laney." Theodore looked proud. "Branch taught me that."

Branch looked at me, but I avoided his eyes. Suddenly, yesterday's events flooded my thoughts—how Branch said love can't be controlled, my anger, the kiss. What was I thinking? I felt my cheeks turn pink, and I looked away, pushed to my feet, and folded my sheet. Maybe Branch was right about love. It was definitely capable of making people crazy.

I walked to Theodore's pack—still untouched since last night—and pushed the sheet into the largest pocket, around my paper book, hiding it from view.

Branch popped another handful of berries in his mouth and then gathered some crumbled leaves and dirt from the ground, heaping it on top of the fire. "You guys ready?"

Theodore nodded, wiping his stained hands on his pants. He reached for the pack, but I stopped him.

"I got this today. It's my turn."

Theodore looked at me. "Are you sure? Laney, I can take it. I don't mind."

"Yes, I'm sure. You do too much. On top of your leg being hurt still."

Theodore smiled, balanced his weight on one foot, then the other. "I can barely feel it anymore."

I hoisted the pack to my back and looked over at Branch. He was watching me, for the third time this morning. I shifted the pack once more. "Ready?"

Branch looked at Theodore, then at me again, and nodded. He started off into the trees.

I stepped slowly at first, realizing this was the way I had gone in my dream. I shook away the thought—the tangled brown hair, the yellow, rotten skin—from my mind and instead tried to focus on the blue-and-purple bug that fluttered past, up into the sky.

The sun crept into the sky like fire—slow and white-hot. It wasn't long before my skin was damp, my brown hair sticking to the back of my neck. I reached into the side pocket of the pack and pulled out a hair tie I had stashed there, gathering my hair in a loose bun on my head.

Ahead of me, I could see Branch push up the edges of his already-torn sleeves, thin trails of sweat trickling down his biceps.

"We'll walk all day today and then turn back tomorrow." Branch spoke loudly, his voice drifting back to me and Theodore. "That sound good to you guys?"

"Sounds good!" Theodore chirped. Then his voice came from just in front of me, too quiet for Branch to hear. "Everything but the all-day part."

I held back a laugh.

We walked most of the morning in silence, and on a constant slope upward it seemed. This mountain, as Nash had called it so long ago, was a never-ending path of trees, grass, and tiny insects swirling in the air. I breathed in deeply, and for a moment I wondered why we couldn't walk downhill instead. Why were we even walking anywhere in the first place? It's not like we were actually looking for a new field to live in.

But then I saw the brightness of Theodore's face, the hunger in his eyes. Even if he joked about it, he couldn't deny it—he loved being out here, exploring the world. Each day he saw things he had never seen before.

"Branch, what was it like the first time you smiled?"

Theodore's question surprised me, and by the silence in front of us, I could tell it surprised Branch too.

"It was like air, like I took my first breath." Branch's voice was soft. "I can't imagine life without it. What was it like for you?"

I had never heard it described like that before. I blinked, and I could tell Theodore was smiling before he answered.

"Same. When was it? Mine was by a fire, when we were reading books we found in a house. Alese said to think of something happy, and I thought of my mother singing." His voice trailed off, and he was silent.

My footsteps crunched on the ground. Branch didn't turn his head.

"I— Mine was—" He stopped. "I don't remember."

I looked up, at the back of Branch's head. He didn't remember? Smiling for the first time was like a first handhold, a first laugh. How could he forget?

"Look, the trees are opening up ahead of us!" Branch's voice cut through the air again. "I think we found a field of wildflowers—maybe water too."

Wildflowers. The word hung in my ears like leaves.

We rounded a fat gray tree trunk with a grassy green layer twisted around the wood and stepped out into fresh air and a light breeze.

Branch was right. The small clearing was dotted with flowers—white and yellow petals, rounded at the ends, sticking up from green stems and pointed leaves. On the other side of the flowers I could hear water trickling past stones. Long tree branches stretched out over the top, covering all the flowers but the very middle in a light blue shade.

Theodore breathed in quickly, then looked at me. "Laney, look!" His eyes were bright, and he turned to Branch. "Flowers remind Laney of her mother, so I planted some for her by her tree."

Theodore whirled around and smiled right at me, like we were sharing a secret.

Branch turned and looked at me, but I kept my eyes on the flowers.

"Come on. I hear water!" Theodore turned and stepped carefully into the flowers, and Branch followed.

I moved slowly, remembering the time when we first saw hundreds of wildflowers on our journey in the world above and Nash had taken my hand, helped me through it. I remembered crying for my mother. I swallowed. But she was gone. We had the people now, the eighty-eight. We had the world. And we had colors, and touch, and love.

I heard Theodore's voice, heard him splashing into the water, and then laughter. Branch was with him. I pressed through the flowers, letting my hands fall and my fingers brush against them as I passed.

I wish you were here, Mother. To see all of this.

Thoughts can be controlled as much as love can.

I set my pack down in the middle of the flowers, made sure Theodore and Branch were still behind some bushes to my left, next to the water. I made sure I could hear their voices before I pressed my hand in the pocket, moved my sheet to the side, and pulled out the paper book. I reached to the bottom and my hand touched the black rock I had found by my tree. I sat down, and the heads of wildflowers bobbed against my legs as I wrote:

A Smile:

The curve of the wind, the slope of a breeze. It's there, swirling through trees and the chubby heads of flowers, lifting leaves and brushing against blades of grass.

Breathe it in, deeply—a first breath, and a last.

After just one, you won't need to breathe again.
It will be your air.

29

ELSEWHERE

History: Entry 16

She was breathing deeply last night, short breaths and thick pasty-white skin.

Her chest was moving in and out, in and out, like the clouds in the sky.

Gray. Pressed against the blue. But not enough to cause a storm.

Her eyes were wide, her hair tangled in a lump on her head.

It's almost time.

30

HERE

It only takes a little while before you start getting used to the world. Not *getting used to it*, like it's boring. This world could never be boring. You start being able to recognize things—the curve of a tree trunk, the shape of a leaf, the way a field of flowers usually means water's close by. How long this path might be, how deep that pool of blue might go.

There is a strong beauty in being able to identify pieces of the world, because in a way, you're identifying with the world. Relating to it. Speaking with it. And to touch fingers with the colors—the greens, the blues, the purples, the reds—is to touch something so relatable, so understandable, and yet something so mysterious and unpredictable and erratic, all at the same time.

So when Theodore found something that was not predictable and not relatable in the least, it left us without words.

"What is it?" Theodore lifted up the large square, twice as long as a tree trunk and as thin as a fingernail, and pushed back his wet hair.

We stood on the side of the water, a long and thin line filled with rocks and bugs and blue. Our water containers sat full next to us.

"I think it's a sign." Branch took the square from Theodore, held it out in front of him.

It was made of some sort of hard, gray material that *pinged* when water dripped on it. And on it, sprawled across the front, were large letters, deeply faded, but I could tell that they had once been a vibrant red.

"What's a 'sign'?" Theodore reached out and touched the front of it again, ran his finger across it.

"It tells what something is." Branch squinted his eyes, looked at it more closely. "Or where it is." Then he looked up, at Theodore. "I think it says, The North Pole. Where did you find this again?"

"'The North Pole?'" I couldn't help but jump in. "Isn't that some place really cold?"

We weren't taught geography in our studies in the Dome, but Delma was taught it as a child, remembered where things were in the world. She had mentioned it once.

"Yes." Branch looked at me, surprise on his face. He didn't think I knew. "But that doesn't make sense."

"I found it caught between some rocks, farther up that way." Theodore answered Branch's question, pointing along the water, farther up the slope.

"Things that flow down usually come from up." Branch looked at Theodore, then me, his mouth twisting in a playful grin. "Let's go!"

Then he swung his pack on his back, grabbed one of the containers of water, and took off beside the trail of blue, following it farther up the mountain. He was still holding the sign.

Theodore looked at me with wide, smiling eyes. He followed Branch immediately.

"Branch, wait!" But he didn't turn around. I grabbed the other container of water and hurried after them before they disappeared in the trees.

We walked for ten minutes, maybe fifteen, and I lost them a few times, then caught Theodore's red head bobbing between the green. When I finally caught up to them, they were standing completely still, staring at something in front of them. Branch was leaning against a tree, clutching his pack.

"Seriously, guys? I almost lost you!"

Branch looked back at me, that ever-present sparkle in his eyes. "Look at this."

I bent for a moment, catching my breath. Then I stepped closer to Branch and Theodore, pushing back a tree branch that was blocking my view.

My throat tightened. I blinked, felt my heart freeze in my chest.

A large clearing stretched before me, filled with patches of grass and tall, thick plants that stretched over dry leaves and dirt. And in this clearing—I took a deep breath—were things humans had made.

A few small papery buildings stood in the middle of the clearing, with walls missing and no doors. Faded red paint was scraping off the edges. And next to the buildings were things I had never seen before—tall, wiry tracks clung to a wooden structure, once painted white, like the flowers. It circled around, going uphill and down, then stopped where it began. A large structure shaped like a wheel stood farther in the clearing, with seats like we ate in while we were in the Dome fastened to the spokes of the wheel. Beyond that, under a caved-in roof, were cars—dozens of them, but much smaller and funny-looking. They had long spokes sticking up out of the backs of each one. Dozens of other structures wound up the mountain behind these—I could see tips sticking out between the highest branches farther up. There was even more that we couldn't see up in the trees.

"Look!" Theodore pointed ahead of us, to the front of the closest building. Painted on the front many years ago, thick letters spelled out the words Welcome to the North Pole. Just like the sign.

"What is this place?" I touched a tree trunk behind me, made sure I wasn't dreaming. I'd never seen anything like this before, or heard about it in any books.

"I think it's an amusement park." Branch was staring at everything, just like we were. "At least, it used to be one."

"An amusement park?" Theodore looked up at Branch, who was looking thoughtfully at the large wheel with seats.

"I've heard about them before. Never seen one." He leaned down, placed the sign by his feet. "It's where people used to go to have fun."

Theodore looked even more perplexed now. "There were places like that? Just to have fun?"

Branch was torn away from the scene in front of us for just a moment. His eyes fell on Theodore, at the way he was looking longingly at the half buildings and broken structures before him.

"We have half a day left." Branch's voice pulled Theodore's eyes away, to his. "We might as well spend it here." Then he winked.

"Really?" Theodore's eyes lit up, and he looked at Branch gratefully. Then he took off, into the dirt and broken-off pieces that scattered the ground.

I set down my pack slowly, pulled out the water I had pushed in just moments before.

Branch looked back at me. "You coming?"

"I'll be right behind you."

Branch nodded, then followed Theodore to the structure with the funny cars.

I took a long drink, then pushed myself to my feet. A place where people went just to have fun. I couldn't imagine it. It was a beautiful thought.

I walked into the clearing, one foot after the other, as if I were walking into the past. I could almost see it—a little girl shrieking as she held hands with her mother, pulling her toward the bright white wheel as the yellow bow in her hair streamed behind her. A little boy, running toward the cars while his mother shouted his name behind him. And a couple, young, wide-eyed, hanging out for the first time and sharing a first kiss, right here, in this amusement park in the mountains. Just thinking about it took my breath away.

I found myself in front of the closest building, and I stopped. The top part of the front wall was open, with the bottom enclosed by a ledge of some sort. Broken chairs and boxes of different sizes littered the ground. And on the inside, filling the back wall from floor to ceiling, was a painting of a face.

It was large, round, with fluffy yellow hair sticking straight up from its head, white-painted cheeks, and a big red nose. It was smiling, with thick lips and bright white teeth. It looked like it was trying to be happy, but something about it made a chill slide down my neck. Is this what happy used to look like?

"Laney, come look at this!"

Theodore's voice jolted me out of my thoughts. I turned from the strange face and saw him and Branch standing at the end of the clearing, looking at something in the trees.

When I reached them, I looked up. Two long lines of wire stretched above in the air, near the tops of the trees. The wires ran parallel to the clearing, much farther than I could see, hidden just enough in the green that we couldn't see it when we had first stepped out.

"Branch said people used to ride it." Theodore's head was tipped to the sky, and I could barely see his forehead.

"Ride it? How?"

Branch looked at me. "I could tell you. Or"—he grinned again. I could tell he was enjoying this—"I could show you."

Branch ran off into the nearest building, one with three walls that looked like it might collapse any second. He returned with three long piles of rope.

"Theodore, come here."

Then, while I watched, Branch wrapped the rope around Theodore's legs, looped it around his chest, then up and under his arms.

"Sit back." Branch held the rope firmly above Theodore's head and Theodore sat back into air. But the rope held. Branch's lips curved, and his eyes were bright. "Perfect."

The end of the wire was a few hundred feet away, past other strange objects sticking out of the ground, covered in ash and dust. A large faded red-and-white-striped building shaped like a cylinder stood next to a tree, and I could see the bottom of a staircase that wound up to a small platform sticking out of the top of the building.

"This is it. This is where it starts." Branch grinned and looked back at us.

Theodore sucked in his breath and walked to the stairs, ducking his head as he bent under the doorframe and took the first step.

"There's no way this is safe." I stared at the tall structure that seemed to be bending slightly in the wind.

"Lesson number one about love, Laney." Branch looked at me. "You have to take a risk."

He set his pack down on the tufts of grass, looked up once more at the wire that wound through the trees, and followed Theodore to the red-and-white staircase.

I frowned. "If I could name off the *hundreds* of risks I've taken in the last few weeks—"

"What? I can't hear you, Laney!" Branch's voice cut me off. "The walls are too thick!"

I reached forward and touched them. The walls were as thin as air—if I touched them any harder, they might crumble to pieces.

"This is crazy! I'm like a bird!" Theodore's voice came from above, and I looked up. He was standing on the platform, holding the wall behind him with one hand.

He looked small from here—it was higher up than I thought. I bet Branch wouldn't even care.

A cool breeze swept past—it was colder here in the shade under the trees. I pressed my hands to my hair, pulled out the hair tie, and let it fall to my shoulders. I should go up there, just to make sure Theodore was safe during whatever Branch had planned.

When I stepped through the door, I had to blink to adjust my eyes to the darkness. I suddenly realized this was my first time inside since the Dome. The wide, sloping walls were a gray-brown, and the floor was cold. There were more similarities to our gray underground world than I would have liked.

I took the stairs quickly, hoping to get out of here as soon as possible. A few of them were missing, and the rest creaked underneath my weight. Dirt was everywhere—on the floors, between the cracks in the walls, on the broken rail that was hitched to the wall by a few rusty nails.

The stairs wound around a center pillar and stopped at the top, next to the platform. As I got closer I could see the sun streaming in through the small doorway that opened up to the sky.

Branch was half on the platform, half on the stairs, securing a rope around himself. "Well, look who decided to join."

I swallowed, the tops of trees coming into view. My head felt dizzy.

"I'll go first, so we know it's safe." Branch tightened the rope once more, then looked out at the platform to Theodore. I could see his red head staring at the trees, the clouds, the sky.

"Can I go first?" He looked back at Branch with wide green eyes. I had never seen them so bright.

Branch raised his eyebrows. "This hasn't been used in a long time, Theodore. We don't know if it will hold."

"So why should you get hurt? My leg is hurt already—well, kind of. Plus, this"—he tugged on the wire that was firmly attached to the top of the building with a thick metal hook—"and this"—his hands closed on the rope around his waist—"seem pretty secure to me."

Branch looked at the wire, then at Theodore. "Theodore, I can't let you—"

"Please, Branch. I never get to be the first, at anything."

Branch fell silent, and so did I. Theodore had just one memory from the world before the Dome—his mother singing, and then being killed because of her song. He was one of the youngest in our class, was the last—next to me—to enter into the world above on our first journey. He was right. I never realized it until now, but I guess he was always pushed behind us because we didn't want him to get hurt.

Branch breathed in, then let the breath out slowly. "Okay."

Theodore's face lit up.

Branch held up a hand. "But make sure you come back here after you make it to the end. If I don't see your smiling, all-in-one-piece face back here in five minutes, I'm assuming something happened and I'm coming after you. Promise?"

Theodore laughed. "Promise."

Branch nodded, grabbed the two ends of Theodore's rope, and held them up, then draped them over the top of one of the wires and tied them firmly together. Once, twice, three times. He pulled the rope, putting his weight on it as he did. It held.

"Okay, sit back. You're going to try to stay like this the whole time—just sitting, like you're in a chair."

Theodore grinned. "Sitting in the sky."

The ends of Branch's mouth creased in a smile. "Yes, just like that. Okay, you ready?"

Theodore stepped to the edge of the platform and looked down, his breaths coming out in short bursts.

"Branch, you're sure it's safe?" I reached out, touched the wire above me. Fear wrapped itself around my chest when I looked down, saw how far Theodore could fall. This was crazy. And dangerous.

Branch looked at me. "He'll make it."

His eyes were strong, sincere.

"He better."

"When I say go, step off." Branch moved back, pushed the wire high over his head.

"Good luck, Theodore!" The words tumbled from my mouth in the moment, and I wished I would have said something else.

"And—" Branch paused. "Go!"

Theodore took a deep breath, looked back at us with bright eyes, and stepped off the platform. Then he was in the air, sliding past the trees with no ground beneath him. The rope above him held, and he was moving past leaves, sitting in the sky. Exactly as he had said.

I realized I was holding my breath, and I let it out quickly. It was amazing—seeing Theodore as high as the trees, getting smaller and smaller as the wire pulled him farther and farther away.

Soon, silence filled the air, and neither Branch nor I said a word. We waited, staring at the ground until we saw a small, red head bobbing excitedly, moving quickly toward us in the grass. I let out another breath, relief filling my arms and chest.

Theodore stopped when he could see our faces and waved his arms excitedly. His tiny face was a dot on the ground, and I could see that it was flushed pink. He was beaming, his eyes wide and wet and bright, and holding his rope in one hand. He yelled something we couldn't understand, then threw his arms up in the air, beckoning toward him.

"I think that's our cue." Branch was grinning widely now, pride in his eyes and on his cheeks. He was ecstatic his plan had worked.

He tightened the knot on his rope one more time, then picked up the last rope that he had dropped on the ground next to him. "Ready?"

I stepped back, into the stairs. "Are you serious? I'm not going. I just came up to make sure Theodore was okay. And he is, so..." I took a step down, then another.

"Laney. This is your *one* chance to do something fun. To see how the people before us used to live. And you're just going to pass that up?"

I stopped on a stair, thought a moment. "Yes."

Branch looked out over the platform suddenly, shock filling his face. "Oh no, Theodore!"

My heart dropped in my chest, and I hurried up the stairs I had just stepped down, looked out over the platform. Theodore wasn't there. I turned around, looked at Branch for some sort of direction. He was standing in the stairway, his arms across his chest, smiling.

"I'm sorry, but I can't let you pass up a chance like this."

My mouth opened as I registered what Branch had done, the trick he had played.

"Seriously? Branch, just let me go. You enjoy your little ride through the sky. Don't worry about me."

Branch was silent for a moment, and his eyes suddenly turned soft at the edges. "I try not to, Laney. Trust me."

I swallowed, words stripped from my throat for a second.

"But when there's someone as *senseless* as you, who will pass up an opportunity like this, I can't help it." He winked.

I frowned.

"You'll regret it if you don't go. Trust me. I've had those moments." Branch's eyes suddenly got lost in a memory, and I wondered what it was—what he was thinking about. Then they turned back to me again. "What if I go with you?"

"With me? How?"

Branch pointed to the wire from his spot in the doorway. "There are two wires. We have two ropes. We can go down together, side by side."

I followed Branch's gaze, wondering why he suddenly cared what I did and didn't do. The kiss suddenly flashed across my mind. If anything, maybe this would help him forget about it—forever.

"Okay. Fine." The words fell from my lips before I let them.

Branch smiled, then moved from his spot. He wrapped the rope around me slowly, carefully, making sure it held when I sat back in the air. Then he stepped out on the platform, and I followed.

The breeze hit me hard, and I shivered. We were next to the tops of the trees, and I was closer to the edge than I had ever been. Before, I had lived underground, constantly looking up at gray ceilings and long walls. Now I was looking down at the world, and the world was looking back at me.

"Ready?" Branch grabbed the rope in front of him with one hand and my rope in the other.

I put my hands around the rope under his hand, clutched it tightly with my fingers. Suddenly the air seemed to create a box around me, and the ground bounced back and forth every time I blinked. With every breath, the air seemed to grow thinner. I took a step back. This was a bad idea. Hoping Branch forgot the kiss wasn't worth dying over.

"I can't." The words squeezed out of me between frantic breaths.

Branch looked at me, his chin curved slightly. "Those words shouldn't exist. You *can* Laney. You always can."

Then he moved his hand from its position above mine and placed it over my fingers. He held them, tightly. I felt a short burst from his touch, but my heart was still in my throat, and I couldn't move. All the anger and embarrassment and wanting to prove myself was gone—now, there was only fear.

"I'm right here, okay? One, two—" He took a step forward, and my feet followed in a clumsy motion.

"Three."

He stepped off the edge, and we were in the air.

31

ELSEWHERE

History: Entry 17

Some people count by seconds, minutes, days.

I count by people.

How many have I taken?

How many are shaking and unsure, eyes wide and fingers trembling, scraping the dirt and asking, Why?

And how many are still out there, delusional, thinking love is the way for humanity to survive?

These numbers are my time of day, my calendar, my distance. They are how long it takes me to get from here to there, from this to that.

The curve of a chin, the wildness of the eyes, the darkness of a laugh—this is how I count.

And this is how I will know when to stop.

32

HERE

When I was five, I imagined I was a bird.

I pictured myself soaring above the trees, white wisps of clouds brushing against my wings, the world upside-down and right-side-up all at the same time, filled with blue—so much pure, beautiful blue. I was free, light as the wind, tumbling through a place with no floors and no walls and no ceilings.

But I never pictured this: Bright eyes, red cheeks, white fingers. Hot bursts of breath, the air thin and deliciously, overwhelmingly thick all at the same time. My heart pounding in my head, my arms and legs losing all feeling because they were just *there*—with nothing to lean against or step on or touch. Trees whispering past, the ground moving below my feet, far below, like the world decided to spin faster and faster without telling anyone it was going to.

I was nothing, a breeze, a tremble in the wind, and yet—I felt everything. I *was* everything. To be nothing, and everything, is a breathless and wonderful thing.

I remember seeing Theodore wave to us as we passed by above, a red-and-peach blur among the greens and browns below.

Color. So much color, all at once, flying past me like the entire world became liquid—the trees and water and grass—

and blended and merged with each other to create one large, watery, perfect mess.

A mess that was all mine, from my place in the clouds.

Sitting in the sky.

After years of living under the ground, with gray walls and stone ceilings, no sun or sky or moon or stars, here I was—sitting in the sky.

Until we slowed at the end of the wire, I didn't notice Branch's hand still on mine, didn't notice that he had been yelling excitedly as we flew past the trees.

Another platform seemed to move toward us, grow larger, and Branch must have put out his legs, because we came to a stop on the worn wooden square. I stood there for a moment, my hands shaking and my head still moving through the trees, the air. My eyes were wet from the strength of the wind—we had tried to race it, tried to push past it. And I couldn't help but think we had won.

"Wooo! That was amazing! I should have done that *years* ago!" Branch was smiling so big it looked like the tips of his mouth were touching his eyes. He was breathing deeply, and he released his hand from mine, started to untie his rope. "What did you think? Worth it, right?"

I released my fingers from the rope, stiff from clutching it, and finally caught my breath. "Definitely. That was definitely worth it."

Branch looked at me as he reached over and untied my rope from the wire. "Lesson number two about love: trust. Without it, you're nothing."

For some reason, Nash's words ran across my mind: *Rule number one in this new world, Laney: don't trust anyone.*

I reached down, untied the rope around my arms and chest, and let it fall from my waist to the floor. I rubbed my legs where the rope had been and knelt. I looked down at the ground once more, reached out and touched a leaf that was leaning against the side of the platform. Then I stood.

Branch was watching me with an amused smile on his face.

"What?" I stepped out of the rope, picked it up with both hands.

"Your hair." There was a glint in Branch's eyes, and his smile finally filled his face. "I don't know if you saw that clown back there, on the wall, but it looks a lot like you do right now."

A clown. That must have been what the painted face on the wall was. I blushed, brought my hands quickly to my hair, tried to smooth it down.

"Here." Branch stepped toward me and reached his hand to my face, brushed a piece off my forehead and smoothed it down, over the top and to the back of my head. When his hand reached the back of my neck, it stopped, just for a second. His golden eyes were on mine, and my throat went suddenly dry. My heart started beating quickly, and my head felt light. He was in front of me now, less than a foot away. I could see the muscles in his arms beneath the torn sleeves, could see his chest, breathing in and out.

And something was different—I could feel it in the air, in the space between us. It was like I was seeing him for the very first time. I tried to swallow, but I couldn't. I tried to understand, but I couldn't.

Branch was the person who pushed my buttons, the person who irritated me until my cheeks were hot. I didn't *feel* things for him—after all, he was *Branch*. The stubborn boy who made my head spin and called me a clown.

"Branch, I have to tell you something." I spit out the words, and they sounded rushed. Unsure.

Branch blinked, then stepped back, away from me. I had ruined the moment. No, I had *saved* the moment. I breathed in, then out, regained my composure.

"Yeah?" Branch gathered his rope from the ground, looped it from his shoulder to his hand.

I avoided his eyes, my own still swirling with colors. "The man with black eyes—the one that killed Eli and took Blakely." I breathed in, slowly. "He's one of the eighty-eight. Living with us, eating with us. He must have joined the group when no one was watching. He's not hiding in the trees somewhere, like everyone thinks he is."

I wasn't sure why I was telling Branch this. Trust. That's what he had said. And aside from Nash and Theodore, Alese and Gavin, Dalia and Delma and Alfred, I think I trusted Branch now too.

Then Branch looked at me, and I looked back. His eyes were deep, pools of sunlight, but I couldn't tell what he was thinking.

"I know." He stepped toward the other side of the platform, and I saw the tips of stairs. "It's getting dark. We should find a place to build a fire."

I stood there, making sure I had heard right. "Wait. You know?"

Branch was on the top stair now, and he looked back at me. "There's a lot you don't know about me, Laney."

He said nothing else, and I could hear his footsteps as he climbed down the second white-and-red-striped building in the trees.

Soon the footsteps stopped, and I heard the chirping of a bird and felt the sharp edge of the breeze. I bunched the rope more tightly in my hands, looked back at the world one more time, then stepped away from the sky through the doorway.

When I reached the bottom, I stepped out and felt grass brush against my feet. I didn't see Branch or Theodore—they must be putting their ropes back in the three-walled building.

I took in another breath, looked at the wire that stretched through the trees once more, felt the weight of the rope that had held me up on my shoulder. Even on the ground, my head still felt the *whoosh* of the breeze, the sunlight on my skin.

And then, suddenly, I was on the ground, pressed into the dirt, my face scraping against the rocks and grass. My mind panicked, and I tried to figure out what was happening.

An arm. A leg. Hair brushing against my neck and back.

A person.

A person was on top of me.

I breathed in sharply, grabbed an arm, heaved the body off of me to the ground. My chest was moving in and out, thick, raspy breaths. The person screamed. A hand searched the ground, grabbed my hair, and pulled. I cried out, thrust my head forward, ripping it from the hand, but the person lunged again, clutched both of my arms and pushed them to the ground. Held them there. I blinked, the face hovering above my own, the back of my head pressed against the ground.

Black hair. Gray eyes. Pale skin.

"Blakely?"

"Stay away from my man! I saw you." Blakely was seething, her eyes dark and focused and angry. So angry.

My throat was aching, and Blakely was pressing her elbow down on my chest, so I could barely breathe. A dozen thoughts ran through my mind at once.

How was Blakely here? *Why* was she here? And why was she on top of me?

I tried to breathe in, but ended up coughing instead.

"I saw the way you looked at him. The way you two held hands, up on that stupid wire in the sky." She was breathing deeply now, heaving in air, and she spat the words down on me. "Don't you *dare* go near him again. Do you hear me? Branch is *mine*."

Branch. This was all about Branch? My head felt dizzy from hitting the ground, but the sight of her here, out of nowhere, made me suddenly angry. What was she doing— following us? This entire time?

I sucked in a breath, then put all my strength into pushing her off of me. It worked. Blakely fell on her side, yelped from pain, and I had my moment: I grabbed her wrists with each of my hands, just as she had done to me.

"If you ever attack me again—" I pushed her farther into the dirt, and the anger in my voice surprised me.

And then, in an instant, Blakely's face changed. Her eyes turned soft, blue at the edges, and her mouth twisted in pain. Her arms and her legs went limp, and a tear appeared in the corner of her eye. A real tear.

I hesitated for a moment, surprised by the sudden change, my arms still pressed onto hers.

"Laney? What are you doing?"

I knew it immediately. Branch's voice.

"Branch, thank goodness. Blakely followed us here, and then she attack—"

Blakely cried out suddenly, like the pain was unbearable. "I can't breathe!" She broke into a fit of coughing.

"Laney, you're hurting her. Get off." Branch's voice was calm, but it cut through my chest. I looked at the girl on the ground in astonishment.

"Are you serious? She was just—"

"You heard him, Laney. Get off me!" Blakely pushed me, hard.

Branch looked at me, then Blakely. I couldn't believe him. Couldn't believe he was taking her side.

I released my hands slowly, stepped to the side, and stood. Theodore was standing next to Branch, his eyes wide. He was holding our packs, one in each hand.

Blakely breathed in deeply a few times before she rose to her knees, very carefully, like every bone in her body was broken. She was trembling. *Trembling.* And just moments ago, she almost killed me.

"Are you okay?" Branch's voice held no sympathy, but he was looking at her. Blakely nodded, brushed a tear from her cheek.

"Okay, then." Branch crossed his arms. "What are you doing here?"

Blakely looked around nervously and wrapped her arms around herself. "I—I wasn't following you. I would never do that. Things were getting weird, so I left. I hoped I'd find you—I guess fate does that sometimes." She tried to smile at Branch, and I felt sick to my stomach. But I had to respond to what she had said.

"Weird? What do you mean weird?"

Blakely didn't look at me. She was staring at Branch, and she didn't respond. She only talked to him, back in the clearing. Funny how that hadn't changed.

"Answer the question, B."

B. He still called her B. And in that moment, I was glad he hadn't kissed me, if that were what he was about to do. I was glad I had taken control, had stopped him before he did.

Blakely smiled, looked at Branch while she answered. "Of course. Alese is sick. Arsen's in charge now. I'm not big on Arsen, so"—she shrugged—"I left."

"Sick? With what?" A panic rose in my chest as I remembered the dream—the lumps of yellow and brown, like mold.

Blakely crossed her arms, let out a breath. "Will you *please* tell Laney that I have no idea what she's sick with? The flu? What does it matter?"

Branch looked at me, then back at Blakely again. "Why don't you tell her yourself?"

Blakely's face grew suddenly serious, her black hair plastered on her head as she shook her head back and forth, slowly. So she wasn't going to budge with that, even though she had just talked to me—*warned* me—a few moments ago. I shook my head in disbelief.

"Why is Arsen in charge?" Branch looked back at Blakely, his eyebrows creased. "Why not Gavin, or Dalia?"

"Dalia is caring for Alese, which is a full-time job right now," Blakely answered immediately. "And Dalia sent Gavin to find you."

"Gavin's out here?" Theodore took the words from my mouth before I could say them. He glanced around him, his eyes touching the tips of tree trunks, the tops of grass.

Blakely said nothing.

It felt like my mind was tumbling in my head.

"Branch, we have to get back." The words came out of me, breathless. Worried.

Branch looked at me, and his eyes were wide. He was worried too. He nodded, then looked at the sky. "We'll get nowhere in the dark. We can't risk it."

He looked like he regretted every word, like he wished we could go immediately. I shook my head desperately, but I knew he was right. We would get lost at night, and that wouldn't help anyone.

"We'll go at first light, okay? The moment the sun starts coming up." He was looking at me, and for some reason my heart skipped a beat.

I nodded. "First light."

Branch looked back, at the trees. "We need to get a fire going. It's getting late."

Blakely immediately perked up, brought her hands to her hair and smoothed it back. It was down to her shoulders, pulled loose from the tight bun she had on the hill.

"I'll help."

Branch looked at her and nodded. Blakely smiled weakly at him, then followed as he stepped into the trees. And a moment before she and Branch disappeared from view, she looked back at me, her head hovering above some bushes, and grinned.

33

ELSEWHERE

History: Entry 18

I saw it today.

Fear.

I saw it in the corners of their eyes, in the creases of their faces.

It's a funny thing, fear. It can change a mind, prevent an idea, sway a thought. It can cause someone to do something, or not do something. It can create followers and like-minded heads, people who will always be by your side and behind your back.

It can do all of these things, like the wind blows through the trees.

Or it can break you.

But the funniest thing about fear?

You only need it until the breaking is done.

34

HERE

I stood there, in the amusement park in the mountains. I watched the tops of Branch and Blakely's heads disappear in the trees.

Trust, Branch had said. *Without it, you're nothing.*

Well, he hadn't trusted me. He had trusted Blakely, of all people. But not me.

Theodore was staring at me with those large green eyes, and everything Blakely had said came back. Alese was sick. Gavin was out here, looking for us. And Arsen was in charge now.

Arsen.

I remembered how he made the people laugh in my group what seemed like ages ago, but I still didn't trust him. The fact that he was leading them made my head hurt. The last time he was in charge...I shook my head. I didn't even want to think about it.

I walked closer to Theodore. I wondered if he was thinking about that too.

"Theodore, we can't trust her, okay?" I nodded toward the trees, where Branch and Blakely had gone.

Theodore nodded. "Did she hurt you?"

Something flooded my head, and tears sprang to my eyes. I swallowed, grateful. Branch might have been blind to it, but Theodore wasn't.

I nodded.

Theodore's eyes stayed large, and he looked toward them, through the trees, then at the clearing around him. "I won't trust her. We'll stick together, especially until we're back. Okay?" The words came out of him slowly, but confidently.

I swallowed again. "I'd like that, Theodore."

He smiled, but then his eyes grew nervous. He leaned down, set the packs on the ground, unzipped one of them. He looked around, once more, to make sure no one was watching.

And then he pulled out my paper book.

My throat went dry at the sight of the slick red square in Theodore's hands.

"I found this—I was getting water after the ride in the sky, and my hand brushed against it, and I didn't know what it was. I didn't open it. I didn't know if I should. I've never seen anything like it."

His words were coming out quickly now, all his sentences blending into one. Then he looked up, at me. "Do you know what it is?"

I hesitated for a second. Swallowed, my throat dry. But this was Theodore. Out of all the people I could trust with this, it would be him.

I nodded. "It's mine."

Theodore didn't move. He just waited for more.

"Nash gave it to me—he found it in the Dome. It's filled with paper. For writing."

Theodore's green eyes turned bright. "Paper?"

We had all heard about it, since it was banned from the Dome. Paper, and anything to write with. During our first week in studies, we had to memorize all the items that were banned.

I stepped forward, and Theodore held the paper book out to me. I took it, felt the smooth red in my fingers. Then I pinched both sides and opened it.

Smooth white pages fanned from one side to the other, and Theodore gasped.

"I don't think anyone should know about this. At least not yet." I closed the book. "I trust you, Theodore."

The boy with red hair and bright green eyes nodded quickly. "Of course. I won't tell anyone. That's—" He paused, his eyes still on the red, then looked at me and smiled. "That's amazing. Nash is a good guy."

I smiled, surprised at those last words. "He is, isn't he?"

And suddenly a wave of something ran over me—some feeling I couldn't name. Maybe this is what Nash was talking about when he said he missed me—this hole in my chest that continued to grow. Maybe this is what it felt like to miss someone.

"We should get to the fire." I took my sheet out of the pack, shook it, then wrapped it around the paper book, nestled it back in the pack. "So we'll stick together, then?"

Theodore smiled again. "Always."

I grabbed one of the packs from Theodore, swung it on my back, and we walked out of the clearing, into the trees. A broken line of gray was drifting above them, toward the sky, and I knew it was smoke. They had already started a fire.

Theodore rounded the bush first, and when I followed, I saw them sitting on a large tree stump next to a roaring orange-and-yellow wave. Blakely's eyes were glowing, and she was saying something to Branch.

He laughed.

Blakely looked up at me. She scooted closer to Branch, less than an inch between them now, her eyes on mine the whole time. Then she reached up and plucked a leaf from his golden hair, hovering just a moment too long in front of his face.

I looked away, grabbed the straps of my pack and set it on the ground. I reached my hand in for some food and touched a small plastic-wrapped square from one of the pockets.

Delma's cookies.

I had completely forgotten about them.

"Theodore, look." I smiled, unwrapping the square. They were broken, chipped, barely cookies anymore. But they were glorious.

Theodore looked at the square, then up at me in surprise. And when he tasted it, it looked like he was in the sky all over again.

Theodore stood and passed some to Branch, who gave a piece to Blakely.

"Courtesy of Delma." I said, and my voice came out cold.

Blakely closed her eyes and smiled. "*Mmmm.* These are amazing! Who knew they were hiding all the decent-tasting food?"

"It's Delma." Branch smiled. "She does what she wants."

Blakely's hand was draped casually over Branch's shoe, touching it with her fingertips. She shivered suddenly.

"Branch, the fire's getting smaller already, and I don't think we have enough wood to last too long." She looked at him with wide, innocent eyes. "Don't you think someone else should get it, though? Since we already took our turn?"

Branch looked back at the large pile of wood sitting behind the stump. "I think we have enough—"

"I'll go," I volunteered, suddenly.

Branch stopped and looked at me.

My eyes flitted to Blakely, then back to Branch. "There's actually nothing I want more right now." I stood, wiping my hands on my pants.

"I'll come too!" Theodore shoved the last piece of cookie in his mouth.

"No, it's okay, Theodore. I got this. Thank you, though." I did all I could to smile at him.

Then I turned and walked quickly into the trees, a voice and then Blakely's laughter filling the silence behind me.

Darkness and cold air swallowed me, but I still felt hot. How could he be okay with that? With her?

I breathed deeply, stilled my shaking hands. Picked up small sticks and chunks of trees as I walked.

The sight of her—straight black hair, almond eyes, twisted lips—and him, Branch, with his wavy blond hair, that curved chin, those straight shoulders, and the way his mouth curved into a smile, little by little, until it took over his whole face—filled my mind, and I shook it away.

It would all be over soon. I would be back with Nash, and then I wouldn't even notice them.

I breathed in, then out. I couldn't believe I had even let Branch hold my hand over the trees.

A small brown ball rushed over and then stopped in front of me. A squirrel stared for a moment, its nose twitching and its small black eyes darting back and forth. Then it was off again, running through dirt and leaves and skittering up the nearest tree.

I sighed. "What I wouldn't give to be you right now."

My voice sounded small in the darkness, and it was engulfed by silence.

When my arms were full a few minutes later, I headed back. I pushed past a bush with my elbow, since my hands were full, and heard Theodore's voice.

I stepped into the light, just in time to see Blakely laughing at what Theodore had said. *Laughing.* She grew suddenly silent when she saw me, and Branch and Theodore looked over.

"I didn't mean to interrupt you guys."

Even Branch could hear the sarcasm in my voice.

"You're never interrupting, Laney." Theodore's voice was genuine, and his green eyes looked soft in the light of the fire.

I just stood there, holding the pile of wood in my arms. Blakely's fingers were on Branch's shin now.

"We should go to bed." Branch stood suddenly and walked the few steps over to his pack. He pulled out his sheet, hesitated for a moment, then held it out to Blakely.

"Here. Since you don't have one."

Blakely smiled widely, surprise filling her eyes. It was fake. Everything about her was fake. Why didn't he see that?

"Branch, it's already freezing. When the fire goes out, it will be even colder. You can't go without it tonight." She grabbed the tip of it. "We'll share."

I was silent. We all were. For a brief moment, I wondered why we hadn't brought the coats we had taken from the Dome. Stupid.

Theodore was the first to move. He already had his sheet in his hands, and he held it out.

"Branch, take mine. I'll be fine."

Branch shook his head. "I can't—it will be cold tonight. You need it." He paused, breathed in for a moment, then looked at Blakely. "She's right."

A smile filled Blakely's cheeks.

My head pounded, but I looked away. It didn't matter. I would be back with Nash soon. It didn't matter.

I took my sheet out of my pack carefully, making sure the paper book didn't show. Then I wrapped it around myself and moved to a small patch of grass close to the fire on the opposite side of Blakely. Before I lay down, my eyes moved across the orange and red flames one more time.

Branch was looking at me, and his eyes met mine for a second. I looked away.

I fell asleep quickly, dreaming of sparkling blue skies and trees whizzing past below my feet. I flew across the sky over and over again, and every time, a hand was holding tightly to mine.

And when I woke, the air was black and my hands were cold.

The fire was gone, all except for a few coals in the dusty ashes that were glowing purple. I saw Theodore a few feet away from me, a blob of gray cotton and red hair. And then my eyes turned to Branch, his eyes closed, his chest rising and sinking slowly, his hair falling over his forehead. Blakely was next to him, one arm draped over Branch's chest and the other in his hair. The gray sheet was covering their waists and legs.

My chest tightened at the sight of them, there, together, tangled arms and feet.

I tried to breathe in, but my throat was raw. Air. I needed air.

I unwrapped my sheet and dropped it in a pile next to me, then stood and walked into the trees, avoiding looking at the tangled mess on the other side of the fire.

I didn't understand this feeling—hot and cold, empty and full, all at once. You couldn't feel things for two people at the same time, could you? And Branch was the last person I wanted to feel something for right now. But every time I saw Blakely touch him...I shook my head. I was with Nash. I had Nash.

"Jealous much?"

I jumped at the sound, at the voice. I whirled around quickly, my hands in fists.

Blakely was standing there, next to a tree, her eyes on me. "Chill out, Laney. It's just me. No need for dramatics."

"Oh, so you're speaking to me now?" The words came out of me quickly, white-hot.

Blakely didn't say anything, but a smile pulled at her lips. She stepped closer to me, humming that same sound I had heard when she killed the squirrel.

"I saw you, you know. Snap that poor animal's neck."

Blakely's eyes didn't move, didn't blink. "You think I'm stupid, Laney. But I'm not. You should actually be *terrified* of me."

"I'll tell Branch." The words came from my lips, hard. "I'll tell them all what you did. What you really are."

"Oh?" Blakely stopped humming, her mouth still in that small smile. "And what am I, Laney?"

I tried to find words, but couldn't. I didn't know what to say.

"Good answer." Blakely laughed a short, bubbly laugh. "Anyway, I thought you'd say that. Which is why I'm saying to you—" She paused, waited for a moment. She was enjoying the anticipation. "If you tell anyone anything about the squirrel, I'll tell them about your little book."

I froze. The paper book. The blood in my veins felt like ice.

"What book?" The words came out of my lips thickly, and I tried to sound confused. But it wasn't enough.

"Don't be stupid, Laney. The book in your pack, filled with paper."

I just stared at her, my head pounding. "How do you know?"

She smiled again, pleased with herself. "Theodore told me."

"No. He wouldn't."

Blakely's mouth dropped a little, upset that I didn't believe her. "He might've. You'll never know."

I blinked, and a picture of her arms wrapped around Branch's chest filled my mind again.

"What do you want with him, Blakely?"

The air was dark, cold, and Blakely stopped walking. She stood beneath the trees, her hair as black as the night.

"Branch?" Blakely looked offended and stared back at me. Then one word came from her lips, a word I never expected to hear.

"Love."

I blinked.

"Your friend is here." Blakely looked at me once more, then disappeared in the trees.

My friend? I heard a stick snap to my right, then feet rushing across the grass and leaves, growing louder. I didn't even have time to think before a boy pushed through the trees, breathing hard. Tall, dark hair—brown like the trees.

He looked up at me, and relief flashed across his face.

Gavin. It was Gavin.

"Laney!" Gavin's eyes were bright, but his face was creased. He looked exhausted.

"I saw the smoke. I've been walking all night—" He stopped, put his hands on his knees, took a deep breath, then stood. "I'm so glad I found you."

I stepped up to him, gave him a hug. He held me tightly, then turned, looked for the others.

"Over there." I pointed through the trees.

The air was blue-gray now, the sun just starting to touch the edges of his face.

Gavin nodded. He stepped back, his eyes on mine. They were large, serious. And they were worried.

A hand reached into my chest, pulled at my lungs.

"They know the person doing all these bad things is one of us."

I tried to swallow. "What do you mean? How?"

Gavin shook his head. "I don't know how, but they do. Everyone."

The hand pulled harder, squeezing out all the air in my chest. My head pounded. But if they knew that the man who's been taking people is one of them...

"It's chaos." Gavin was breathing softer now, but I could still see his chest moving in and out. "No one trusts anyone; everyone is afraid. We need to get back. With Alese hurt, it's been—" He stopped. "I need you guys."

"And Arsen?" I saw his eyes widen, wondering briefly how I knew. I didn't feel the need to explain—he would see soon enough.

"He was doing fine at first. Honestly, I was shocked. But it's all going downhill. He says he's okay, but I know he's not. I don't trust him, Laney, don't trust what he'll do—"

"Gavin, slow down." I put my hand on his arm. He looked so tired. "What happened?"

Gavin stopped, breathed in and out a few times, then looked at me, his eyes dark under the fading moon.

"Brooke is gone."

35

ELSEWHERE

History: Entry 19

Out of all the colors of eyes, green is my favorite.

It's bright, strong, like the tips of trees when the air is warm and they're alive and not dead.

In green, you can see every feeling that flashes before an eye blinks and it's gone.

Anger.

Fear.

Pain.

And exhaustion—when a person can't take it anymore, their nails scraping the leaves, and gives in.

When this happens, the green is not as bright, not as vibrant—a morning fog over a grassy field.

Blond hair, tangled across her neck, her ears, her cheeks. And green eyes, not so green anymore.

She is my next victim.

36

HERE

Gone is a word that has so many meanings.

Gone to the next room, gone on a walk, gone to bed. It could mean someone left for a second, an hour, or years. Temporary, permanent, or disappeared from existence. Gone can mean one more thing, and in this meaning you'll never know how long the *gone* will be or where it is or what they're doing:

Taken.

In this case, you'll only know when they're back.

I looked at Gavin with wide eyes, my head pulsing. Fear. That cold, pointed feeling that seems to turn your insides to ice and heighten all the senses of your body.

There was no telling what the imposter did to a person when he took them, no way we would ever know unless we found the person or were taken ourselves. And we could all do without another Blakely.

I looked up at the sun that was slowly turning the sky from black to gray and creating a faint white mist on the ground, making the grass look blurry. It was light out. We needed to go.

A bush came to life next to us and Branch pushed through with his pack already slung on his back. He was blinking the sleep from his eyes, and surprise flashed across his face when he saw Gavin.

"Gavin! It's good to see you, man. You found us."

Gavin nodded a quick thanks, then looked behind Branch, at the trees. "Is Theodore ready?"

Branch nodded. "Theodore and B. I just woke them up."

Gavin's eyebrows rose at the second name, but he said nothing. I had a feeling he didn't even want to ask. We had all seen how she clung to Branch, how he was the only one she would talk to. Maybe Gavin wasn't even surprised.

Silence fell over us for a moment, and Branch's eyes landed on me. I avoided looking at him.

"Brooke was taken." I left out the fact that everyone knew the imposter was living among them. Since Branch was best friends with Blakely now, I didn't need to tell him everything. And he didn't trust me, so why reciprocate? He would find out soon enough.

Branch didn't move. "Isn't Arsen in charge?"

Gavin nodded.

Branch pulled tightly on the strings of his pack. "Well, all the more reason to leave immediately."

Finally, something we agreed on.

Theodore stepped into our little opening in the trees, followed by Blakely. His eyes grew wide, and he ran up to the boy with brown hair.

"Gavin!" He held up his hand, motioning for Gavin to slap it. "It's a high five! It means I'm glad you're here."

Gavin smiled. "It's good to see you, Theodore."

His eyes fell on Blakely for a brief moment. Her black hair was loose at her shoulders, disheveled from the night, and her arms were hanging loosely at her sides. I couldn't tell what he was thinking. Then he looked back at Theodore, at me.

"You guys ready? Is there anywhere to get water before we go?"

I nodded. "We found some water right before the amuseme—"

"The amusement park!" Theodore's eyes lit up, suddenly remembering where we were. "Gavin, we have to show you the ride in the sky! I know we're in a hurry, but it will only take a second. It's worth it."

"Ride in the sky?" One side of Gavin's mouth curved into a tired smile.

Theodore was wearing the pack today, and he insisted he packed my sheet and our water containers, so we headed out of the trees and into the clearing.

When we first saw the grass, a little less blurry and a little more green, my heart skipped a beat. I didn't know why I was excited to see the amusement park one more time—it was basically torn apart, unusable. But it was a glimpse of the world before, a world with love. When people went places just to have fun.

I stepped by the last tree and a breeze swept past my face, through my hair that was in a heap on my back. The caved-in roof to my left that used to be filled with small chipped cars was now filled with broken glass and steering wheels littered across the ground. Large pointed sticks were puncturing the bodies of the cars.

I stopped. Swallowed. Something was wrong.

"Guys?" Theodore's voice came from behind me, small and confused.

I walked quickly to him, the picture of the cars still in my mind. Theodore was standing in the middle of the grass and dirt, unmoving. He was looking up, at the tops of the trees.

I followed his gaze, and I wish I hadn't.

The wires that used to be stretched across the trees, long and black and perfect, the wires we had ridden across the sky, were cut. Shredded. Pieces hung down like spikes on the leaves.

It was ruined. Our ride in the trees, the place I had felt like a bird, soaring across the waves of blue and white and yellow, was ruined.

I swallowed back a hot, thick moisture that was coming from deep within my throat.

I looked at Theodore. His face was white, shaken, and he was blinking back tears.

"What happened? We were just...here." The words came from Theodore's lips, so soft that I barely heard him.

Gavin, Branch, and Blakely were gathered next to us now, looking up at the sky.

There's only one person who could've—who would've—done this.

Blakely.

My eyes snapped to her face, and my breathing quickened. Her cheeks were pale, her eyebrows raised in concern and confusion. Pretending. She was pretending it wasn't her, when it was. It was always her.

Suddenly, Blakely let out a sigh. "And I didn't even get to ride it."

She looked down, and her eyes met mine. She reached her arm toward Branch's, grazed her fingers with his. Just like he had done with me, up in the sky. Up on that wire. Branch's face was completely still, his eyes a sadness I hadn't seen before.

Heat flashed through me, and my heartbeat sped up. She attacked me, she stole Branch away, and that was fine. I could live with that. But *this*.

I looked at Theodore, at his bright red hair and the way he was trying to smile, trying to push back the tears. At the way he was apologizing to Gavin, and saying at least now we'll get back to everyone faster. At the way he was hurt, but trying not to show it.

This was a hit on my friend. And this was too far.

Everything in my mind and heart seemed to leap out of the way, seemed to abandon me as I lunged toward Blakely. It was like one of those photographs we had found another lifetime ago in the house—I was looking at myself, and I was looking at Blakely, and it wasn't real. I was watching it happen, watching my body push hers to the ground. I wasn't in control anymore, wasn't aware of any other feelings but pain and anger. And I let them win.

"Laney!"

I heard a voice come from a blur to my left, but I didn't stop. Didn't slow when I saw the flash of surprise in Blakely's eyes. Didn't pause when she screamed—fake terror, fake pain—and tried to push me off of her.

Energy pulsed through me like fire, and I felt as though I would never need to stop.

"Laney! What are you doing?"

I understood them this time, the words. Branch's voice.

Strong arms grabbed mine, sent another pulse of heat through my veins from the touch. They pulled me into someone's chest, held me there tightly, firmly. I struggled, but the arms didn't let go.

I blinked, and the world started to come back into focus again. Green and yellow leaves. Theodore's wide eyes. Branch's arms, wrapped around me. Holding me close.

I gasped, breathed in and out, as deeply as I could with Branch's arms across my shoulders.

"It was her! She destroyed the wire."

In and out, in and out.

"What? Laney, we don't know that. There's no way to know how this happened!"

He sounded frustrated, and slightly pained.

Blakely was picking herself up off the ground, her face wide and her eyes pricked with surprise. And for the first time, I think the surprise might have been real.

You underestimated me, didn't you?

Gavin and Theodore both stood, unmoving. Neither of them went to help Blakely up. Gavin's face was expressionless. And for once, Blakely said nothing.

I wasn't struggling anymore, and Branch's grip loosened. He let me go, slowly, gently, and then moved so he was in front of me and his eyes were looking into mine.

"You don't have to like her, okay? But please, just tolerate her." He paused, took a breath. His eyes were searching mine, and they were upset. Confused. "We have more important things to worry about right now."

He looked at Blakely, then back at me, ran a hand through his golden hair. "What's gotten into you, Laney?"

I was silent. I didn't know the answer to his question.

His eyes left mine, and I was cold. He stepped over to Blakely, who was crouched on the ground, watching us.

"Are you okay?" Branch held out his hand. Blakely paused, then took it. And when she was pulled to her feet, next to Branch, she clung to it for a moment longer. But Branch let go, looked at both of us, and walked out of the trees without a word.

I didn't move for a moment. And then I pushed past Blakely into the clearing and across the grass, trying not to look at the punctured cars and walls, now lying on the ground in a heap, as I walked.

But when I passed the building in the center of the grass, the one that still said Welcome to the North Pole in crooked, painted letters, my eyes turned one more time. This was the only building that was still standing. And I could just see the picture on the back wall, staring back at me with big white eyes. The face was torn through the middle, the yellow hair sliced in two and the smile a jagged Z shape, curved up, then down, like it couldn't decide if it wanted to be happy or sad. One world, cut into two.

"Laney?"

I tore my eyes away, startled by the sound. Red hair, bright green eyes. Theodore.

He looked up at me, his hands holding tightly to the straps of the pack. And then he let go, and he held one hand out to me.

"Me and you. Always."

I blinked, a flood of relief and gratitude and exhaustion filling my chest so suddenly that it made me dizzy.

What did I do to deserve a friend like this? I didn't want to think too hard, didn't want the moment to fall away in front of me, a dream.

I took it.

37

ELSEWHERE

History: Entry 20

Sometimes I think about touch. About holding hands.

They're starting to do it—starting to touch. What does it mean if someone touches your hand, holds it in theirs?

In my first week in the world above, I used to hold someone's hand. Used to clutch it, fingers laced in fingers, palm to palm. Breath to breath.

I'll hold it again someday, when the time is right and the air is dark, like the space two hands create when they come together.

And this time, I won't let go.

38

HERE

I said nothing the rest of the morning.

I didn't look at Branch or Blakely anymore. I walked in the back of the group, next to Theodore, Gavin in front of us.

I was furious at Blakely for everything she had done. And I was still angry at Branch for playing along with Blakely's little game, for helping her.

I almost couldn't remember the moment I had lunged at her—it was a blur in my mind, a picture from an album. I had lost control, different from before. And it scared me a little. Isn't that the reason the world was destroyed, why we were all here in the first place? I had never felt so many feelings before, had never been consumed by so many different thoughts and temperatures—hot and cold, fire and ice. I didn't understand it. I was overwhelmed by it. Maybe this is why people banned them.

I pushed my hair back behind my neck, my breath puncturing the air with hot bursts. We were walking quickly, and the sun was directly above us in the sky. Even the leaves seemed to fold, to decide they weren't going to give us shade today.

"Gavin, how's Dalia?" Theodore's voice came from behind me—we were on a thin path now, trees and bushes creating a thick wall on either side.

Gavin looked back and smiled, then hurried to catch up the few steps he had lost just for doing that.

"She's good." He kept his head forward as he spoke. "And I know she'd hate this hike, so it's probably good she's not here." There was a hint of laughter in his voice when he said that. Then, softer, more serious. "I miss her."

The words I had thought about Nash. I wonder if he was thinking it about me.

"You and your *lovers*." Theodore looked from Gavin to me and stuck out his tongue.

I laughed from surprise. Theodore kept going.

"Remember when you didn't even know what love was? When the thought of touching someone like that was *gross*?" He paused, and there was a glint of playfulness in his eyes. "Well, it still is to me."

Gavin laughed now too. "You'll get there, Theodore. You'll find your girl—a little redhead, the absolute love of your life."

Theodore looked at me and gagged.

A smile stretched across my cheeks. Thank goodness Theodore and Gavin were here.

Gavin slowed in front of me, and I could only guess that meant Branch was slowing too. We emptied into a small circle of space with a few large gray tree stumps in the middle. Blakely was sitting on one of them, sucking down water.

"Three-minute break." Branch stood next to her, looked at the sky, then back at us. His shirt was clinging to his chest, and I could see that it was damp with sweat. Still, his breathing was even—he was the least tired of us all.

Theodore set the pack on the ground gratefully, taking a seat on one of the other stumps. I reached down, took out a container. The water we had gotten by the amusement park before we left touched my tongue, and it was cold. I couldn't remember anything feeling better as it slid down my throat, hot and dry from the walk.

Blakely stood suddenly, pushed the water into Branch's hands. Her face was expressionless, her eyes on the trees.

I tried not to pay attention to her, didn't want a repeat of this morning to happen again. Getting back to the others was the only thing on my mind now.

"Blakely, what are you doing?" Theodore was holding my water now, his hand poised in the air in an almost-drink.

"Shh!" Blakely held out her hand and kept it in the air, her fingers fanned out, pointed to the sky. Her face suddenly turned white. And then she lunged at Branch, her expression a mix of anger and disbelief.

I stood, couldn't believe what was happening. She was attacking Branch now? My heart thudded in my chest, and in that moment, with everything happening quickly, in a blur, one thought ran through my mind—*What if she killed Branch?*

Terror filled my veins and I jumped forward, could hear myself scream, "Blakely!" as I prepared to pull her off of him.

And then he was on the ground, and she was on top of him, and both of them weren't moving.

I couldn't breathe.

"Blakely? What are you—?" Branch's voice, and he sounded angry. Relief filled my head at the sound. He was alive.

Blakely moved off Branch, pushed herself to the ground beside him. Her eyes turned forward, at a tree that was directly behind where Branch had been standing.

"Look."

I peered closely. Some sort of rock was sticking out of it, carved sharp with a pointed tip. A knife.

My blood turned cold.

Branch had turned now too, stood slowly to his feet. He stared at the knife for a moment, then gripped it with his hand, pulled it from the trunk. The wood made a slight splitting noise as he removed it. He looked back at Blakely, who was still on the ground.

I didn't move. I didn't know what happened.

Branch looked at the knife again, then around the trees, at all of us.

"I don't understand."

A tree rustled behind us, and I jumped. Turned.

Three circles were looking back at us from the trees, dirty and peach and pointed. Three faces, with gray clothes that hung loosely around their thin bodies.

They were with us! They were part of the eighty-eight.

It was a girl and boy about our age, and an older woman with orange hair, so dirty it looked brown. They were frozen, and their eyes moved to Branch, wide and so white I couldn't see their pupils. *Fear.* It was all over their faces, their expressions. They were terrified.

And they had tried to kill Branch.

They suddenly came to life, took off in the trees with such force I didn't know if I had seen them or imagined them.

"Wait!" I heard the word come from my lips, but they didn't stop. The tops of their heads disappeared in the green, and the leaves stilled, and all was quiet again.

Theodore stood slowly, his eyes like the moon. He looked at the knife, then at Branch, then at the trees. He blinked and slowly turned to the tree again, the punctured wood, the blade in Branch's hand.

"What is that?" His voice was quiet, and his chin trembled slightly.

But he knew the answer. We all knew. The knife glinted slightly from the light through the leaves—it was as if it had sliced the sun in half instead of Branch.

"They were ours," Gavin spoke, his eyes on the trees. "I recognize the woman—she helped me set up the blankets during our celebration."

The blanket-table. The memory seemed years ago, and it stabbed me in the heart.

"She must have been taken. Changed. All of them. They wouldn't leave otherwise." The words rushed out of me like water. None of us were like that. None of us would try to kill one of our own.

"Yeah." Blakely's voice pierced the air, loud and confident. She was still sitting on the ground, and she propped one hand behind her back. Raised an eyebrow. "Unless they're just terrified because they don't trust anyone. You don't see *me* trying to kill anyone."

And there it was. She finally admitted what had happened to her.

I took a step forward, my head pounding. My legs wobbled slightly, and I tried to push the thought of Branch lying on the ground, the knife in his chest, from my mind.

"What did he do to you, Blakely? *Who* was it?"

Blakely said nothing. She brushed her fingers against a few tufts of grass that were growing next to her, scraped the ground slowly, and gathered a ball of dirt in her palm. She didn't look at me, but she spoke. "That person told me to forget about them. Forget their face." She let the dirt rain from the fingers to the ground, a spray of brown dust. "So I did."

"Come on, Blakely. No one's believing that. You have to remember *something*." I was growing frustrated. If she would just tell us who it was, tell us what he did to make everyone act differently, to make them change—

"I must have forgotten when my head hit the ground this morning while I was being attacked." Her voice was high and clear, like a song.

I could feel it again—a thick, icy cold, slowly taking over my veins. She was being sarcastic. After all of this, after everything that had happened and had yet to happen because she wouldn't tell us anything, she was being *sarcastic*.

"We could change everything! We could fix it, save everyone, if you would only—"

"*Laney.*"

I stopped abruptly. Branch's voice. I looked at him, still clutching the knife in his tanned, strong hand. He looked at me, and for a moment it took the breath from my lungs.

"She saved my life."

The air grew quiet. Blakely didn't move, just breathed in and out, her eyes on Branch's. Her tangled black hair was a mess from pushing him to the ground.

Branch paused for a moment, seemed to think. He ran his fingers down the stubby brown handle of the knife, traced it lightly. Then he gripped it tightly, raised his fist, and thrust the knife down into the tree stump that Blakely had been sitting on when we first came into the clearing. The tip of the knife lodged into the wood, the rest sticking out, pointed to the sky. It was like the trunk had been diseased, and it grew a knife instead of a tree.

Theodore, Gavin, and I all watched in silence as Branch's eyes lingered on the knife for a few seconds longer, and then he turned. He looked at Blakely and held out his hand.

Blakely blinked once, surprised. She rubbed the hand that was still brown from the dirt on her pants once, then looked up again. Took it.

Branch pulled Blakely to her feet slowly, and when she was standing, she used her free hand to push her hair out of her eyes, smooth down the mess that it was.

Branch's mouth curved—just barely, but I could see it. "Here, let me help you."

Blakely's hand stopped, fell to her side. Branch lifted his hand from hers and brought both of them to her face, touched her hair, smoothed down the black strands. They were standing inches away from each other, face to face. Breath to breath. Like he had done with me, up in the sky— smoothed down my hair slowly, that crooked smile on his face.

My cheeks felt hot, and suddenly I wanted to be anywhere but there. I felt like I had been punched in the chest, the face. *Nash. Think of Nash.*

Branch's hands returned to his sides again and Blakely's face was pale, her eyes bright and round and open.

"Thank you."

Branch didn't move for a moment. "Thank *you*, B. Really. That was—that was amazing."

And then Blakely blushed, a circle of reds and pinks in her stark white cheeks.

Gavin moved, swung his pack onto his back. Thank goodness for Gavin. "We need to get going. From what we just saw, things have gotten even worse back home."

Home. I hadn't heard that word in years—had only seen it etched in my dreams, heard it in the stories that were spoken from mouth to mouth, decade to decade. Forbidden stories. And I realized I had never thought about the clearing like that, our place in the woods that we called our own—small compared to the rest of the world. It was our home. *My* home.

"Shouldn't we follow them?" Theodore looked back at the trees, at the place where we had seen the three circles of peach and orange.

"If we head back, we can find out what's going on. Where they went. We would have no idea where to start right now." Branch turned from Blakely to his pack, grabbed the straps with his fingers.

"He's right." Gavin nodded. "And they tried to kill him. So, there's that."

I swallowed, glanced at the knife again that was puncturing the trunk. I tried to push the three faces from my mind—the dirtiness, the determination, the terror. The pure, unbroken terror.

"Let's go." Branch stuck the water into his pack, zipped it, and swung it on his shoulders. "We're not stopping until we get there."

He turned and stepped into the green and brown, his feet crunching the ground as he did.

"Branch, what about the knife?" Blakely's voice, and Branch turned, still walking.

"We leave it."

That took us by surprise. What if we needed to defend ourselves? What if someone tried to kill one of us again?

Blakely shrugged and ran to catch up with Branch.

Theodore looked at me. "At least she's talking to you now."

Blakely. He was talking about Blakely. And I realized he was right—she had talked to me today, in front of the others, for the first time. She had slipped up.

I nodded slightly, then turned to Gavin. "We can't just leave this here. What if—"

"I was thinking the same thing," Gavin cut in gently. He looked once more to where the people had been standing. Our people. "But it was used to almost kill Branch. Maybe it's a reminder to him—maybe he doesn't want it near him."

"And maybe it will save someone else's life." I looked at Gavin, held his gaze. "Branch isn't in charge here."

Gavin shrugged. "We all know you do what you want, Laney." He almost smiled, just for a moment.

I walked to the knife and pressed my fingers to the handle, pulled it from the stump. Theodore was watching us, and I called him over. I slid the pack from his back, unzipped it, and dropped the knife inside. Theodore's eyes were wide.

"I'll carry it. Just so you don't have to have anything to do with this."

Theodore hesitated for a second, then nodded.

I shrugged it onto my shoulders, and the black fabric was cold against my back.

Branch wasn't thinking straight. I would never turn to violence for no reason, not in a million years—after all, this is how the world was destroyed in the first place. But if someone was coming at me with a knife in their hand—well, I would rather fight than die. If Branch didn't understand that, then he was weaker than I thought.

Love is worth the fight. It's what Lander had said, before Mr. Dabir slit his throat. What he had said before his brilliant blue eyes turned a shallow, dull gray. And if he had a knife on him when Mr. Dabir grabbed him, maybe he wouldn't be dead right now.

"You ready?" Gavin nodded toward the trees, where Branch and Blakely couldn't be seen anymore. Theodore glanced at the pack once more, then started walking in the way they had gone.

Gavin moved, and I fell into step beside him.

"She knows something, Laney. I can tell."

I looked at Gavin, surprised. "Blakely?"

He nodded. Finally, someone on my side.

"If she knows who it is, who's been taking our people, causing all of this, everything could be fixed. Just like you said. And if she won't tell us voluntarily...then, if it comes to it—" He stopped. Looked up once, at the sky. "Then we might just have to use that."

I stopped for a second. I couldn't help it. I could feel the heavy steel blade through the fabric, cold against my back.

I looked at Gavin, and he took a long, deep breath. But he was calm. Calmer than I had ever seen him.

39

ELSEWHERE

History: Entry 21

I was walking through the forest yesterday, a haze of green weeds, brown dirt, and dry leaves. Every step I took I could hear the *crunch* of a leaf breaking beneath my foot, a thousand pieces grinding into the thirsty ground.

Something, once whole, now crumbled to nothing.

A green-and-yellow life now different—changed, ugly. Dead.

Some might wonder how I do it.

I brought a knife from the Dome—snuck it in my pack before we left. In case I needed it, I remember thinking.

Now I wonder why I ever thought about it at all. I need this knife—need it like I need air.

40

HERE

I remember a few things from my time in the Dome—a hazy blur of grays and whites and blacks. Memories come back to me sometimes, slowly, in dreams. That's what those thirteen years of my life feel like: a dream.

But when we came aboveground for the first time, and then the second time with everyone, it's like we had finally surfaced from a thick, murky pool of water. Memories are like pricks of light, a breeze that dances in the flowers on a hillside, the red stain of berries on a white palm. From the moment we saw the sun, I remember everything.

For the rest of the night, when the sky turned a deep blue and the ground was a shadow, Gavin, Branch, Theodore, Blakely, and I walked in silence. And at some point, between the blues and grays, my mind filled with a memory. It was the moment we had found our clearing, the day Alese had everyone take a vote, and everyone voted *yes*—this small piece of the world, in all its green and yellow and blue splendor—would be our new place to live. Here, we would start our lives all over again.

. . .

"It's beautiful, isn't it?" Delma was sitting next to me, and Alese had just announced the news. The old woman with wrinkled hands had tears in her eyes.

I nodded. I looked around me, at the eighty-eight people including me who filled the small clearing—at the spots of gray in a field of green. I still couldn't believe it. They were here, with us, in this world. The Dome was in the past, for good. Now these people would know love—they would know everything.

I looked to my other side, at Nash. He was grinning. He took my hand and squeezed it, then dipped his head and brought his lips to my ear.

"We did it, Laney."

Four words, whispered so quietly the world couldn't hear them. But to me, they were the loudest and most beautiful words I had ever heard.

"Where do we sleep?" A voice from the crowd broke the silence.

Alese looked at me and smiled. "The trees."

There was silence, and then another voice: "What if there are things out there? Things that want to kill me? I saw something today—some sort of small brown thing, alive. I was told it was an animal. What if there are more of those?"

I turned my neck, followed the voice. It was a girl, about Theodore's age. She must not remember anything from her time before the Dome.

Alese's smile softened a little. "That was a squirrel. They won't hurt you. And the birds in the sky won't hurt you either. We have seen nothing out here that poses a danger to anyone. If we do, we'll reevaluate. But right now, there's nothing to be afraid of."

Another person shifted. "But I've never been...in a tree before. Isn't it high up? I don't know if I can do that."

Alese opened her mouth to speak, but someone else beat her to it.

"What if I step on a sharp stick? Hurt myself?"

"What if I get lost? I never needed to pay attention to where I was going in the Dome, because we all walked together. Are you saying we're not going to do that anymore?"

And then the first girl again: "What if I die?"

Alese held up her hands, seemed at a loss for words. Her eyes swept the crowd, but she didn't know what to say.

Nash shifted next to me. He released his hand from mine, the cold air brushing against my fingers suddenly, and stood. He walked next to Alese and smiled at her—I remember feeling weak inside when he did. He made everyone feel like the most amazing person in the world, lit up the sky with that smile—and yet he chose me.

"Let's take a poll." Nash's voice sounded strong in the air that was slowly turning from blue to black, day to night. "What are your greatest fears?"

The air was still—everyone was still. His question took us all by surprise. I gathered my hair in a ball and pushed it behind my back.

Then, slowly, the first girl that had spoken stood. She had red hair that ran in tangles of curls down her back. Her face looked young, younger than she must be. But her eyes looked like they held years of wisdom.

Nash nodded. "Emily, right?"

The girl blushed, and I immediately wondered how Nash knew her name. I liked him even more in that moment. Details. He always cared about the details.

The girl tucked her hair behind her ear. "Um—animals. Wild things that I can't predict."

Nash nodded again. "Anyone else?"

Someone coughed. "Being high up, with nothing to catch me."

Nash narrowed his eyes, looked into the sea of gray, and spotted the person that had spoken. "Ms. Geena. Thank you. We'll take one more."

I heard an insect in the distance, chirping low tones that swept through my skin and made me shiver. And then I saw someone else stand. Her body was in shadow, and her voice was a tremble—quiet, small.

"Death."

No one else coughed, no one shifted. The air was stiller than I had ever seen it.

Nash didn't move. He just watched, with confidence in his eyes.

"Animals. Heights. Death."

His words seemed to hover in the air for a moment before they vanished. He held up three fingers and brought each one of them down as he spoke. "One: the men with black eyes were worse than animals, and you survived them. Two: you just climbed hundreds of stairs to get here, and I didn't see any of you hesitate. You're higher than you have ever been. And three—" He stopped. Looked back at the girl in the shadow. "Every day that you're out here is a day you conquered death. That gray—the motionless, feelingless, loveless people that we were for so long—that was death. And I can promise you nothing will be worse than that."

I remember the sun dipped behind the clouds when he said that last sentence. The light was gone, the air a milky blue that made his face seem a little darker, a little rougher.

And someone behind me let out a cheer.

I smiled, my eyes still on Nash, and he winked at me. I saw the girl that was in shadow sit down, the one who had said death was her greatest fear, and her face wasn't in shadow anymore. It was Blakely.

"We have nothing to fear." Nash held up his hands, palms outstretched. "We've already conquered it all."

. . .

"I can see the clearing!" Branch's voice jolted me from the memory, from my thoughts.

We had been walking for hours, days, for all I knew. The sky was black, slowly turning a watery gray with yellowed edges. And he was right. I saw a space in the thick wall of trees, a hole that didn't fit.

Theodore looked back from where he had been walking in front of me and grinned. The smile lit up his eyes. "We're home!"

When I pushed back the heavy branches in front of me, I saw Branch, Blakely, Theodore, and Gavin standing on the side of the clearing. And I saw nothing else. The clearing was empty.

Theodore pushed his hands into his pockets. "Where is everyone? Nash! Alese!" His voice was loud against the air. "Delma!"

Something moved out of the corner of my eye, and I turned to the bottom of the clearing, my heart pounding in my chest.

"Gavin!" The word rushed from my mouth and the boy next to me raised his hands, bracing for whatever was there.

The figure at the bottom of the clearing was moving slowly, twisting and swaying with the wind. It was a single person, I could see that now, and it was like that person didn't even notice us. Gavin lowered his hands, and Branch's voice was soft, a single note.

"It's Erika."

My feet moved down the slope, closer to the gray figure, and I stopped when I was a dozen feet away. The space around her was empty, silent. It *was* Erika, though she looked slightly different. She turned in circles, clumsily, her arms and hair swaying around her like water. And for a moment, I wondered if all the bones in her body had been replaced with the limbs of trees.

Her eyes were on the ground, the air, the sun that was slowly melting up into the sky—anything and everything but us. She seemed to be listening to something, some sort of silent song that was coming from around her. A chill swept up my neck.

"Erika." I heard a voice behind me, saw Branch step to my side.

She stopped abruptly, but she wasn't surprised. Her eyes looked amused when she saw us, like she had known we were there all along. There was something else though—a glint of wild, a speck of something not quite right in her head. I didn't step forward anymore, felt the comfort of Gavin and Theodore at my back.

Erika's head turned sharply, suddenly, toward us. Her body stayed facing the other direction. She looked like a doll that had its head put on backward.

"Where is everyone?" Branch's eyes were on her, and his voice was gentle. But I could tell he was a little taken aback.

Erika looked at us for a moment, and then a smile spread across her face. "Gone."

An ice-cold finger stroked my heart.

"What do you mean, 'gone'?" Branch never took his eyes off her. "Where did they go?"

Erika shrugged, then giggled, like we were playing a game. Like this was all a joke.

Gavin stepped forward. "Erika, if you know where they all went, you need to tell us. Now."

Erika's face fell slightly. Gavin's voice was stern, with no give. Then the trees behind her moved, and a person appeared. He was laughing.

"I found you! Erika, I've been looking for hours. You were supposed to make it a little bit easy—" The man, Erika's age, stopped suddenly when he saw us. Erika didn't even look at him. Her eyes were on us.

And then she lifted her arm, pointed to the trees in front of her. And now, in the light, I could see that her fingertips were stained with something red. Red, like berries. Or blood.

"What's on your hands?" The question rushed past my lips.

Branch didn't move. I could hear a small breath burst from Theodore's mouth.

Erika's mouth curved slowly, and she lowered her arm. Then she walked to the man who had come from the trees, put her hands on his face, and kissed him. After a moment, she moved back.

His cheeks were stained red, and he smiled.

41

ELSEWHERE

History: Entry 22

There were four more today. Four.

They all had gray eyes, and gray hearts, and I knew they would be simple.

It's chaos now. My chaos.

It will always be my chaos.

There's not much time left. So, I make time. I twist the secondhand on the clock, pinch the seconds in my fingers, stretch the minutes like they're made from the sap in the trees.

I have time. The more I twist, the harder I pinch, the longer I stretch—I will have time.

42

HERE

When I stepped from the Dome into the world for the very first time, I remember the world was terrifying.

It was huge, and bright, and colorful—all things foreign to me, things I had been taught were dangerous, that I should stay away from at all costs. It was beautiful.

And to me, beautiful was terrifying.

But here, today, staring at Erika and her red-stained hands and hollow eyes and limp bones, terrifying had a whole new meaning. I never thought the world would give me a reason to want to run, hard and fast, and never look back.

Branch was still staring at her—at the laughter in her eyes and the red cheeks of the boy next to her. They were like the tiny figurines in the black box Theodore had found in the house in the woods—twisting and turning, but with terrifying grins instead of painted-on smiles. They didn't belong.

"Forget her." Gavin's voice was low, so Erika couldn't hear. "Let's go find the others."

I was surprised how quickly everyone followed him, silent feet padding on the yellow-green grass that led to the forest. We all wanted to get away.

We heard nothing as we walked through the trees to the water. That's where Erika had pointed—a little to the left of the water, but to the water all the same. It was just a short walk; we would be there soon.

"That woman needs help," I found myself saying as we pushed through the green, and my words hit the air like stones. "Something's not right with her mind."

"Oh, come on, Laney." Blakely pushed aside a leaf with her forearm. "She's just having a little fun." She looked back for a moment, cocked her head. "But then again, you and *fun* have never been used in a sentence together. You probably have no idea what I'm talking about."

My blood got hot. "This coming from the person who cut apart the wire at the amusement park. You *destroyed* some of the only fun I've ever had."

Blakely whipped back her head, obviously offended.

Gavin touched my shoulder. "She's not worth it."

I took a deep breath. He was right.

Blakely opened her mouth to respond, but something beat her to it. Something pounded the air, soft at first but then louder. Footsteps. Someone was running—and they were coming right at us.

The knife flashed in my head, and I swiped at my backpack blindly.

A body burst through the trees.

I saw a flash of blond hair, tanned skin, deep brown eyes before I was swept up into someone's arms. My head was pounding, and my heart felt like it was falling. *Nash.* It was Nash.

I wrapped my arms around his neck, breathed in his scent—wood, fresh grass, gray stone. There, in his arms again, I felt safe. I had never felt so safe.

Nash pulled away, his hands still gripping tightly to mine. His eyes were sparkling—dark brown, like the sky right after sunset before it turns black, when the stars are just starting to come out. *With the brightest star shining for me.*

"Dalia said she saw people—I thought, had hoped, it might be you." His chest was rising and falling quickly, his breaths short. "Are you okay? What happened out there?"

Out there. I swallowed, but suddenly my throat felt dry. The fake kiss, the ride in the sky, the almost-real kiss. Everything suddenly seemed ridiculous, and a hot flash of shame filled my stomach. *Embarrassment*, was that what this was called? It was the second time I had felt this way—felt this feeling. There we were, having fun and exploring the world, while they were all here. Terrified. Afraid for their lives.

"Someone tried to kill Branch." Gavin stepped in, and Nash's eyes turned to him. And I could see now—the sparkle, the brightness I had thought I'd seen, was tiredness. I could only imagine what he'd been through while I was gone. What *had* he been through?

Nash seemed at a loss for words for a moment. But he didn't seem surprised. And that scared me more than anything else.

"Come on." His eyes swept across the group slowly, tiredly, lingering for a second longer on Blakely. "We need to stop Arsen."

Nash released one of my hands, but held the other firmly.

"What is he doing?" I looked at Nash again, fear turning my blood cold. He just looked back at me.

Branch moved first, and I saw his eyes look a second too long at my hand in Nash's before he pushed through the branches and out to the water. My cheeks felt hot.

My feet felt like they were someone else's as I followed—mechanical, a leaf moved by the wind. And when I was suddenly in open air, the water to my left and a large stretch of sand to my right, they didn't move anymore. This wasn't our water—our pool of blue, bordered by browns and yellows and greens. No, this was something else.

A large fire crackled and groaned in the middle of the sand, filled with scorched wood and red, burning rocks, like eyes. It stretched from the trees to the water—four times the size of the fires we always made at night, at Collaboration. The water was churning, blue and black twisted together, and at the edge, a dozen feet from the fire, was some sort of hole—a pit—dug deep into the sand and rocks. The edges were the only thing I could see, and I couldn't tell how deep it was. But that wasn't what made it so different, so unlike our world before.

I blinked.

People. *Our* people, sitting at the far end of the water in three rows, like this was some kind of game. They were unmoving. They all sat next to each other, completely still, their legs crossed in the dry sand. Their eyes wide and frozen, like they had always been in the Dome, but so much more—horrified. Like they had seen something they would never forget.

Arsen was standing in front of the two groups, his hands on his hips, paused like he was in thought. And on him—I blinked in disbelief—draped across his shoulders, like a heavy coat, was the brown, furry skin of an animal. It was a bearskin. And it was the same color as the bear I had seen.

Nash's hand was still in mine, and I felt his eyes on me.

"What is this?" Branch whirled around to Nash. Next to him, Blakely looked intrigued. It made me like her even less, if that were possible.

I looked at Nash, and his eyes were still on mine. "Laney, someone found that bearskin in the trees a few days ago. It looks like your bear scare...well, it might not have been a bear after all."

A joke. Is that what he was saying it was? Some sort of sick joke where someone pretended to be a bear and tried to scare me? I couldn't find the words to respond.

"Nash, what's going on?" Theodore now. I looked over at the boy—small, wide-eyed, confused. His words were soft, but everyone was looking at Nash now, ready to listen.

Nash didn't speak for a moment. His eyes didn't move. "Apparently, Arsen's been setting up for something all morning. You guys arrived just before—well, right when he's about to start."

"You didn't stop him?" Gavin stepped forward.

"I've been with Alese and Dalia all morning. We thought he was just building something, thought it was just Arsen being Arsen—except a little crazier, because of what happened to Brooke. Then he brought the people here, and that's when I realized it might be serious. They won't leave, though." He paused, breathed in. His voice sounded desperate. "I need your help. This can't be good—for anyone. Help me stop it."

Branch breathed out sharply, like he was about to say something. Then he turned around and took off on the sand, jogging over to Arsen. Blakely, Gavin, and Theodore followed.

Nash didn't move, and I hesitated for a moment, then squeezed his hand. He looked down in surprise. I tried to smile.

"We all know how impossible it is to change Arsen's mind about something." I looked at him again, at the boy with eyes as light as the bear skin. "At least we got here before he...destroyed something."

"Or someone." When the words came from Nash's mouth, without hesitation, they caught me off guard. Then his eyes snapped back to mine again, softened.

"Are you okay, though? It seems like you were gone for months." His sandy blond hair, like the wildflowers, ruffled slightly in the breeze. I felt my heart squeeze in my chest.

"I'm fine. I just wish we wouldn't have left." I looked back at the people, sitting in three straight rows. The flames of the fire barreled into the sky, and from the direction we were at, it almost looked like the people were *in* the fire. I shook my head at the thought.

"Me too. I missed you." Nash squeezed my hand back, bent down slightly, and kissed me on the cheek. His lips were soft, and I felt suddenly dizzy. I wanted to say them back, wanted to voice the words I had been thinking since I had been gone, in the trees. But for some reason, they didn't come. I heard voices in the distance. Branch had reached Arsen.

"We should hear this." I tightened my hand around Nash's and pulled him with me across the sand.

I heard a sound as we passed the large hole that was dug into the ground by the water. At first, I thought it was just the water lapping against the sides, reaching to the edges. But then it grew louder, unmistakable—a soft, low hissing sound. I slowed to a walk, stepped to the side and peered in.

Snakes.

The hole was filled with four or five snakes, that I could see, slithering in the shallow water, trying to climb out the sides. Arsen had a pit of *snakes*? I tried to stop my hands from shaking. This was much, much worse than I thought. I had never seen a snake before, had only heard about them in our studies. But everything I had heard about them was bad. Snakes could kill.

When we reached Branch, Arsen, Theodore, Gavin, and Blakely, the world wasn't quiet anymore. Arsen was speaking, his words moving fast, like the water. And I could see it plainly in his eyes: fear.

"He changed four more last night. *Four.* Brooke came back with them. I saw them, this morning, in the middle of the clearing, sitting there in silence like nothing had even happened. Like Blakely." Arsen paused for a moment, but Blakely didn't say anything. His eyes hardened, his face twisted slightly in pain. "And then she looked at me, in the eyes, turned to the guy sitting next to her, and kissed him. I don't even know who he was, but *Brooke kissed another guy.*"

Branch blinked. Blakely reached for his hand, and he let her take it. I forced my eyes back to Arsen. I knew Arsen had gotten close with the girl, but I didn't know he was that close.

Gavin breathed out. "So what does this have to do with—"

"And then Brooke stood, her eyes still on mine, and said they're leaving. That they don't need us anymore. And they left." He didn't move, didn't breathe. "So I'm weeding them out. I'm going to find the guy who changed her, whoever it was, and have him change her back. That isn't Brooke. I know it's not—" His voice broke, but he quickly regained his composure.

"I still don't understand how *this* is going to help with that." Nash gestured to the fire, the pit, the people. "You're going a little overboard, you know that?"

"I'm not!" Arsen shouted the words, and his chest was moving quickly, in and out, in and out. "The imposter, he has to be among us still, plotting his next victim. And only someone as sick and twisted as him would be able to get through something like this."

Nash's hand tightened in mine, and his face looked pained. It was whiter than when I first saw him.

I spoke for the first time. "What do you mean, *get through something like this?*"

Arsen's eyes brightened, and for a second, he looked honest. Genuine. Like he was honestly, truly trying to help.

"It's a challenge. A game. If a person can walk through the fire, climb from one side of the pit to the other, and then climb that tree, the one over there, with no branches"— Arsen pointed to his left, and I saw a tall, thin tree sticking out of the ground, like a horn—"get the blanket, and bring it to me, they're our guy—the imposter. He's taking people, every night. Doing who knows what kind of sick and twisted things to them. This shouldn't even phase him."

I hadn't noticed it, but there it was. There was a blanket attached to the top of the tree—tangled against it, the top of the tree poking through the corner of the fabric like a knife. The wind must have blown it there during the storm.

Branch crossed his arms, nodded at the people. "Why would they even do this? This"—he gestured around him—"is insane."

Arsen's mouth curved slightly at the edge, and his face flushed. With pride?

"They think that if they win, if they complete the game, they get to be in charge. Of everyone. They're the new leader."

Branch opened his mouth in disbelief. "You're lying to them."

Arsen shrugged. "Everything's chaos now that they know the imposter lives among us. Everyone has different ideas of how things should be run."

Nash stepped forward. "This is ridiculous."

Arsen shook his head and smiled, a full smile this time, one that reached his eyes. "It's brilliant. Because of the little poll you took, Nash, I'm playing on their greatest fears."

"Arsen!" A voice came from our left, in the trees. I turned immediately to the sound and saw two girls emerge—one with blond hair, one with brown. Dalia and Alese.

Alese looked thin, her skin as pale as the bits of foam on the water. She was leaning on Dalia as she walked, using her as a crutch. One of her legs wasn't touching the ground.

Still, relief rushed through me at the sight of them—my friends, safe. When they reached us, I gave both of them a quick hug. Theodore ran over too, wrapped his arms around Alese's neck. Alese smiled, but her eyes were sad.

"I'm so glad you stayed safe." She put her hands on my and Theodore's shoulders, squeezed them.

I nodded. "Alese, what happened? We heard you were hurt, or sick—"

"Hurt." Alese's eyes creased at the edges. "It's my leg. Someone—someone pushed me in the water. I didn't see who."

Theodore looked crushed, said, "Wait here!" and then took off into the trees. Before I could answer, Dalia was speaking to Arsen.

"*What* do you think you're doing?" She looked around with large eyes, but her voice just sounded annoyed. "Bring the people back to the clearing. Now."

As she was speaking, Dalia sidestepped over to Gavin and gave him a hug. It was the first time I had seen him smile all day.

"I can't do that, Dalia." Arsen's voice was quiet now, calm. "Time is running out. We need to find out who the guy is, the one who doesn't belong."

Alese was leaning on my shoulder now, and she stood up straighter.

"Dalia's right, Arsen. This isn't going to help anything. Please, clean this mess up. I'll take them back myself."

Arsen frowned and moved to his left, angled himself so he stood between the people and us. It reminded me of me, so long ago in the Dome, standing between Theodore and Arsen. Except this time, Arsen wasn't trying to save them— was he?

"Please, just trust me. Do you have any better ideas?" Arsen's voice was soft now. He was pleading to Alese— pleading to us.

The words he had said before Alese and Dalia appeared out of the tree replayed in my mind. *I'm playing on their greatest fears.* And suddenly, it all made sense. Animals. Pain. Death. Each of the three obstacles he had added to the game represented one of the three greatest fears of our people— the fears Nash had pointed out that very first day in the clearing. Blakely had said death was her greatest fear, but she had jumped in front of Branch—in front of a *knife*—like it was nothing. She wasn't scared anymore.

Maybe the changed didn't have any fear.

"Wait." Everyone looked at me. I could still see our people a few dozen feet away, sitting cross-legged, their eyes staring forward. I swallowed. Licked my dry lips. But I couldn't say it here, not in front of Blakely.

I pulled Alese from the group, to a tree a few feet away. Dalia followed.

I wrung my hands out in front of me, tried to make sense of it all.

"I remember when Nash was asking everyone's fears, Blakely said death. And today, in the trees, she jumped in front of a boy who was about to be hit by a knife without hesitation—without a second thought. Maybe changing her made her get over her fear somehow. Maybe somehow, whatever the imposter is doing to them…it's making them not afraid anymore."

Dalia crossed her arms. "And how exactly is that a bad thing? Maybe we need less fear around here. It would help us survive—get rid of this chaos."

I shook my head. "Not like this."

I thought of Blakely, of the way her eyes changed when she was slicing the squirrel's throat. She was smiling. Humming, even.

"The people with black eyes weren't afraid of many things, and look where that left us. If someone's not afraid of *anything*…well, they won't be afraid to hurt. To lie. To kill."

"But these people…these people don't have black eyes, Laney." Alese's words were quiet, and she looked tired.

And she was right. They were different somehow. Lived too fiercely. Laughed too openly. Loved too hard. Smiled when they killed. Everything about them was a little too much, a little overdone. And because of it, our world—the order, the knowledge, the peace, and piecing this life back together—was falling apart. Who could have known that once we defeated the people with black eyes, there would be another enemy?

Alese shifted, looked at Arsen, then back at me. "What if they get hurt, Laney? I could never forgive myself."

"*Our* people won't. They're terrified. They're afraid, and Arsen made sure these challenges were their greatest fears. And because of it, they would never even try to complete something like this. Arsen's right." I sucked in a breath, couldn't believe I was saying the words. "Only the imposter would be able to win this game, because he doesn't have fear. And maybe we need to find out who it is, before things get even worse."

Dalia said nothing. She was looking at Alese. The girl with long brown hair and soft eyes didn't move for a moment. Suddenly Theodore burst from the trees, carrying the large stick he had used as support when his leg was hurt. He spotted Alese and ran over to us, held it out to her.

"Here." He was breathing hard, like he had run a long way. "This will help you."

Alese looked surprised, and she smiled. Took it. "Thank you, Theodore."

Theodore smiled back. "Of course." And then he saw us, saw the silence on our faces. "What's going on?"

Alese took her arm from Dalia's and leaned all her weight on the heavy stick. Then, without another word, she moved back toward the group. They had been watching us. Arsen's eyes had been on me the entire time I spoke to them.

I could hear the water hit the sand like a palm slapping against a tree.

Alese looked up, at Arsen, at the others. She nodded.

Arsen let out a breath he had been holding the entire time. He grinned. "Let's get the guy."

43

ELSEWHERE

History: Entry 23

This has always been a game. A race to the finish line.

I get rid of the other racers as I run, pulling and slicing and then getting back up, running again.

Soon it will be just me, and I won't even have to reach the finish line to win.

That's the difference between me and them—they race to save each other.

I race to save myself.

44

HERE

Alfred was the first to go—the first to compete in Arsen's game. He didn't even look at us as he passed, walked slowly across the sand to the fire. Arsen had filled a pail with water and threw it on the fire just a moment before, extinguishing the flames but making sure the coals were still excruciatingly hot. Branch had insisted—had said no one could survive walking across a raging fire. Nash had tried to stop it again, had tried to reason with Alese. He didn't understand—I would have to explain it to him later.

I broke from the group while Alfred walked, and I ran across the sand to the three lines, in the middle, on the very end: Delma. I gave her a hug. She smiled, but the smile didn't reach her eyes.

"Laney...what is this? You're really having us compete against each other, for a new leader?"

She looked confused, hurt, and I wanted to explain everything to her. But the people surrounding her—they were still staring forward, motionless, like they did so long ago every day in the Dome. I wasn't sure if they were listening, but they could hear everything.

I leaned in, my lips almost touching Delma's ear. "Don't go through with it. Quit before the first obstacle. Trust me."

I knew the imposter wasn't Delma, and I had to make sure she was safe. She should be with us, not in this group of glassy-eyed people.

Delma looked at me once more, and her eyes searched my face.

"Laney! No conversing. Your turn will come." Arsen. He shouted at me from his place next to Alfred. I squeezed Delma's shoulder, then jogged over to Nash again, took his hand in mine. This had to work. It had to.

"Are you guys serious? This is crazy. It will never work." Branch looked at Alese, then me. I didn't look back.

"Ready?" Arsen's voice pounded the air. He was filled with energy again, like he had a whole world to take down and no one to stop him.

Alfred didn't move, didn't even look at him.

"Go!"

The old man with gray hair stepped slowly to the coals and stood at the edge. He thought for a moment, looked into the black smoke and the spotted red glow at the bottom. Then he took a step back and shook his head.

"I'm not doing this."

"No need for words." Arsen checked off an imaginary list. "Just go sit over there, in the square beside the others."

Alfred looked at Arsen for a long moment. Then he walked back the way he had come and stopped in a large square shape that had been drawn into the sand right next to the three rows of people. A box for the people who give up. Or the people who fail.

"Next." Arsen motioned to Delma, and she stood. She did the same thing, did what I had told her to do. And when she walked to the square and sat next to Alfred, I breathed a sigh of relief. The person after Delma didn't try either, or the person after that. This was working, so far.

The girl who stood after Delma was Emily, the little red-head that had said animals were her greatest fear. When she stepped closer and took her place next to Arsen, her eyes were determined.

"We need a new plan." She looked at Arsen, her eyes like stone. "This whole you-as-leader-thing isn't working."

Arsen blinked, and I could tell she took him by surprise. "Well, now's your chance to change it."

Emily nodded and turned her head forward.

Amusement filled Arsen's eyes. He knew that she would never really be the leader, that this was all to weed out the imposter, but she would never know that. And he looked proud of that fact. I turned my eyes from him, focused on Emily.

"Go!"

She was sprinting before the word had even left Arsen's tongue.

When Emily reached the fire, she came to an abrupt stop. It was as though she hadn't thought about how long it was, how hot the rocks might be. She looked up, and her eyes met mine. Her face scrunched, as if bracing for something, and then she moved forward, quickly, without thought. *She was doing it.* She was walking across the coals.

When Emily reached the halfway point, she started screaming. The sound filled the air and shook the leaves, and my head started pounding. Nash gripped my hand so tightly it almost hurt.

"Stop her!" Alese's voice rose up against the sound of the screaming. "Arsen, we're not doing this anymore! We're done."

"Finally," I heard Nash say.

Arsen's voice snapped back in a loud whisper, "What if she's the imposter? We can't stop this, Alese. Would you rather have one person get hurt, or dozens taken and made crazy?"

Alese swallowed, looked at Emily. There were tears in her eyes.

I looked over at Theodore. He was sitting next to Delma, his eyes closed and his hands pressed tightly over his ears. He didn't want to see it—didn't want to be a part of any of it. And I didn't blame him.

Emily reached the end of the coals and collapsed on the cold sand. She was breathing deeply, her shirt drenched in sweat, and she cradled her feet in her hands. And when she turned slightly, the bottoms of her feet facing us, I sucked in my breath. They were black, and they looked shiny, like the glint of the sun on the water.

"Do you give up?" Arsen watched her with narrowed eyes.

Emily slowly raised her head, and her eyes locked on his. "Never."

"Okay, well, I'm sure you'll love this next one." Arsen sounded casual, and he walked over to the pit of snakes.

Emily's mouth twisted in a grimace, but she planted her hands and knees on the ground and crawled to Arsen's side. Her face wrenched in pain. She didn't know what was in there. I immediately wanted to stop her, wanted to pull her away before she even saw it.

But she did. Her eyes froze and her face was gray. She looked at Arsen, then back at the pit.

"Where did you get those?" Her voice trembled.

"Not important, Emily." Arsen looked pleased with himself. "The important thing is you getting in."

Emily didn't respond. She just stared at them, and it took everything in me not to stop her, tell her she didn't have to do this.

She closed her eyes. Seconds passed. And then she opened them, sat on the edge, and slid into the pit.

"I can't believe she did that." Nash let go of my hand and hurried to the edge of the pit, and I followed.

Emily was at the bottom of the hole on her hands and knees, completely still. She wasn't even breathing, for what I could tell. The snakes were on the other side, and they slithered back and forth slowly, not even noticing her. Maybe they weren't so bad after all—I hoped.

There was silence, and then Emily, in barely a whisper— "What do I need to do?"

Arsen laughed, then pointed one finger at the opposite end where the snakes were tangled up with each other. "Just get to the other end. Climb out."

Emily's eyes looked like they were going to pop, like the red and blue berries we had found in the forest. She closed her eyes again. And when she opened them, she moved. It was very subtle, very slow. But to the snakes, it was a change in the atmosphere in their hole. An unknown. A threat.

To the snakes, it was everything.

Multiple *hiss* sounds pricked the air like the sizzling of a large fire. A large brown snake with shiny skin slithered straight to her, and another yellow-and-green snake lunged forward, its mouth open with four white teeth, sharp, like knives.

"Get me out!" Emily fell backward, pushed herself to the edge with her hands and feet. "Get me out!"

Arsen stood there. "Say you're afraid."

Emily was shrieking now, and she pressed herself into the side of the hole, dirt crumbling onto her hair, her face.

"Arsen!" Branch rushed to the side of the pit.

I couldn't believe what I was seeing. I stepped next to Branch and fell to my knees, reached my hand down into the hole. Emily grabbed it, clung to it. Branch grabbed her other hand and together we pulled hard, until she was lying on the sand next to us. I looked back in the pit. The snakes were at the edge now, throwing themselves at the side and trying to reach the top.

"I'm afraid, I'm afraid. I'm done." Emily was sobbing, her arms and legs trembling, her feet still black.

Arsen crossed his arms. "Next!"

Branch looked at him, his hand on Emily's shoulder. "You can't be serious."

Arsen rolled his eyes, turned to me. "This was your idea, Laney. Explain it to him, please?"

Emily turned over, looked at me in surprise. "This was— this was your idea?"

Blood rushed to my head, and the words tumbled out. "No. Well, not exactly. I never thought—"

"Never thought what?" Emily looked at me, and she didn't blink, didn't break her gaze.

I didn't know what to say. Maybe this was all a mistake.

Emily nodded. "I'm done here."

"Emily, wait—"

The girl with curly red hair, now dusted in dirt, stood. She walked slowly and I could tell every step hurt—every move forward had her wincing in pain, tears in her eyes, but she didn't stop. She disappeared into the trees, and I saw Theodore run after her.

Branch shook his head and stood, the sparkle from his eyes gone.

Nash was next to me suddenly, looking at me with those soft brown eyes. "It's not your fault. We never should have done this."

I tried to nod.

"I *said* next!"

The people in the group were like statues now, even more so. They were frozen in time, a group of loveless people who had learned to love, and then lost it all over again. Rows of gray in a green world.

"I did it!" Someone shouted behind us, and I whirled around.

Branch turned too. "Oh my—"

"What are you doing? That's the *last* obstacle!" Arsen's face turned red, hot.

I just stared.

Someone had climbed the tree. Arsen's tree, as tall as the sky with no branches. It was a boy, my age. He looked thin, with the bottoms of his gray pants rolled up to his shins. He wasn't wearing a shirt, and his bare chest caught me off guard.

"I got the prize! I'm the leader now!" The boy with blond hair that touched his shoulders held the blanket in his hand. His legs were wrapped around the tree, and the top looked like it was swaying—like the wind was moving it back and forth.

"No, you're not the leader! Get down from there." Arsen was frustrated, and everyone was watching now. All three rows had heads pointed at the boy clutching the blanket at the top of the tree.

"Please climb down! We'll figure it out down here," Alese pleaded with the boy, and I could tell the game was going to be over after this. It had all gone very wrong.

The boy shook his head and grinned, raising the blanket in the sky like a flag. "Not until you say it!" He took his other hand off the tree and raised it toward the sky too, in victory. "I'm—"

The tree groaned, and he sucked in the end of his sentence, his eyes wide. His leg slipped, and he threw his hands down, tried to grab the tree again, but he was too late. I tried to close my eyes as he fell, tried to look away when his body hit the ground and his head bounced twice before it settled on the sand. But I couldn't.

"I think what he was about to say was—dead." Arsen's eyes settled on the boy one more time before he turned, started throwing sand on the pit of snakes. "I was wrong. This will never work. Why? Because these people are idiots."

No one else said anything. Everyone just stared—the group of us and the three lines of people on the white sand. Arsen threw handful after handful into the pit, piling grains on the slithering animals, and the only sound we could hear was the gentle *splat* of the handfuls of sand breaking against the growing pile.

We were the snakes. And we were slowly drowning.

45

ELSEWHERE

History: Entry 24

If there's one thing I've learned about this world above, it's that it's predictable and unpredictable, all at once.

46

HERE

We buried the boy a few feet from where he fell, between the trees.

It was a silent event, and this time the silence didn't seem strange. The three rows sat still, cross-legged, and didn't move from their spots. Only their eyes moved as they watched us dig with pieces of wood we found, curved and rough, like cups, and then place the boy in the hole.

He was smaller than he had looked when we were below and he was above, waving the blanket in the air like he had just won. Victorious. It made me sad to think that very well might have been the only time in his life he felt like he had accomplished something—the only time he had felt happy— and then he fell to his death. Happiness can be gone in the blink of an eye. We needed to hold on to it.

No one even knew his name—so to us, he was nameless. The boy who had appeared for a brief moment, only to disappear soon after. One of the three greatest fears come true right before our eyes. Right before their eyes.

I wished I had never told Alese to do this.

Theodore and Emily emerged from the tree line soon after the boy fell. Emily stood there, her arms crossed, her red hair blowing in the cold air. Theodore placed the blanket on top of the boy before we covered him with dirt.

"So he can keep it with him. His victory."

I blinked as the boy with red hair smiled after his words, then backed away, step-by-step, as if walking away from all of this would mean it never happened. But it had. Mallory had died, and Lander, and the boy Erika found, and now him.

I couldn't explain this feeling, this deep lump rising up inside of me. I didn't know how humans dealt with this in the past—it was always one of the strongest feelings I felt. Bottomless, fresh, unbearable. Like a dull knife was striking me, again and again, never breaking through but making raw black circles on my skin.

"This is your fault, you know." Gavin spoke, and I hadn't realized he was next to me. I looked over, felt the knife strike again, but his eyes were on Blakely. She blinked.

"*My* fault? You can't be serious." Blakely looked at me, expecting me to defend her, to blame it on myself. But I was silent.

The air was cool, the sun softening at the edges and becoming a deep red. It would be night soon.

"You're the only one here who was taken that hasn't disappeared into the woods somewhere afterward, and you won't tell us anything. If you had told us who it was, none of this would have ever happened." Gavin was speaking softly so the three rows wouldn't notice, but I could hear the anger in his voice. "*Why* are you here, Blakely? If you're not going to help us, just leave."

Blakely's face whitened, just barely. She looked like she had been slapped. "I told you, I don't *remember*. There's nothing for me to tell!"

"You're lying." Gavin's expression didn't change, his eyes didn't move. "Someone took you against your own will, you were with him for an entire night, and he did something to you—something that changed who you are. There's no way you forget about that."

Branch stepped forward, careful not to put a footprint on the boy's fresh grave. "Gavin, let it go. She doesn't remember."

"So you're on the side of the crazy girl. This is great."

"Guys." Alese pushed herself farther up her stick. "Now isn't the time, okay?"

"So when is the time?" Gavin's voice softened when he turned to the girl with brown hair. "Alese, I respect you and consider you a friend, but this is all going to hell. And it's just going to get worse the longer we sit here and wait."

Alese opened her mouth, then closed it.

"He's right," Nash said, and squeezed my hand.

I heard footsteps come up behind us and saw Arsen, his hands stained from covering the snakes with sand and dirt. He had buried the snakes instead of the boy.

Gavin nodded and dropped his piece of wood on the ground, crossed his arms. "So, what do you want, Blakely? How do we get you to talk?"

Blakely crossed her arms too. "This is so ridiculous."

"I have an idea." Arsen's eyes were bright—too bright after what had just happened. His cheeks were flushed with excitement. I realized, too late, that his hand was behind his back. "You tell us where Brooke is, or..." He brought his hand forward, and I felt dizzy. His fingers clutched the knife—stubby brown handle, silver blade—that the three in the trees had used to try and kill Branch. *My* knife. The one that was in my backpack.

Alese gasped. "Where did you get that?"

Arsen smiled. "The correct question is, *who* did I get it from?" He looked at me, and I felt like burying myself in the sand, next to the boy. This wasn't happening. How did he get the knife? I swallowed as a sickening feeling washed over me. My pack—I had thrown it off by the pit of snakes when I was helping Emily get out.

Branch's eyes widened, and Blakely should have looked scared, but she didn't.

"Nice. The knife that someone used to try to kill Branch, that Branch specifically said not to touch. To leave in the woods. I wonder who did exactly the opposite?" Her voice was singsongy, and it made me feel even worse.

"I can't believe you brought that." Branch looked at Gavin, and his eyebrows creased. Gavin said nothing.

"We're not using a knife," Alese jumped in, and she sounded worried. Dalia was holding tightly to Gavin's hand, silent.

Nash was staring at the knife. "Arsen, we can't use that. It would turn us into one of them. Everything we've worked for, everything we've accomplished, gone."

"If we have to become them to beat them—" He lunged at Blakely suddenly, the knife pointed toward her chest. Nash jumped forward and grabbed him by the arms, and Branch stepped in front of her. All this, and the boy's grave was right next to us.

Arsen laughed. "Scared?"

Blakely narrowed her eyes. "Never."

"Arsen!" My voice came out surprisingly strong, and he stopped. Looked back at me.

"Oh, I'm sorry, Laney. You probably want a turn, right? Since this is *your* knife."

The words dropped like lead, and the air went silent. And then Branch looked at me, in the eyes, and held my gaze for the first time since our ride in the trees.

"Tell me that's not true."

I wanted to say it wasn't, wanted to assure him that I would never do something like that. But I couldn't. And when the seconds passed with no answer, I could see the hurt in his eyes.

"It was for protection…" I managed to squeeze out.

"You call this protection? Look what you did, Laney!" His words were sharp, and I couldn't respond. He was right.

Blakely looked from me to Arsen, his eyes seething, and then at Gavin, his fists clenched next to me. The tension in the air was hot, striking—like the coal-eyes from the fire.

"Gavin's right." Blakely clapped her hands together once, and dirt and sand fell to the ground in a cloud. "I think my time here is up." She looked around the group once again, then stepped around Branch so she was facing him. Slowly, she stood on her tiptoes and kissed him. Held his face in her hands. He stood there, unmoving. But he let her kiss him. He let her lips touch his. Then she turned, as if nothing had just happened—as if Arsen hadn't just tried to kill her—and walked into the trees.

"Blakely, wait." Branch's eyes followed, and he stepped toward her.

"I'll see you soon." Blakely turned once more and smiled at Branch—at the boy with golden eyes like the sun. "I promise." She winked once, and she was gone.

"We can't just let her go!" Arsen's eyes were wide, like he had lost his only hope. Nash was still holding Arsen's arms, and Arsen struggled against his grip.

"I'll go after her." Gavin moved toward the trees. "I'll find her."

"Gavin, wait," I spoke, and he stopped. Everyone looked at me. I avoided Branch's eyes. "There's another way."

"Oh? Do you have another knife somewhere, Laney?" Arsen spat the words, and no one tried to defend me. I tried to ignore it.

"No. But I have exactly what the imposter wants."

Gavin was frozen now, staring at me. The rest were too.

"A person. To be taken."

Arsen scoffed. "Are you insane? Who's going to want to *volunteer* to be taken by crazy man?"

I looked at Branch. His eyes were on me, but his face was expressionless. I felt Nash's fingers in mine, felt the warmth of his touch in the cold air, the almost-night. It felt like several long minutes passed before I spoke.

"Me."

47

ELSEWHERE

History: Entry 25

What is sacrifice?

It's watching them, assessing them, choosing one over the other.

It's refusing to stop when they beg you to, it's leaving the dirt in their fingernails when they scrape the ground over and over again.

It's cleaning the blood off your hands every night, because they need you to be new in the morning. White fingernails, scrubbed skin.

Because this is what matters.

What is sacrifice?

Sacrifice is being the only one who is not afraid to see the truth.

48

HERE

Sacrifice:

Like a flower.

Each petal round, dipping, drinking in the sun. The chubby green stalk pressed firmly into the ground, reaching into the dirt like fingers, stretching, closing. The head open, bowed slightly, like in laughter, kissing the rain as it falls.

Then the flower is plucked, torn from the ground by a hand and a greedy eye. And there it sits, on a windowsill, no longer laughing, drinking, dipping. Slowly dying.

But it's okay—for a time, it looked beautiful.

"I see you like the paper book."

I looked up quickly from the page, smudging the last word—*beautiful*—as I did.

"It's okay. It's just me." Nash gave me a half smile. "You can show the others, you know. This doesn't have to be a secret."

"Theodore already knows." I shut the book between my palms and slid it into the pack beside me. The tree trunk I was leaning on was hard, and I shifted, crossed my legs in front of me. "He's the only one I think should know about this, anyway. If the others find out, with the way things are going—they might destroy it."

The half smile from Nash's mouth was gone. He looked around the small clearing in the trees I had found. "What are you doing out here?"

I swallowed, but I knew I couldn't tell him. No matter how many times Alese or Gavin or Theodore protested, no matter how many times I told them I would be okay, that the crazy guy doesn't kill people—probably—they wouldn't be on board with this. Nash would never let me do this—wait outside by myself, all night, in the trees, hoping some unknown person would kidnap me. So they couldn't know. At least Arsen was all for it, and Branch was silent, so that was basically an agreement. All I needed was to be alone.

All night.

"I didn't want the others to see me writing," I said matter-of-factly. Lie.

"Okay, I get it." He studied my face for a few moments. "I'm not leaving your side, you know. Tonight. I can't let you even think about doing what you volunteered for."

This was going to be harder than I thought.

"The tension was getting crazy back there, and it just came out. It was a bad idea." I faked an embarrassed look. "I know that now." Another lie.

Nash didn't hesitate. "Bad? It was a *terrible* idea. The worst I've ever heard."

"Hey!" I almost laughed—Nash's words, always unpredictable. He sat down next to me, and I hit him lightly on the arm.

"Promise me, okay?"

My smile faded, and I looked at him. He was serious. His eyes were deep, and they looked darker in the blue-gray air. The sun was almost down now, and I shivered.

"You don't know what's going on, Laney. This is—this is serious. Promise me you won't be alone, at least until all of this is fixed."

I just looked at him. His eyes—a mixture of protection and fear.

"Okay." I swallowed. Maybe I shouldn't do this. Maybe I shouldn't go through with it. "I promise."

Nash searched my eyes, my face. Then, slowly, relief filled his cheeks. He smiled. "You want to know what a *good* idea sounds like?"

I tried to smile, but I couldn't. "Tell me."

Nash closed the last few inches between us and took my hand in his, slowly, brushing his fingers against mine as he did. "This."

When he kissed me, I didn't expect it—maybe it's because my mind was spinning, my thoughts were going back and forth, tearing each other apart. Maybe it's because Branch's face—pained, hurt—was embedded in my mind. Or maybe it's because I still had the dirt underneath my fingernails—the dirt from the boy's grave we had buried a little over an hour ago. But still, I let him kiss me. And I kissed him back.

Slowly, Nash pulled away. He was silent for a few seconds, and I could feel his chest moving, could feel the faint beating of his heart.

"So you guys didn't find anything? You, Theodore, and Branch?"

He was so honest, so genuine.

"No. I mean, yes. But no."

Nash looked amused, and his eyes lit up in that playful way they always did. I couldn't help but smile.

"We found an old amusement park—you probably don't know what that is. It's a place people used to go, just for fun." I couldn't help but think of the cars, the wheel, the ride in the sky. And I suddenly wished we could go back there. I could see why people enjoyed it—even rusted, beaten down, torn apart, it had made me happy, for a moment.

Nash smiled. "I bet Theodore was all over that."

"He was."

Theodore's large smile under his freckled cheeks, Branch's look of pride when he figured out how to tie the rope to the wire.

"We all were."

Nash was silent for a few seconds. He squeezed my hand. "I wish I could have been with you."

Dark. It was dark now. The black had almost completely closed in on the blue, and the trees overhead made a canopy, so only a few stars poked through. Their light splashed on the grass in lopsided circles.

"Nash, I'm really thirsty." I shifted again, sat up a little straighter. "Do you think you could get us some water?"

Nash looked at me. "Of course." He pressed his hands to the ground and stood to his feet. "Don't move, okay?" He bent and kissed me on the forehead, and then he was gone.

I was alone. I stood, the pack in my hand. The forest seemed different in the dark, and for a moment I didn't know which way was which. I blinked. The imposter only had a few minutes. I hoped he was prowling the forest right now, looking for his next victim. Everyone still slept in the clearing, terrified of being alone when there was a traitor among them. Maybe I should go to the clearing, then walk back into the woods so the person would see me leave alone. Maybe he waited until someone left, and then followed them. Maybe—

"Laney."

I turned, and the sound of a voice that wasn't Nash's sent my heart racing.

A figure stood in the dark, and he was holding a knife. My blood turned cold, and I realized in that moment that I never actually thought about what I would do if the person *did* show up. Fear pulsed through me, so fast I could almost feel it. I couldn't breathe.

The figure stepped forward slowly, like he was unsure if he should be here. I didn't move—couldn't. My feet were frozen to the dirt, and my throat suddenly closed up. He took a step into a small pool of light by a bush.

I looked back at the shadow. Taller than me, strong arms, broad shoulders. Golden hair. I blinked.

"Branch?"

Branch just looked at me, and it didn't seem like he noticed he had just made me more scared than I had ever been in my life. Well, a close second to the time the world was destroyed right in front of my eyes.

Branch didn't move, but he finally spoke. "I thought you might want your knife back. Since you're going to save the world and all."

Sarcasm. He was still upset that I took the knife. I wondered how he ended up with it. Alese had taken it before she brought the three rows of frozen people back to the clearing.

"Branch." My voice broke. "I only took it in case something happened. So we would be prepared."

Branch still didn't move. He was standing a dozen feet away from me, the moonlight touching his forehead and bathing his eyes in shadow. He let out a breath. "I don't want it near me, okay? Just keep it away from the clearing. I don't want Arsen to find it again."

Branch lifted the knife, barely, and threw it toward the ground. It landed almost exactly halfway between us, its stiff blade sticking up from a small patch of grass.

I took a deep breath. "Why do you hate knives so much? They could save a life."

"Or take one." Branch was still, and I grew silent. I hadn't expected him to answer me so fast. A few bugs started to chirp in the darkening air, and he shifted. "I knew someone who died from a knife."

I could hear my heart beat in my chest. The breeze was cool, and it swept my hair behind my back. I immediately regretted taking the knife. It all made sense now. I had brought back a painful memory. I tried to look at him.

"Before the Dome?"

Branch's expression didn't change. He looked at me, then the knife in the ground, and back at me again. "Good night, Laney."

He turned and walked back into the trees.

"Branch, wait!" My heart was turning circles in my chest, and I didn't know why.

He stopped, turned back to me.

"I'm sorry. I didn't know that. I didn't mean to make you upset." The words came from my lips and hung in the air.

He didn't say anything for a second, and I thought he was going to leave. But then he shut his eyes, pushed his hand through his hair, and opened them again.

"You make me crazy, you know that?"

I blinked. What did he just say?

Branch walked forward until he was a few feet away from me, and I could see the creases on his face, in his eyes. "I know you feel something for me too, Laney. I can see it."

He stopped, his eyes wide, waiting.

My heart started beating quickly. "I— What—" I swallowed. "What about Blakely?"

Why did I ask that? Suddenly I felt dizzy.

Branch closed the space between us, reached down and took my hand in his, then locked his eyes on mine. "You do stupid things, and you don't think sometimes, and you randomly kiss people when you're upset—" He stopped, frustrated, but his eyes didn't move from mine. The desire in them was unmistakable. "But I choose you, Laney. No matter how hard I try not to, it's you." Pause. Breath. "Who do you choose?"

Nash. He was talking about Nash.

I stood there, and he stood there, under the leaves that were slowly turning blue from the fading sun. And the answer should have been obvious, shouldn't it? My mind was racing, set in motion by his touch. I tried to say words—to say a word, a name—but nothing came close enough to my lips.

Branch licked his lips, nodded. And I was still standing in the middle of the clearing, my fingers burning from his touch, when he turned and stepped forward into the trees, disappeared behind the leaves.

Another tree shifted, leaves were pushed out of the way. Nash appeared, and his eyes immediately fell on the knife.

"Where did that come from?"

"Branch." It was the only word I could squeeze out of my mouth.

And for once, Nash didn't ask questions. He sat next to me, placed the container of water by our feet, and suddenly I wasn't thirsty anymore. I had never been thirsty, had I?

It wasn't long before we fell asleep, curled next to each other under the tree, on top of grass and chunks of wood and leaves. My mission seemed blurred after seeing Branch, and tiredness and confusion swept over me like a wave.

I woke when it was still night, the sound of crunching leaves disrupting my dreamless sleep. And when I blinked, my eyes focusing in the shadows, I saw slight movement above the bush.

It was Erika's face, peering at us in the darkness.

49

ELSEWHERE

History: Entry 26

It's funny how people never notice when you're watching them.

They sit, hands crossed, staring at the leaves, the butterflies, the tall grass blowing in the wind. Enjoying life. Thinking their day is perfect, that the world is beautiful.

And I sit, behind the leaves and butterflies and grass. Staring at them.

Thinking my day is perfect, and that the world is beautiful.

50

HERE

I woke the next morning, warm from my body pressed against Nash's. His arm was over me, and I could feel his breath on my neck. And the event from last night trickled back into my chest.

Branch. Telling me he chose me.

I tried to swallow, but it stuck in my throat. I couldn't get his face out of my head, his words, his eyes...

Nash shifted next to me. Small, slow breaths. His chest moving, in and out, against my back. The trees were quiet, the leaves still, like fingers poised in the air. A small white butterfly fluttered to a leaf, landed on it, and waited. It looked like a flower now, a white bloom on a red-and-green leaf.

And then I heard a scream.

I jolted up, pressed my hands against the ground. My palm landed on a sharp stick, and I let out a breath, pulled back my hand. Pain shot up my fingers—throbbing, red lines of pain.

"What was that?" Nash was awake too now. A wave of cold washed over me as he pulled his body from mine and moved to his feet. Bright eyes, alert, like he had been awake for hours.

I cradled one hand in the other and, as best as I could, stood. I looked at Nash and shook my head.

We were at the clearing in a few minutes—wordless, breathless, both of us jogging through the trees into the open grass.

"Erika," Nash breathed the word, and I followed his gaze. And I had to blink to make sure I wasn't dreaming.

Erika was in the middle of the stretch of grass, Arsen and Gavin on either side. She was kneeling, her knees pressed against the green, her hands behind her back. I saw a stubby gray piece of fabric hanging from behind her to the ground— a blanket? Erika's hands were bound with one of our blankets. Another blanket was tied stiffly around her thighs. And I remembered her face last night—small, black, eyes wide as she stared at Nash and I above the bush. The traitor—it was Erika?

I tried to swallow, but we were still running.

Alese stood off to the side, arms crossed, with Theodore. I could tell she was doing everything she could not to look, doing everything she could not to hear Erika's shrieking. Theodore, the redheaded girl Emily, and Dalia were next to her. And so was everyone else. All the people sat in the clearing, scattered around Erika. Staring at her.

"Well, look who decided to join us." Arsen grinned when we stopped next to them. "I'm guessing crazy man didn't get you last night?"

"What's going on?" Nash pushed past Arsen and stood in front of Erika. And for the first time, I realized Branch wasn't here.

Arsen whirled around, obviously not pleased that Nash had ignored him. "Ask him." And then he turned and pointed to Theodore.

I sucked in a breath. "Theodore?"

Theodore looked small, his red hair a mess on his head. His eyes met mine, and wet streaks covered his cheeks. He had been crying. What did Erika *do*?

"I saw her last night, watching you and Nash."

So I had been right. Theodore's voice broke multiple times. It sounded like he had to force every word, otherwise, he might start crying again. Nash looked at me, surprise written on his face.

Theodore took a deep breath. "I asked her what she was doing, said she should get back to the clearing. And she said—" He stopped. Shook his head, squinted from the tears in his eyes.

"She said she knew where the others were." Arsen stepped in, his mouth a line across his face. "And then she tried to take Theodore with her."

My head pounded. "What?"

"I got away," Theodore spoke again, and Alese put her arm around him, brought him close to her. "I—I kicked her. I'm so sorry!" The last words came out in a rush, and he choked back another sob. And I couldn't help but wonder who he was saying sorry to.

"So...so she's it, then. The traitor." I felt like I was hearing the words instead of saying them.

"We don't know that," Nash said. He looked at me, at Erika. "Just because she said she knows where the others are doesn't mean she's the one we're looking for. Come on, guys—let's think rationally here."

Erika let out a groan and goose bumps pricked my arms. "I'm not—I'm not him," she managed to say, and then louder: "Let me go! I was trying to help!"

"Then you can help us now." Gavin. He had been standing silently next to Erika, his expression unreadable. His voice was calm. "Where are the others? Where do they all go?"

Erika grew completely silent, her body slumped on the grass. No one spoke, and I could hear a bird chirp in the distance. Three long notes. Like the three lines of people that had watched a boy die yesterday.

Then, slowly, Erika looked up. She turned her head toward all of us, her face streaked with dirt and tears. Her eyes grew suddenly bright, empty. Haunting. She opened her mouth, and she started laughing. It was quiet at first—low, short bursts. And then it grew louder, until it was as loud as her shrieks had been just moments before. I realized that I would much rather hear the shrieking than this.

Arsen took two steps forward and kicked her in the stomach.

"Arsen!" Alese's eyes were wide, but her arms were still wrapped around Theodore. "I said don't hurt her."

But Arsen didn't listen. He kicked her again, and then again. "Where is Brooke?" He screamed the words, his breath hot against the air. And I could tell he was losing it. Like he did before, when he tried to kill us in the Dome. And it all came back to me, in a single moment. If I couldn't see the sky, couldn't hear the leaves rustle against each other on the trees, I wouldn't be able to tell if we were in the world, or in the Dome. It was all—slowly, painfully, hopelessly— becoming one and the same.

"Arsen, stop!" Alese was screaming now.

"Don't you see? This is what he wants! To make us all crazy!" Nash pushed Arsen to the side, stepped in front of Erika. "This needs to stop, now—"

Arsen punched him across the face, clipped his jaw, sent Nash to the ground. I gasped, tried to breathe, lunged forward, and fell to my knees on the ground next to him.

Theodore was wailing. And I could feel the eye of every person in the clearing on us. Gray, glassy eyes. But no matter how gray, no matter how empty and lifeless they were—they could still see.

"The Dome!" The two words struck the air, louder than the shouting and screaming and crying. And it took me a moment to realize they had come from Erika.

Arsen backed away, breathing heavily, the back of his gray shirt soaked in sweat. "What did you just say?"

Erika was doubled over in pain, but she bit her lip, closed her eyes in a squint, and straightened her back. Nash and I were standing now, his hand pressed to his nose. Blood on his cheeks, his lips. He turned toward her, his palm still on his face.

Where in the world was Branch?

Erika didn't smile this time. Her face was white, her eyes wide, staring forward into nothing. Her thin lips pressed firmly together. She blinked once.

"They went to the Dome."

My throat felt tight. The air was still—water before a stone had been dropped. She couldn't be right. Why would they go back to the Dome? That was everything we wanted to get away from—gray and silence and death.

"We can't—we can't go back there. You don't understand." Nash. He sounded scared. I was scared too.

"If they're there, they need us. They can't survive on their own. They don't know how…" Don't know how to love. Alese spoke, but the words were much quieter than they should have been.

"That doesn't make sense." Arsen was breathing deeply, his eyes still on Erika. "Why would Brooke go to the Dome?"

Erika said nothing else. Her eyes were fading fast—she was retreating into herself, emotionless, lifeless. So she wouldn't have to deal with the reality in front of her. So she would be here, but not really here. Like all of us were taught to do when we first arrived in the Dome. Eyes were gray for this very reason—because sometimes it was easier not to feel.

Gavin reached down and pulled the strand of fabric around her legs, untied her wrists. "Go."

"No," Arsen said. "What are you doing?"

Gavin just looked at him. "She told us what we wanted to know." His eyes fell on Erika again. "Go."

Erika looked up, but there was no surprise on her face. Her emotions were gone the moment she decided she didn't want any. She stood slowly to her feet and didn't even clutch her stomach, wipe the blood from her arms. Pain was a dream to her now.

She stepped forward, slowly at first, and then broke into a jog, and soon she was sprinting to the trees at the bottom of the clearing. She looked back one more time, but I was too far away to see her face. Her eyes looked like holes in her head. And then she was gone.

And for a moment, I wondered where the man was. The one that she had kissed.

51

ELSEWHERE

History: Entry 27

Oh, the Dome. Gray, dark, confining.

Walls like hands that push against each other—corner to corner, edge to edge, until they push against you.

Who knew a human could live in a place so deep the worms can't even reach it?

And the way silence would echo—louder and louder, until you couldn't tell if you were hearing nothing, or everything.

Blank eyes, square teeth, white skin stretched over weak bones. Dark, so dark the lights need to breathe to survive.

We never should have left.

52

HERE

The Dome.

The memories, once foggy, blurry, were getting clearer.

Stairs, endless stairs, going down, down, down. So deep the air seemed like it would disappear forever with each breath we took.

Dark, always, shadows on corners and corners on shadows. Black and gray the only colors that existed.

And silence. Everywhere, silence. Except once. When I woke to Adrian screaming. Adrian, the man with black eyes who lived next to the boy with eyes as bright as a cloudless sky. Adrian, the man who had died because he had nothing else to destroy, so he had nothing else to live for.

I shook my head, forced the memories out. No. We weren't going back. We couldn't go back.

"We have to go back." Alese wrung her hands in front of her. Theodore was still next to her, but he had wiped the tears from his face.

"We can't." Nash spoke softly so the people surrounding us wouldn't hear, but shook his head firmly. We were huddled in the middle of them now. He swiped his hand across his face again, wiped the last bit of blood from his cheeks. "We can't go back, Alese. We're not going back." He gestured to the people. "You really want to go back to where this all began? Take *them* back to a loveless world?"

Alese shook her head. "We can't just leave them in the Dome. And we're not splitting up again." Her face filled with pain, and she looked down. She was thinking about the boy who died. The one who had fallen from the tree. "We stick together."

"Okay, say we go with your idea." Dalia stepped forward. She was next to Gavin, her hand in his. "Who's to say they would even come? They're *terrified*. And sleeping in a deep, dark forest for a few nights, where we're even more vulnerable, is not going to sound appealing to them."

Nash looked from Dalia to Alese. "She's right. This is crazy, Alese. The Dome is the last place we want to be."

"Well, I don't care what you decide or how long it takes you to do it." Arsen was picking up the blankets on the ground, balling them into his hands. "I'm going to find Brooke."

"But, it's the Dome..." Theodore spoke softly, and his eyes were large. He looked like I felt.

Nash nodded. "I agree with Theodore. It's *the Dome*. It will ruin them. They're not even close to being ready to face that again. Not like"—he hesitated, his eyes going to the people around us—"this."

Nash was persistent. He was fighting hard for this.

"We're all going." Alese's voice was more confident this time. "I'm sorry, but I'm going to make this decision. I want to have my eyes on *everyone*. It's my fault if we split up and someone gets taken. Or dies."

I looked at Alese, at her guilt-ridden face, and it was the first time I realized she must have taken responsibility for everything that had happened—every death that had happened—since we came aboveground the second time. We all had voted her leader, after all. But it wasn't her fault. It had never been her fault.

Theodore shifted from one foot to the other. Nash said nothing and shook his head, frustrated.

Arsen whirled around suddenly, faced the people. "We're going back to the Dome! The others are there. Everyone okay with that?"

"Arsen," Alese whispered his name harshly, and her cheeks turned red. No one in the scattered crowd moved.

"See?" Arsen turned back to us. "They're fine. Let's go."

But they weren't fine. I could tell. Their eyes grew a little larger, faces turned a little paler. Delma and Alfred stood, stepped over to us.

"What is it?" Alese turned to them.

Delma looked tired, but her eyes were still less gray, full of life.

"I thought you should know—" she began, looking at Alfred like they shared a secret. Alfred nodded, encouraging her to go on. "The people, they talk sometimes, late at night, when no one can hear. And, well, to keep it short, the Dome is currently number one on their Greatest Fears list."

I swallowed, hard. Dalia was right.

"I want us to all go together." Alese tried to stay confident, but it looked like she was running out of ideas. "How do we get them to come?"

Delma shook her head. "Unless there's some sort of miracle…"

Miracle. That was a word I hadn't heard in a long time. *An event that is so different, so unlike this world, that if someone has the opportunity to see one, they won't recognize it.* The words my mother had told me when the men with black eyes were almost to our town, would almost destroy us all. She had hoped for a miracle then.

"This is stupid." Arsen threw the blankets on the ground. "We're wasting time. Let's just force them to go."

Alese folded her arms. "I'm not doing that, Arsen. That is not even an optio—"

"Hey, guys." A voice, from behind us. "What's going on?"

I turned, and my eyes stopped on Branch. My heart started beating quickly before I realized it. He was standing between the people scattered on the ground, breathing hard, like he had just come from somewhere. His arms were full of color—yellow, green, white. Wildflowers. He was holding dozens of wildflowers.

"You found them!" Theodore grinned suddenly, his eyes on Branch's arms.

"Yes, right where you said they would be." Branch hesitated, his eyes still on us. He raised his eyebrows in question.

"Erika said the others are at the Dome." Alese half smiled at the sight of Branch full of color, but it didn't last. "We need to convince everyone to go with us. They're—they're scared to go back."

Branch was silent for a moment. But he didn't ask questions, didn't ask how we got Erika to tell us or where she was now. I was glad he didn't. But I couldn't take my eyes off his arms, wrapped around green stems and white petals. And it dawned on me that the people here—sitting in the grass, staring with blank eyes—hadn't seen flowers yet, not since we came to the world above.

My heart was pounding, but I silenced it.

I stepped forward without thinking, released my hand from Nash's and walked over to Branch, stopped in front of him. I could feel everyone else's eyes on me. But most of all, I could feel Branch's eyes on me.

I looked at him, and he looked back at me, and I couldn't tell what he was thinking. Something trickled into my chest, quickly, like water.

He was right. There was a feeling there, something I couldn't explain. Every time I looked at him.

But instead, I dropped my eyes to the flowers. "Can I?"

Branch said nothing at first. And then he nodded.

I plucked a single flower from his arms, a yellow one, with petals that looked like large round tears. I stared at it for a moment, thinking of the sun and dancing and my mother. And then I took a deep breath, turned, and faced the people.

I heard someone suck in a breath—a few feet in front of me and to the left—and that was all I needed.

"Branch brought these for you." I took a deep breath again and tried to still the slight tremble in my voice. "They're not from around here—as you probably know."

I could see a girl in front of me staring at the flower, her chest moving faster than normal, her eyes brighter. I stood up straighter.

"There's one for each of you. And as long as you have it, it will keep you safe. You don't have to be afraid—of anything."

I thought of the field in front of my house, seeing the hem of my white cotton dress swirl behind me as I twirled from flower to flower, weightless, the sky above me and below me. I felt safe. In the flowers, I was always safe.

The girl in front of me stood. And then she hesitated, like she was unsure what she was doing. I stepped forward, smiled. Held the flower out to her, between two fingers.

"This one's yours."

Her eyes rounded, fascinated. She couldn't tear her gaze away. And she took it from my fingers, held it in her own.

"I didn't even think these existed anymore." Delma was smiling. She walked over to Branch. "May I?"

Branch held his arms out, and Delma took a handful. She stepped into the crowd, began handing one to every person. Dalia, Alese, and Theodore did the same.

I just stood there, watching the people show emotion—if only a little—for something that had always been a part of my story. Something that had always brought back my few memories of the world before the Dome.

"Did you get one?"

I forced my eyes away. Branch.

"No, I..." I paused, at a loss for words. I didn't understand why—didn't understand why this boy made the words in my mouth turn to dust.

My eyes fell on him, and he was standing there, that twinkle back in his eyes, bare arm outstretched, holding a flower. Yellow petals, like the sun. Like my flowers.

"Here."

"No, it's okay. We need to make sure everyone else gets one." I swallowed, but I couldn't pull my eyes away.

"I got plenty," Branch said. "You like yellow flowers, right?"

My head felt light. He remembered. And then he leaned forward, whispered words that no one else could hear.

"I'm not giving up just yet."

I paused, looked at him. And without thinking, I took it.

Branch turned and handed out flowers to the rest of the people, his lips curved in a smile.

When everyone had a flower, they stood—slowly, one by one—but they were there, ready to leave. Ready to go back to the Dome.

The clearing looked like something that didn't belong— gray people, gray eyes, gray hands, now clutching white and yellow and green. Small dots of color on a gray canvas, flowers on stones.

The clearing—suddenly so different, so unlike this world, that for a moment, I didn't even recognize it.

53

ELSEWHERE

There's an old rhyme my mother used to say when I was a child as she lay me down each night and rocked the crib with crooked fingers. She got it from a book, one with wrinkled pages and the binding ripped at the bottom edge, so when she was holding on to it her fingers poked through to the other side.

It went like this:

> There was a man, he went mad,
> He jumped into a paper bag;
>
> The paper bag was too narrow,
> He jumped into a wheelbarrow;
>
> The wheelbarrow took on fire,
> He jumped into a cow byre;
>
> The cow byre was too nasty,
> He jumped into an apple pasty;

The apple pasty was too sweet,
He jumped into Chester-le-Street;

Chester-le-Street was full of stones,
He fell down and broke his bones.

Jump, my friends, jump.

54

HERE

The first time I saw everyone walking side by side in the Dome, I remember thinking they all looked the same. They looked like one person, and then ninety-six replicas of that same person.

Legs, moving back and forth, striking the ground at the same moment. Arms, swinging back and forth like hands on clocks, the perfect angle and width and length as each second ticked past. And eyes, staring forward—at first, it looked like, at the walls, the turns in front of them. But then I realized they were staring *into* the walls, beyond them. At something neither I nor they could see.

It was only when they passed that I saw they were each a different person, only the different heights and hair colors—brown, red, blond, black—that gave it away.

But each time I walked with them, and the days in the Dome started to blend together, so did the hair colors. And I began to think that maybe I had been right, after all. There was only one of us, and all the others were copies, shadows—marching next to and in front of and behind the original so he wouldn't feel so alone.

And today, in the trees, I started to see it again. Blended hair and legs and arms marching in the green, crunching on leaves and dry grass. An army of one.

"Let's stop for the night," Branch called, a dozen feet in front of me. At Alese's encouragement, because of her leg, Branch had taken the leadership position again, just like he had with Theodore and me.

"Yes, we're sleeping here! Everyone stop."

But then, there was Arsen. He couldn't let anyone else be leader. He always thought it should be him.

I stepped into a small clearing, much smaller than ours, and set my pack on the ground. Theodore let out a large breath beside me and sank to the ground. I didn't blame him; we had been walking all day.

Theodore looked back at the people. "Didn't anyone tell them they don't have to walk like that anymore? It's creeping me out a little."

I couldn't help but smile.

"At least they're moving, one giant parade of robot people or not." Emily came up behind Theodore, a pained look on her face. She knelt on the ground, rubbed her feet with her fingers. She didn't even glance at me.

"Emily, I—"

"Save it, okay?" Emily looked at me, finally. "I didn't die. That's all that matters."

I said nothing. It seemed like making people mad was becoming a specialty of mine lately.

Emily looked at Theodore again, and her eyes brightened. "Want to help me start a fire?"

Theodore smiled at her and nodded. He started to follow, but looked back at me apologetically. I managed to give him an encouraging nod. It looked like he had found his red-headed girl after all. And lucky for me, it was the one person who didn't like me. Well, her and Arsen. But Arsen didn't like anyone.

A hand slipped into mine, and I felt warmth run through me like water. Nash appeared next to me, his light brown eyes on mine. "Should we snag our spot?"

I nodded, grateful for the interruption from my thoughts.

The fire—it was always by the fire. Down in the Dome, fire was destructive, something to avoid. It destroyed things, one by one, placed into it by Mr. Dabir and the other teachers. It had destroyed everything of color in the Dome, leaving it the dull, flat gray that it was.

But here, the fire was color—oranges and browns and yellows and whites. It burned when everything else went to sleep, full of breath, panting and crackling, while the stars filled the sky. Here, the fire didn't destroy. Here, the fire was life.

I pulled my blanket from my pack and flicked it in the air, securing it on the ground next to the cold wood—and a busy Emily and Theodore, scraping for sparks—with a small gray stone. I zipped my pack up quickly, sat, and shoved it between my legs. The paper book, its shiny red cover and pages stuffed between, sat snugly inside, right next to the yellow flower. And next to that—the knife.

Theodore whooped as a spark turned into a flame that slowly began eating the pile of grass, devouring the wood, and Emily held her hand up for a high five. Theodore's thing. He slapped her hand and flexed his arms, one after the other, puffing out his face while he did. Emily burst out laughing, and I felt a smile fill my face. In the growing light of the fire, I could see him smiling too.

"I said we're *sleeping* here, not looking at the scenery." Arsen's voice filled the air. "Sit down already."

My smile faded and I looked up. The rest of the people were standing in rows, in the trees, staring into the darkness around them. They hadn't moved since we'd arrived. I hadn't even noticed.

I stood, but Branch had beat me to it. He was laying down blankets, one by one, in the small clearing. Then, as I watched, he guided the people to their own. They were all clutching their flowers tightly, their eyes as wide as the moon. Scared. I started to think Nash was right—that we shouldn't have all come. But Alese had insisted. *It's everyone or no one*, she had said. And we were all in this together now. We had been from the moment we stepped out the Dome's door. We couldn't abandon someone, even if they had gone back to the world of gray.

Abandon.

I blinked.

There had been a girl while I was being taken to the Dome when I was five. While my town was getting destroyed. My age. Blond hair that looked almost white. A white face, pink at the cheeks and orange at the edges, like she had tried to get a tan but the sun only touched the ends of her skin. She was in a house we had passed, and I remember she was clutching a small stuffed bear, staring out the window, screaming. Screaming for us to take her with us. Screaming for us not to abandon her. And then someone hit her on the head with a chair—one of those heavy wooden ones with the curved legs. And I saw her release her bear, fall to the ground, before I was torn away. If we had still known how to love, maybe we would've stopped, tried to help. But as we walked away, as my feet scuffed the dirt and ashes and broken streets, I remember feeling glad that I couldn't hear her screams anymore. I shivered.

The night was growing darker, but the fire was warm. I wondered if the people scattered around the clearing could feel it. Everyone had a place now and was sitting or lying on a blanket, thanks to Branch. He was sitting on his own, across from the fire, his legs stretched out in front of him and hands pressed behind him on the ground. Gavin was next to him, saying something. I saw Branch smile and then nod. Theodore and Emily were a dozen feet away from us, drawing in the ground with a stick and laughing. And for the first time in a long time, it was kind of peaceful. Like I didn't have to be afraid anymore.

"Can I borrow your flower? I left mine in the clearing." Nash spoke suddenly.

I didn't answer right away. He left his? I thought of the yellow flower Branch had held out to me, and the way he had looked at me, the way his eyes had sparkled. But this was Nash. I was being ridiculous.

"Sure." I unzipped my pack slowly, pulled the flower out between two fingers. Carefully, so I wouldn't break the petals. Nash took it, and my hand felt cold. Nash stood, and I wondered why he wanted it. Why he hadn't brought his own.

"Why do you need it?" My voice stopped him and he turned.

"You'll see." The smile on his face appeared and vanished, all in a second. And before he spun around again, I could see his face—white, fear plastered to his skin like the cold air.

I kept my eyes on Nash as he walked around the fire and into the blue-gray darkness. He stopped in front of all the people, their blankets pressed next to each other like chairs in the Dome. He bent, slowly. He was talking to the old woman in front of him, gray hair that curled on the tops and sides of her head, too short to pull into a bun. I could see his mouth moving.

Nothing happened for a few minutes, and my eyes drifted away from Nash and to the fire again. Every time the flames grew hot, reached into the air, and then shrunk down again, I could see Branch. Flickering, in and out, like the fire. He was talking to Dalia now, who was seated on the other side of Gavin. Dalia's lips pressed together like she was thinking, and Gavin jumped in, said something. Dalia and Branch laughed. And then Branch's eyes met mine, the smile still on his face.

My heart pounded and I looked away quickly. He had caught me staring at him. I could feel my cheeks get red, and I hoped he would just think it was the heat from the fire.

"Laney, you can join us, you know." Dalia's voice. She had moved from her place and sat down next to me on Nash's blanket.

Her statement caught me off guard.

"I know, I…I'm fine. Where I am. Over here."

Dalia laughed and gave me a strange look. "If you say so. Where's Nash?"

Nash.

"He's—"

Someone let out a cry. I forced my eyes up to where the sound had come from. The old woman with gray hair. Nash, his hands up, like he had done something to upset her.

I jumped to my feet and rounded the fire, stepped over to the group of people. Dalia followed.

"What's going on?" I stopped next to Nash and looked down at the woman. She had tears in her gray eyes. And then I looked at Nash. He was holding two flowers—mine and hers.

"I didn't mean to make her cry. I was trying to help. See?" He turned to me, stuffed a flower in my hands—a white one, the old woman's, I guessed—and held my flower out in front of him. "Laney, you look beautiful today." He motioned for me to take the yellow flower, turned his eyes back to the old woman as he did. I didn't know what was going on—I took it.

"Nash, what are you—?"

"Now Laney says something nice about me, and gives me her flower—the white one. And then we both have a flower again. *And* we showed some love in the process. It's that simple."

"Everything okay here?" Branch, behind us.

The air fell silent. Dalia said nothing next to me. I looked from the woman to Nash, and back to the woman again. Her eyes were almond shaped, and her face was twisted into an expression of betrayal and pain. And sadness—a deep, deep sadness.

I held the white flower out to her, placed it in her hands that were spread on her lap. The expression on her face immediately retreated, her eyes dried, until she was staring ahead again, calm. She closed her fingers around the stem of the flower.

Branch's eyes moved from the woman to Nash. "Why did you take her flower?"

Nash's eyes flitted from Branch to me. "I was trying to help. They need to learn how to love again. We can't—we can't take them to the Dome like this. You don't understand. We can't. It's suicide."

"We're already on our way. We'll be there soon." Branch's voice was calm, but I could see his eyebrows crease slightly, like something wasn't right.

"Yeah, but we shouldn't be!" Nash's voice came out loud, and I stepped back without meaning to. I hadn't expected it. "They're terrified, and they don't talk, and they forgot everything we taught them about how to love, and we're just taking them back? Back to where it all began? This is a mistake." He was breathing hard now, deep, frantic breaths.

"Nash." I reached over and took his hand in mine. What was going on with him?

Branch took a breath too. He spoke in a calm, low voice so the people in front of us couldn't hear.

"We'll get the others, the ones that left, and bring them back. Get them to tell us who the traitor is and get rid of him before he takes anyone else. But we can't go back to normal until we find the traitor, get rid of him for good, and the people don't have to fear anymore. We're not staying at the Dome. You know that, right?"

Nash said nothing, and I could feel his chest move, in and out. The air was cold over here—the warmth of the flames from the fire didn't reach this far. I could just make out the people, most lying on their blankets now, eyes closed in the faint light of the stars.

He turned, and in the slight darkness, his eyes were white.

"Laney, take them back with me." His voice was almost a whisper now, and goose bumps pricked my arms.

I didn't understand—we had all agreed on this. I almost didn't recognize the boy in front of me. He still had blond hair, like my wildflowers. Like the flower I held in my hand. But his face was pinched in all the wrong places.

"Nash, we'll go back the moment we're done. Like Branch said, we're not staying at the Dome."

His brown eyes looked at me for another second. Then he released his hand from mine, looked at the woman with gray hair one more time, and stepped back to his blanket by the fire.

Branch was looking at me, but I didn't know what to say.

Later that night, as the fire burned low and I drifted in and out of sleep, I felt Nash put his hand on mine. Warmth, a blurry flower, a brief thought that he was okay again. That the woman's face—wrinkled, gray, eyes squinting through tears—was just a dream.

And then the warmth lifted, cold touched my fingers, and it was dark.

55

ELSEWHERE

History: Entry 29

I remember when I realized the color gray was the same color as tears.

She was sitting there—pale skin, glassy blue eyes, hands crossed in her lap. Hair curled in front of her cheeks. Trembling.

A breath, a swallow, and then a single tear, sliding down her cheek like blood. Like her eyes were bleeding.

Except it wasn't red.

It made me excited, and I wondered why. And then I realized—it was the color of the Dome.

The color of home.

56

HERE

When the edge of the sun wobbled into the sky the next morning and the air turned blue gray instead of black, I opened my eyes.

I could see the tops of the trees, their leaves twisting in the air, blowing in the wind that had picked up overnight. The smoke from the fire was on the tip of my tongue.

I planted my hands underneath me and angled up, pushed my hair behind my back. The old woman with gray hair was standing a hundred feet from me, her blanket in her hands. She was facing me, her eyes on what used to be the fire. Or were they on me? Her white flower was tucked firmly in her sleeve.

I looked away and stood to my feet slowly. I grabbed my pack and turned, opened my mouth to tell Nash to wake up, but there was only dirt and grass next to me. Nash—and all his things—was gone. And where he had been sleeping, there were two words written in the dirt with a finger, barely visible because the wind had almost swept them away.

I'm sorry

My heartbeat quickened. I looked around at the trees, the people, thinking he must have gotten up already. He was here

233

somewhere, he had to be. I looked down again, and my throat filled with some sort of thick liquid. Sorry—sorry for what? Where was he?

And then a realization pricked at me—something so terrible I almost fell to my knees, heaved the liquid from my throat.

He had been taken.

Taken, by the traitor. And the traitor had the audacity to write this in the sand next to me. While I was sleeping.

I couldn't catch my breath anymore, couldn't see anything but the words scratched in the dirt.

"Laney? Are you okay?" Alese and Dalia had been laughing about something, and they came up behind me.

I shook my head, heaved in a breath, pointed to the dirt next to me.

"He took him. He took Nash." The words came out in a jumble, and I couldn't tell if they made sense or not.

Their faces went cold.

"Are you sure he's not here somewhere? He might have just—"

"Alese, he's gone." I felt like crying. He was so worried last night, so desperate to teach the people how to love again. That was probably why he was chosen—because he, of all of us, was trying to fix things.

Alese's eyes were wide. "We'll find him, Laney. Maybe he was taken to the Dome, where we're going..." Her voice trailed off. It was the first time I had seen her look helpless, like she didn't know what to do.

"He won't change." Dalia's voice was stronger. She held her chin up. "He's too strong for that. He's one of us."

I tried to nod. She was right. And it was only then that it hit me that he was the first one of our little group to be taken. Theodore, Dalia, Gavin, Alese, Nash, and me. Before, it hadn't meant as much. I didn't know Blakely or the others. But I knew Nash, knew him better than anyone.

"Branch." Dalia called his name as he was passing, a bundle of sheets in his arms. He stopped, and Dalia spoke softly. "Nash is gone. He might've been taken. Keep an eye out for him today, okay?" Dalia's voice was tight, like she was trying not to sound worried.

Branch didn't move. His eyes met mine, and I turned, lifted my pack from the ground.

I looked at Alese and Dalia. "The sooner we get going, the sooner we find him." I tried to swallow.

Alese hesitated, her wide eyes still on me. She nodded. My hand was shaking, and I balled up my blanket, shoved it inside, and pushed the pack onto my back. When I looked up, Branch was gone.

The lines were marching through the trees again in less than ten minutes. At least Branch had done his part as leader—rallying up the people so we could leave as soon as possible. To find Nash, and the person who took him.

I couldn't think, tried to push back thoughts of what the person was doing to him right at this moment. Nash was the best one of us all. He was always trying to help, and he was repaid in the worst way possible.

"Water!" Branch called from the front.

"Water!" Arson echoed.

I slowed, pushed back the tree branches in front of me, and the world opened up to a stretch of dirt and grass and hopeless plants trying to spiral up under rocks. The dirt was next to a winding wall of water, a hundred yards wide, rushing down the slope of the mountain on sharp rocks and flat stones. They looked like they were made of glass—shiny on top and smoothed by the water. And from where I was standing, I could just see it—the water, twisting and turning to the edge of the grass, and the beginning of a canyon. Brown walls that dropped a hundred feet below us. The door of the Dome was in a canyon. This was it. And this explained why the canyon flooded during the storm—there was a swirling trail of water hundreds of feet above it.

Branch was standing fifty feet from the water, looking left and right for the end or beginning of the winding blue, but it was nowhere to be seen.

I walked over to him, stepped into the conversation he was having with Alese, Gavin, and Dalia.

"There's no way we can cross this. Yeah, most of the people will probably make it, but not everyone. *Someone* will slip and fall." Dalia looked at the water again.

"We have to." Branch shook his head. "Going back up, trying to find the end of it, will take days. And we can't go down." He pointed at the cliff next to the water.

"We walked from the Dome to the clearing and didn't run into this, so we know there's another way. Let's try to find that way."

"Dalia, we're already here." Branch held up his hands. "We cross it, or we add days to our hike. Days that the others—that Nash—might not have."

Dalia blinked, noticed me for the first time. She didn't say anything else.

"Okay." Alese looked at the water, then at us. "We'll do it."

No one spoke. I could see the frustration on Branch's face—frustration from taking us the wrong way back to the Dome. Alese wrung her hands in front of her, bit her lip. Dalia was staring at the water.

I tried not to think of Nash, tried to think of the dilemma in front of us, but it was becoming harder and harder. His eyes on mine, pleading with me to take the people back with him. His game where he said something nice to the old woman, tried to get her to say something nice back. His hand in mine, clutching my fingers, and then all I felt was the night.

His hand.

I looked at Branch, and this time I didn't take my eyes away.

"I have an idea."

57

ELSEWHERE

History: Entry 30

Touch is like fire.

It's fine at a distance, the warmth and breath on your skin. Stretch out your hands, let your fingers brush against the air, feel the flame. But don't get too close—

Someone will always get burned.

58

HERE

People, breathing. The mist in our hair and the sun in our eyes. Feet spread, placed firmly on the smooth rocks—not too slippery and not too sharp. Water, lapping over the edges of gray and soaking shoes, feet, legs. Hands outstretched, clasped to other hands, and to other hands, from one side of the water to the other.

Wrinkled, small, smooth, large, firm. No matter the size, no matter the roughness, a hand is a hand. And that was all that mattered right now.

"Keep going!" Branch's voice, spoken loudly so it could be heard over the sound of the water. He was three people away from me.

I took a deep breath, clutched the hands of Emily and Delma tightly. It wasn't the water that scared me—purple-blue and foaming every time it touched a stone or one of us. No, it was the rocks. There were only so many spread across the water, and they were our path. A miss, one foot slipping, would take us all in. But without our hands holding tightly to one another, like a rope, we would have gone in already.

We moved from one rock to another, slowly, Branch choosing them carefully, making sure they didn't wobble or slip. And it was working.

I looked back at the line, could see the people, hands holding hands, many of the flowers pressed tightly in their teeth so they wouldn't lose them. And, despite the spray of water in my eyes, I almost smiled. Nash should have seen this. The people didn't hesitate when they heard my idea. It was like they remembered what it was like to clasp hands in the Dome, to raise them up together in victory.

"We're almost there!" Theodore's voice, on Emily's other side.

I sucked in my breath, stepped to the next rock, and let the relief rush over me when my foot stayed firmly in place.

I heard a bird cry from somewhere far above, but I kept my eyes on the water. The sky was a bright blue today, with white wisps scattered down the center. No storms, no wind. We were going to make it.

Emily moved forward next to me, half stepping, half jumping to the next rock. I had to grip her hand hard not to lose it. She regained her balance, and I mentally prepared myself.

Three feet to my right. Position my foot on the very edge of this rock, inch by inch. Okay, on three. One. Two—

"I'm sorry, Laney."

What? I was imagining Nash's words again, written neatly in the dirt.

"I never really forgave you, you know.

I hesitated. It was Emily, speaking low so I could barely hear her over the sounds of the water and the birds.

I was already in position. I couldn't stop now.

Three.

I jumped, and her hand released mine, and Delma's fingers grasped the air, and I saw water, rocks, the look on Emily's face as I fell—eyes focused, eyebrows creased, mouth parted slightly in a smile. And then I saw nothing.

. . .

A warm breeze touched my face, grazed my lips. I blinked. A field—flowers, full and golden and smiling. A butterfly twirled in the air, its wing almost brushing against my cheek as it fluttered by. And my hand—it was in someone's hand. His arms around me, his head by my head, next to my ear so I couldn't see his face. I could feel his breath on my skin, and it tingled. Could feel him pull me gently around the flowers. In, out, in, out. We were dancing.

"Nash?"

I smiled, pressed my head against his, melted deeper into his arms. We were safe. Somehow, some way, we had made it out of all of this. We were dancing in a field of wildflowers.

"Grab my hand." His voice.

I turned my head slightly. What? My hand was already in his. I threaded my fingers more deeply, and he pressed his lips to my ear, whispered the words.

"Grab my hand."

"I already have your—"

"I said grab my hand!"

I jerked my head back, looked into the person's eyes— wide, frightened. Golden. It wasn't Nash. It was Branch.

"Laney! Grab my—"

Water. Water on top of me, below me, inside my chest and nose and lungs. The flowers vanished and I saw only blue—a wall, bricks, pushing on top of me and sucking everything from inside.

I gasped, but there was no air. Only more water, water pressing, water suffocating. I tried to cough it out of my lungs, but then I was choking. Air. I needed air. Which way was up and which was down?

Light, so bright I almost closed my eyes. I gasped, gulped in breaths as I pushed myself over the top of the water wall. A face. A hand, reaching.

And then water again, pulling me down, down. My body hit against something, hard. The bottom. Small rocks scraped against my legs and I cried out, but no one could hear me. Everything was muffled down here, mute. A different world.

I opened my eyes. Saw gray and light, murky light, from somewhere far away. Water, so much water. My lungs were gasping, choking, coughing. I needed air, but there was only water.

The wall grew darker, pressed against me harder, harder.

I took in a breath. And then another, again and again. I was desperate for air. Desperate for my mother. Desperate to be in a world that loved.

My limbs were heavy, and I stopped fighting. I couldn't win.

I felt something on my arm, cried out in pain. I was going up, up, up toward the light. And then I surfaced, was pulled from the wall of blue and pushed onto something hard—dirt, rocks. Water heaved from my lungs, and I turned, clutched the ground, coughed until I could breathe again. I sucked in breath after breath. Air. Fresh, beautiful air. I blinked hard, could feel tears in my eyes.

"Laney, what—"

"Thank God. How did that happen?"

Voices, everywhere. I coughed again, turned slowly on my back. Blinked. Branch's face. Theodore's. Alese's.

"Are you okay?" Branch still had his hand on my arm, was kneeling next to me, his eyes wide. He was soaking wet.

I opened my mouth, but instead of words, I heaved in air again.

Branch, in the field of wildflowers. Branch, right here.

"I didn't think you had her, Branch. We almost— She almost didn't make it." Alese sounded like she was about to cry. "This was stupid. Maybe we shouldn't have come."

"Emily, what happened? Did your hand slip?" Theodore's voice, innocent, worried.

A pause, and then Emily: "Yes. I'm so sorry."

I placed my hands behind me, pressed myself to a half-lying, half-seated position.

"Hey, take it easy." Branch took my other arm, held me up against him. "You must have hit your head pretty hard when you fell in."

"What's going on?" Gavin. "Was that Laney?"

"What happened?" I heard Dalia come up behind him.

"Let's give her space, guys. Once everyone makes it across we'll all gather over there." I saw Alese point to some trees a hundred feet away, cast another glance in my direction. "Branch, stay with her? Until she can get up?"

Branch nodded.

I squinted, and the water came into focus. Half of the people had made it across, were still holding hands and stepping from rock to rock, one by one. And then, finally, on the other side—when they reached it—they released hands and walked, eyes forward, to the trees. Just like they had walked this entire trip so far.

"Everyone else made it?" The words came out heavy, thick, like a wall of water was still inside my stomach.

Branch shifted and let me lean onto him more completely. Even if I wanted to move, I couldn't. My legs and arms were still lead.

"Yes."

My head was against his chest, so I couldn't see his face while he spoke.

"I heard you, calling to me. Telling me to grab your hand." Why was I telling him this? "It was in my dream."

Branch chuckled. "Well, apparently it didn't do any good."

It was the first time he had laughed at something I said in a long time. I felt a warmth fill my chest.

There was a long silence. I could see everyone make it to the other side of the water, step over to Alese and the others. They were waiting in the trees, behind the green, and it reminded me of the time we saw three faces in the bushes. Three faces that tried to kill Branch.

"Laney, I'm sorry about Nash."

His voice pulled me from my thoughts. I swallowed. In the near-drowning, I had almost forgotten.

"We'll find him. Okay?"

I could feel myself take a breath. I nodded.

I could feel his chest underneath his wet shirt against the back of my arms, my neck. It was warm, and I was shivering.

Branch was silent. I closed my eyes. I wanted to stay like this—my back against his chest, his chin resting on my hair. The sound of the water wasn't so bad now. Next to Branch, it was calming.

Alese's voice carried over to us on the wind, and I opened my eyes. It sounded like she was telling the people to get ready—to start walking again.

"Do you think you can stand up?" Branch slid his hand down my arm and grasped my fingers in his. I felt a warm chill spread up my back.

"I—I can try." I tried not to show my disappointment, tried to ignore the feeling of his hand in mine.

The air felt cold against my wet clothes as I planted my feet underneath me and straightened my wobbly legs. Black started to tunnel into my eyes, and I shut them, could see stars. My head felt dizzy.

"Easy." Branch put his arms around me and held me up so I didn't fall down again. My cheek was pressed against his wet shoulder, and I looked up.

"Hey, thank you. For saving me."

Branch looked back at me, his eyes golden and strong and soft, all at once. "I'm just glad I got to you in time."

No—I couldn't feel this way. Not while Nash was gone, taken, being tortured somewhere. I couldn't let a simple thing like feelings get in the way. I couldn't.

But I didn't understand why my chest felt heavier than it did when I was underwater.

I tried to swallow, tried to move. And I tried not to, all at the same time. His face was inches from mine, and my heart was pounding. I could feel bursts of red and yellow and green, fireworks in my chest. And I didn't understand, because I hadn't kissed him yet. Couldn't kiss him. But I wanted to, more than I had ever wanted anything.

"You guys coming? You look fine to me, Laney!" Arsen's voice called from the trees.

I looked over at him, and my eyes slowly came into focus. Dirt. Grass. Thin trunks, fat leaves.

"I think I'm okay now." I released my hand from Branch's, my face still next to his. His eyes were on me, and I could feel his breath—a little faster than normal.

I pushed them back, the feelings.

"Are you sure?"

I nodded. Took a few steps, to test it. As long as I went slowly, I was fine. Branch was still watching me.

"If you need anything during the rest of the way, just...call for me at the front, okay?"

I paused in my walking. "I will."

"I should get back to the group, figure out the direction we're going." Branch looked at me for another long moment. "You'll be okay?"

"I'm right behind you."

Branch nodded, turned toward the trees.

"Oh, hey, Laney?" He turned back, and I stopped. "Don't forget your pack. It was still on your back when I grabbed you. It should be fine, it just might need some time to dry out."

Branch pointed to the black bag that was on the ground a few feet from where we had been sitting and gave me a half smile. Then he turned and started walking again.

Panic rose in my chest, and I stepped over to the pack. I picked it up and a stream of water trickled from the bottom to the ground below.

No.

I unzipped it quickly, stuffed my hand in and found the flower, soaked and missing a few petals, but still a flower. The paper book, though, was anything but.

I pulled out the stack of sopping wet paper, opened the cover, and the book fell apart in my hand. The words on the page were a blur of black ink. My very first entry was a blob on the white—*Love* distorted now, with black bubbling out and filling the rest of the page.

I tried to flip the rest of the edges, but they were melted together in one thick, messy page. A book with one page. I felt like laughing and crying at the same time.

I held up the lopsided book, changed from the inside out by the water, and watched it drip from the corners. There was no saving it. Once again, any proof of love we had in a book was gone.

I stood slowly, holding the stack of wet paper tightly in my hands. I walked to the edge of the water, knelt down on my knees. Saw the wall of blue, the light from the sun winking on the colorless surface. And I pushed the pages in, watched the water run over the edges and take them down, down, down to the bottom. White in blue. Words in a world where air was water, and water was air.

59

ELSEWHERE

History: Entry 31

There is one more.

We are the only people in this world—she and I.

Her eyes, watching, waiting. Her hair, like water. Her face, focused. Determined not to die.

I wait by her side, my hand in hers. She feels protected by me. Loved by me.

I did love her, once. The first time I stepped out the Dome's door, I didn't see grass or canyon walls or the sun, so bright it hurt my eyes.

I saw her, staring at the world.

I saw her face.

I told her I would protect her. Told her I would be there, by her side, no matter what happened.

And I will.

I'll be by her side. I'll hold her hand—fingers laced in fingers, skin to skin, breath to breath—while I kill her.

60

HERE

When I think back to that moment when the eight of us saw the world for the first time in thirteen years, I remember everything.

Emerald grass stretching in front of us, swaying in the soft wind—the first wind we had felt since before the Dome. Strong canyon walls, brown and yellow and black, as thick as the Dome's walls but not gray. No, they were everything but gray. And the sun—so bright, I could feel my eyes burning, and tears formed. Real tears. I hadn't felt tears in years.

But when I think back to that day that changed everything, the beginning of it all, there is one thing that will always stand out to me the most: the look on his face. Theodore's face. The way he was standing just inside the Dome's door, his hands over his eyes, trembling. The way he looked at me, terrified at what was through that door. Terrified of the world beyond our own.

And I realized something that day: we're all like that. We all have fears—heights, wild animals, death. And we can either wait inside the door, our hands over our eyes, trembling. Or we can still our shaking hands, put them over our foreheads to shield the light, and walk through that door without looking back. Like Theodore did. Only then will we find it—the sun in our eyes, the wind on our faces.

Only then will we learn that everything we want is on the other side of fear.

But today, as we stand in the middle of the browns and yellows and blacks of the canyon, I can't help but think that we're about to walk through the wrong door.

"We made it." Branch's voice. Then silence.

All of us—however many we were now—stood on the canyon floor, the walls on all sides rising hundreds of feet into the sky. Brown stretching up to meet the blue.

I had gotten used to their staring, the mute eyes that looked straight ahead into something no one could see. But I was staring now. And I could see it.

The wall on the far end of the canyon had a large square cut from it, the edges around the square jagged and brown. And inside the cutout was a door. Massive, gray—a dozen people could fit through at once. It almost didn't look like a door, with no handle or knob, just a smooth, flat surface. It was like someone wanted a piece of the canyon to be gray instead of brown, so they chipped the wall away and replaced it with stone.

I was breathing slowly, deeply. I could feel my heartbeat thudding in my chest. It seemed years ago that we had stepped out this door, once with eight and then with eighty-eight. And yet it didn't seem long enough.

"Crazy that there's a whole world behind that door." Theodore spoke softly beside me, and his voice was followed by more silence. Emily was next to him. If only he knew what she had done.

The wind had grown stronger down here, and goose bumps pricked my arms.

"Okay, then. The Dome's not coming to us!" Arsen spoke suddenly, hitched his pack on his back, and started walking across the canyon floor.

Gavin and Dalia stepped by me, their mouths in a line.

"Let's just get this over with." Dalia tried to smile. "For Nash, right?"

I tried to smile back, but ended up nodding instead.

For Nash. This was all for Nash. We would find him, and the others, and then we would leave. And never come back.

"Out of all the places in this world, why did they have to pick here?" Branch came and stood beside me. Brought his eyes from the Dome's door to me. "Are you okay?"

I thought of my thirteen years of life here, of the nights in my indent and the days of silence. The gray. I tried to nod. "We find the others, we leave." I turned back to the canyon, to the people walking across the floor to the cold gray door, and Branch followed my gaze.

"Well, I'm here, okay? If you need anything."

I blinked. "Thank you."

I watched Arsen reach the Dome's door, motion for us all to come join him.

"I guess we should head over."

Silence.

If I didn't force one foot in front of the other, I never would have moved.

While we were crossing the canyon floor, I wished I could grab Branch's hand. Hold it tightly. This canyon, the Dome's door—this wasn't something I wanted to experience alone. But I kept my hands by my sides.

"Anyone have a hammer? A knife?" Arsen was standing in front of the door—so much larger now that we were right in front of it—kicking it with his feet. The wooden planks we had nailed to the door were gone, with no nails or scrapes to prove that they had even existed. It was as if they had just disappeared, like mist into air.

"There's no way to open it from the outside, remember?" Gavin crossed his arms and looked at Arsen with part amusement, part annoyance. "We're just going to have to wait until the others come. Open it from the inside."

"And what if they don't *want* to open it?" Arsen stopped kicking, stood and faced Gavin. "What if they don't want us to find them at all?"

"Let's hope they do." Branch looked at Arsen, and Arsen held his gaze and then dropped it, started kicking the door again.

"Brooke! I'm here! Come open the door!" Arsen yelled the words, and they made a few people wince.

I closed my eyes. This was going to be a long night.

Theodore came up next to me. "What did we do when we came back the first time, Laney? Pound it with our fists, right? Maybe we should try that again."

"Maybe we should." I smiled, and then Emily's face appeared. She was always by Theodore now.

My eyes locked on to hers, and she looked away.

You almost killed me, I wanted to say. *I almost drowned because of you.*

And then I saw Theodore—eyes bright, grinning as Emily helped him pound the door with her fists. He looked so happy. I didn't know if I could break his heart, didn't know if his heart could even handle it.

I took a deep breath.

I would tell him, just not now. Not here.

Alese, Gavin, and Dalia joined in on the banging. The air was a mix of "We're here to save you!" and "You better open the door or I'll kill you! Not you, Brooke, but—the rest of you!" It wasn't hard to guess who said which.

After fifteen minutes of pounding the cold gray door, Arsen whirled around and faced Branch. "You're the leader here! Shouldn't you have a plan B or something?"

Branch looked up at Arsen from his place a dozen feet away, in the corner of the canyon, out of the wind. He chuckled, gestured to the fire he was trying to start from the wood he had gathered on our journey. "This is plan B."

Arsen rolled his eyes, turned and faced the people who were standing in the canyon, staring at the door. "I hope this is proof enough that you should vote me leader next time. And every time."

The smile was still on Branch's face.

"Nash, if you're in there, please open the door!" Alese's voice.

I flexed my cold fingers. Imagining him inside, gray shadows and light from the walls flickering in and out, in and out, his face barely illuminated—I pushed the thought away.

I stepped up next to Gavin and Dalia, started hitting the door with my fists.

The air turned colder and the day grew hazy, blurry. The sun was behind the canyon wall already, and Branch had a roaring fire going where two of the walls connected. Most of the other people were sitting in front of the fire, their sheets wrapped around them.

I was sitting with Dalia a few feet from the door, throwing rocks from the floor at the large gray square. Every time a rock hit, it bounced off the door, clattered to the ground, and there was silence. Another rock, another clatter, silence. Theodore and Emily were by the fire now, Emily's idea of course. Only Gavin and Arsen were banging on the door now, though more slowly and not as hard.

"Do you think Erika was lying? Someone would have heard us by now." Dalia threw another rock at the door, and it bounced off into a shadow.

"Who knows?" I grabbed a small rock close to me—black, with three edges—and tossed it at the door. "There was something weird about her."

"You know she said her mother abandoned her? She lived for months alone in the trees when she was fifteen, before the world was destroyed."

I held the rock that was in my palm, didn't throw it. "What? That's crazy."

"I know, that's what I said." Dalia smiled and rolled her eyes as she threw another rock. "That explains how strange she is, even though she wasn't taken."

I didn't say anything for a moment. Who knew someone could be so different from everyone else, just because she was abandoned. Just from a decision her mother made years ago. Maybe everything around us—every person we came in contact with and place we saw and decision we made—affected so much more than we thought.

"I'm going to call it a night." Dalia cast another glance at the boys and then looked at me. The moon lit up one side of her face, but left the other in shadow. "You coming?"

I nodded. I hadn't realized how exhausted I was. Apparently almost dying and then pounding on a door all day took a lot out of you.

Gavin looked back at me as I stood. "I'm right behind you guys."

"You're just giving up?" Arsen whirled around. "Apparently, I'm the only one who actually *cares*."

"We'll start again first thing in the morning." Gavin stood. "No one can do this all night, Arsen."

"I can!" Arsen turned back, hit his fists on the gray. "I'm not giving up on you, Brooke! I promise."

I could still hear the pounding when we walked over to the fire, sat next to the orange flames. Dalia sat by Branch and I joined her.

The wind was only a quiet breeze over here and the fire made pictures on the canyon wall behind it—shadow flames, reaching up and then back, dancing across the brown. The night was quiet, no trees rustling or water lapping against the edges of sand. And it almost seemed right that no one was speaking. The Dome was silent—silent walls, silent floors. And it was only a few feet away.

I could see the moon high up in the sky, the walls like a frame bordering the night. I lay down on my back and put my hands behind my head, let my eyelids close.

But I couldn't sleep. Thoughts ran through my head, and I didn't understand them. I had never felt feelings tear up my chest before, pull me one way and another until I couldn't stop, couldn't breathe. I sat up.

"Branch."

He opened his eyes, surprised. Pushed himself to a seated position, slowly. He was still sitting on the other side of Dalia, just a few feet from me.

The others were spread out, a dozen feet from us. Still, I didn't want to wake Dalia up.

"I'm sorry. Did I wake you?" I was whispering, half wondering why I even said his name in the first place. What was I thinking?

Branch shook his head slowly, nodded to a spot a dozen feet from us by the canyon wall, away from the others. Before I knew what I was doing, I nodded. I stood quietly and stepped over to the wall.

"Everything okay?" Branch's eyes were still partly lit up by the flame, and they looked even more golden. Even more like the flower he had given me. I shook my head.

"What is it?"

My mouth was dry.

"Don't tell me—you were dreaming about me again?" The corner of his lips curved up in a smile.

I almost laughed, and the nervousness drained out of me. "Seriously?"

He shrugged. "I'm not holding it against you. You can't help what you dream."

"I almost drowned, and you're making a joke out of it."

His smile stayed, but his eyes grew soft. "Never."

The light from the fire flickered off the walls behind us, making the world seem slightly off. The shadows were wider, the curves of Branch's face and his hands softer. It almost didn't feel real. Like a dream that I would wake up from the next day. And suddenly, I didn't stop the words that came to my lips.

"You were right."

Branch was still for a moment, and a breeze pushed through his hair, then settled again. "Right about what?"

"About...everything." My heart was pounding, but I clenched my fists. "I don't know what's happening to me. I always thought it was Nash. It was supposed to be Nash. But then you showed up, and—"

I stopped. His eyes were focused on mine.

"And you were right."

Branch blinked. He lifted his hand, touched my cheek. In one moment he closed the space between us, his face inches from my own. I could see the creases of his eyes, the smudge of dirt on his chin. And that feeling—that one, untamable feeling—pressed against my chest, and it made me breathless.

Branch opened his mouth, but hesitated. He looked at the fire, then back at me. "There's something you should know."

I tried to swallow, tried to focus with his arm laced around my back. With his lips so close to mine.

Branch was quiet again. He looked at me for a long moment. "It's about me."

My heart started to thud a little faster, and I took a step back. Branch's eyes didn't move—they were watching me. I waited.

"Laney." He shook his head, like he hated himself for ruining this moment. "I want this. I want it more than anything. But I can't kiss you without you knowing the truth. I'm not who you think I am."

I waited for more. Waited for an explanation. "What do you mean?"

He took his hand off my cheek. Laced his fingers in my own. It still felt like a dream—hazy, blurred edges. But something cold was trickling through the warmth in my chest.

Branch swallowed. "I'm—"

A long, loud scraping sound filled the air. It was like the canyon walls had pushed against each other, scraping rock against rock, and would crush us at any moment.

"Hey, guys!" Arsen's voice.

I turned toward him, to the sound. The scraping made the canyon floor move slightly beneath me. I could feel it. I released my fingers from Branch's, felt the cold fill them back up. I didn't want to—but I tore my eyes away. He was right behind me as we ran to Arsen, ran to the door.

The rest of the people were standing quickly, eyes open wide, woken from their sleep. They followed in lines—one big blob of black moving to the source of the sound.

Before I reached Arsen, I stopped. His eyes were bright, and he was grinning. I turned to the wall behind him, could just see it in the darkness.

It was the door.

Slowly, painfully, the door was moving away from the canyon wall, little by little, disappearing inside.

"What did I tell you?" Arsen crossed his arms and smirked.

The bottom of the door scraped against the ground for a few more moments, but it was like it was scraping the air. The sound made me cringe. When it stopped, the complete silence almost screamed louder than the door had.

No one moved. There was no door anymore. In place of it was a deep, black, square-shaped hole. Darkness—even more darkness than the night.

We watched it, dozens of eyes on the square of black, but nothing happened. There was no movement inside. I thought Arsen would step over, would jump at the chance of going in to save Brooke, but even he stayed still, his eyes on the space where the door used to be.

I let out a breath. Theodore shifted next to me.

Footsteps. I could hear them, softer at first, but then stronger. They were coming from inside.

And then I saw someone—shoes, black from shadow. Gray pants, long legs. The person stepped to the door, stopped, and then put one foot out into the world, then the other. And in the light of the moon, the fire dancing on the canyon walls, I could just see his face.

"Welcome back. We've been expecting you."

Mr. Dabir smiled.

61

ELSEWHERE

History: Entry 32

It's over.

I'm standing outside the Dome's door.

The sky is black, the door in front of me gray, like the world. My world. The world inside.

Today is the day—the day that I belong again.

62

HERE

The air was hollow, empty, pounding.

The sight of the shadow in front of me, standing in the door, made it feel distorted—fake. Like a dream. Maybe I was dreaming. Maybe this entire night had been a dream.

But my heart was still beating too quickly in my chest.

"Mr. Dabir?" Alese's face was white.

The shadow smiled even wider.

"Well, don't just stand there in the cold. Come in, come in."

Silence.

Gavin shifted next to me. "We thought you were—"

"Dead?" Mr. Dabir took one more step out the door, so I could see his eyes. Dark, like his hair. "Of course not. I'm doing better than ever here in the Dome."

No one moved. Out of the corner of my eye, I saw Branch turn toward me.

"That's Mr. Dabir?" His voice was a whisper, and I barely heard it over the silent air. The softness of his voice and the sparkle in his eyes were gone.

I couldn't take my eyes away. Mr. Dabir was just standing there, a shadow in the door. He made the hole look even darker. And then a thought stabbed my mind—how did Branch not know who Mr. Dabir was?

"Please." Mr. Dabir motioned inside, to the darkness.

"We're not staying." Alese stepped forward. Her cheeks were still flushed. "You know that, right?"

"Of course." Mr. Dabir looked offended she would even ask. "You have your home now. I have mine."

"The others? Are they with you?" Arsen stepped from the shadow, just a few feet from the man.

Mr. Dabir looked at Arsen for a moment. Nodded. "They are."

"And if we go in with you, we can take them back?" Alese crossed her arms. "You don't care?"

Mr. Dabir's eyes were wide. He looked different tonight. Different from when we had last seen him, before we thought he was dead. And the difference gave me chills.

"They're yours. Take them."

Alese didn't move. She looked at Mr. Dabir for a long time.

"Gavin, take Branch with you and go inside. Find them. We'll wait here."

I noticed Branch clench his fists. Gavin nodded, started to walk forward, but Mr. Dabir looked at Alese.

"There's a storm coming, you know." He lifted his eyes from Alese to the sky. "The canyon will flood again. It does every time."

Alese followed his gaze. Dark clouds were moving in slowly, covering the gray-blue and making it black. The air was getting colder, the night darker. And it looked like he was right.

I swallowed, could feel the tension between them. Alese, the girl who taught the people how to love, and Mr. Dabir, the man who stripped love away from everyone and everything.

Alese finally nodded. "We stick together. No one leaves the group."

Mr. Dabir smiled again. "One moment, please." He stepped from the doorway for a moment, leaving the gaping hole alone. He returned a minute later, holding two long, thick sticks with cone-shaped pieces of wood on the tops, wrapped with rope. The tops were on fire, licking at the edge of the Dome's doorway. Torches.

"One for the front, and one for the back." He handed one of the torches to Alese. "I'll lead the way, of course."

Alese took it. "So lead. We're ready. And if you try anything..."

"You know me too well." Mr. Dabir's eyes were lit up from the flame. It danced back and forth, making his face too light and his body too dark. "But I'm quite happy here on my own. I'll let them leave, if they so choose. You have my word."

Before he turned, he looked out at the group. At all of us. His eyes swept across, slowly, and stopped on me. He smiled. Then he turned and walked into the darkness.

"Branch, can you be the last? Make sure no one gets left behind or lost?" She held out the torch Mr. Dabir had given her.

Branch hesitated, nodded. "Of course."

Alese looked relieved. "Thank you. I trust you." She took a deep breath. "We'll be out of here soon. Twenty minutes, tops."

She looked worried for a moment, like she wasn't sure why we were doing this. She shook her head, turned, and followed Mr. Dabir through the door. The group followed, one by one. Lambs to the slaughter. I shook my head. No. We would be out of here soon.

"Laney." Branch was staring at the door, the gaping hole. Something about his face had changed. The spark from our conversation was gone. "Your knife." Branch turned from the door, faced me.

"What?"

"Do you have it?"

I felt something move inside my chest. "Yes." I swallowed. "Why?"

"Where?" Branch's hands, clutched to the torch, were white.

I looked at him. "My pack."

Branch held the torch out to me, and I took it. Then he reached behind me, unzipped my pack, pulled the knife out just as the last few people were stepping through the door. He took the torch from me again. Held the knife in one hand, the fire in the other.

"I thought you hated knives." I said the words slowly, carefully. Something wasn't right.

"I do." The flame was shaking, but his hands were steady.

Branch slid the knife into a pocket on the side of his pack and followed the last person past the gray door.

I watched him. The air was eerily quiet out here—the wind had stopped blowing, and I couldn't hear a sound. I wrapped my arms around me, and, staring at the door, I felt like crying. After everything, it had all come back to this.

I took a deep breath, remembered my mother, the trees, Lander. Then I stepped through the Dome's door, from one world to another.

I had to blink to see anything—it was so dark in here, darker than I had ever seen it. Where were the lights fading in and out on the sides of the walls? I could just see Branch's flame, bouncing on the walls of the stairs, going down, down. I followed it, hurried to catch up. This was the last place I wanted to be alone, and especially now, in the complete black.

When I saw the back of Branch's golden hair, white from the flame, I breathed with relief. No one was talking, but the air was filled with footsteps, stepping down one gray stair after another. Only seconds had passed, but it felt like we had been walking for hours.

I looked at the walls as I passed and I saw one of the lights. Broken, the glass jagged, empty. It was as black as the air surrounding it. I wondered what had happened here in the few weeks we were gone.

The floor leveled out below my feet, and in the light of Branch's flame, I recognized the ground floor. Long, with footsteps echoing on the cold gray walls. We had walked this floor to get to studies, to meet at Collaboration. I couldn't shake the feeling that, aside from the complete darkness, nothing felt different. We walked in groups, in rows, side by side. No one was speaking—the air was quiet except for the occasional *drip* of water from the stone walls. And Mr. Dabir was leading us.

"Where is he taking us?" My whisper sounded too loud, and I looked at Branch. He shook his head. His face was stone.

I noticed my hands were shaking, and I tried to still them. Thirteen years of silence and gray and glassy eyes. Thirteen years.

I stepped through another doorway into a large room. There were torches placed along the walls, flickering in and out, eating the air. I watched the people stop as a group in front of me. The walls were tall here, sloping toward the ceiling on all sides. In the light from the fires, I could see chairs in the center of the room, one next to the other, in a circle. Dozens of them.

This was the center of the Dome. The place we held Collaboration.

Mr. Dabir turned, faced us all. His voice echoed on the walls. "Well, don't be shy. Have a seat."

I saw Alese cross her arms. One by one, the people sat in the chairs, hands clasped on laps and noses pointed forward to the cracked wooden platform that we always passed for a stage.

"Where are they?" Alese stood behind the chairs, her eyes on Mr. Dabir.

Mr. Dabir turned. "They're coming."

I stood next to Branch, watched the dozens of heads wait silently in their chairs. I heard a sound behind me, and I whirled around. The door creaked open, slowly at first like the Dome's door, but then it swung open, hit against the wall behind it.

Blakely stepped in first. She did nothing—didn't turn her neck, didn't sweep her eyes from row to row, looking for Branch. She just stared straight forward, walked to the front row, but turned once before she sat down. She was grinning. Another followed, and another. Brooke was last. She walked into the room after the rest of them, her long hair pulled back in a loose bun at her neck. She was smiling too, had a look of pride on her lips. Pride that we had come to save them. There were seven. Seven heads sat, one by one, in the front row, their hair facing all of us.

Relief touched my chest. Well, at least they wanted us here. Their expressions showed it—they were happy we had come. This would be easy. Tell them we had come for them, leave together. Never come back.

Arsen jumped up from his chair. "Brooke! I'm here to save you!" His eyes were wide, a nervous smile on his lips. He stepped toward her, pushed past chairs to get to the front, stepped on the stage. He threw his arms around her in a hug. "Why did you leave?"

Brooke stood there. She didn't hug him back, but she didn't push him away. When he pulled away, the smile never left her face. But from here, in the back of the room, it looked off, like the fire had melted it to her cheeks.

"Take them." Mr. Dabir nodded to Alese. "They're yours."

Alese didn't move. "Why are they here? What did you do to them?"

"Me?" Mr. Dabir chuckled. "They came here on their own. I gave them shelter. That's what I did for them."

Alese stood there for a moment. The silence pounded the air, and I could tell she was deciding whether to believe him. Then she nodded. "Okay. We're leaving."

"Nash." My voice stabbed the air, water on stone. "Is he here?" I tried to push back that feeling—the feeling that I had betrayed him.

Mr. Dabir's eyes snapped from Alese to me.

"Yes. The boy. Is he not with the rest?" He looked at the front row, seemed to do a quick count. "Oh. He must have gotten lost on the way to this room."

I could hear my breath, hot on the cold air. My pulse quickened. He was here. We could bring him back.

Mr. Dabir stepped away from where he had been standing next to the wooden platform and moved to a door on the far side of the room.

"Come, Laney. We'll find him together."

I watched his back walk away from me, and I hesitated. This was Mr. Dabir. I still didn't trust him. But I knew one thing for certain: we couldn't leave Nash down here.

"I'll come with you." Branch looked at me, gripped his torch. "Just in case."

I nodded, grateful.

The people in the chairs watched us as we walked— turning their heads slowly at each step we took, their eyes wide with fear. Mr. Dabir's torch was bobbing across the cold gray floor. Up, down, up, down. A burning light in a world of black. We followed it.

63

ELSEWHERE

History: Entry 33

Black. Everywhere, black.

The lights move on the walls, up and down, like they're terrified. Like they're trying to escape.

Gray walls, black air, yellow lights.

But every time I close my eyes, I see red. I see her blood.

64

HERE

We said nothing as we walked.

I watched the walls as we passed—looked from doorway to doorway, indent to indent. Empty beds, a gray shirt in a lumpy ball on the floor. One of its arms was out, pointed, like it was waving at us as we walked by. I shut my eyes and looked away.

"Where is he?" I focused on Mr. Dabir's flame. I didn't want to look at the back of his head. I didn't want to look at him at all.

"No *hello*? No *how have you been doing, Mr. Dabir? I'm so glad you're alive.*"

I swallowed, kept myself from saying something I would regret.

Mr. Dabir looked back at me, but instead of anger from my silence, he smiled. "It's good to see you too, Laney. I'd hoped this moment would happen."

His gaze shifted and he seemed to notice Branch for the first time. "I don't think we've had the pleasure of meeting. Did they find you in the world above?"

Branch said nothing, stared straight ahead.

"He's one of us." I said, not wanting to talk anymore. "Just take us to Nash, okay?"

Mr. Dabir looked at me, then back at Branch again. "Whatever you say, Laney."

The air was cold down here, and I hugged my arms around myself. It was probably the same temperature as it had always been the thirteen years I lived here. But I had felt the sun on my face now, the warmth of the air. I had never known it was cold because I had forgotten what it was like to be warm.

"Well, that's not right." Mr. Dabir stopped by a room that we had passed, flicked the switch on the right side, and the door slid open, the only sound in the empty hallway. He stepped inside, righted a small gray dresser that had fallen on its side, and came out again. He smiled at us, brushed his hands on his shirt. "That's better."

I let Mr. Dabir fall in line in front of us, and I looked at Branch. He was staring straight ahead, hand gripping the bottom of the torch. He wasn't himself—being back here again was affecting him hard. I touched his hand, tried to reassure him.

What was he about to tell me?

He drew back in surprise, like I had pulled his mind from somewhere. Then his face went forward again, his eyes hidden in darkness.

Laughter came from ahead of us, down the hallway, and at first I thought I was hearing something. I looked forward, past Mr. Dabir. Three faces appeared in the darkness, plump cheeks and white foreheads. Their gray shirts were torn, slathered in mud. They weren't wearing any shoes. More laughter, and in the silence of the hallway, the sound gave me chills. One of the three opened a door in front of them, and the last turned her head, looked at me. Wild red hair. Eyes, wide and terrified.

I stopped, felt dizzy for a moment. It was the girl who had tried to kill Branch.

"Oh, yes. They came here as well." Mr. Dabir chuckled, like seeing three strangers in a dark hallway was the most normal thing in the world. "You can have them back too, if you'd like." He turned to us and winked.

"Branch, it's them."

Branch turned to me, and from the look in his eyes, I could tell he knew.

"Go." He motioned toward them. "See if you can stop them. Alese would want to bring them back with us."

I looked at him, surprised. But he was right. I nodded, spoke loudly so Mr. Dabir could hear. "I'm going to get them. Wait here."

Mr. Dabir stopped. I turned once more, saw Branch watching me as I jogged toward the sound.

The door they had gone into was dark gray, heavy. I pulled it back with both hands and found myself in a hallway, blacker than the one I had just come from. I should have taken the torch. I stopped, listened. There was no more laughter, no more faces watching me. The hallway rounded a corner in front of me, disappeared in more darkness. This was hopeless without the torch—I would never find them.

I let out a breath, opened the door behind me that I was still holding with one hand. I walked back through, saw the light of the torch at the end of the hallway.

"Branch, I need your—" I stopped. Something was wrong. The torch was propped up on the floor. The flame looked like it was melting against the wall.

I walked closer, saw a body in the darkness next to the flame. Tall, thin, like a tree. Mr. Dabir. But where was Branch?

Mr. Dabir's body looked like a board—straight, unmoving. Tense. And it was only then that I saw the knife against his neck. Branch's arm across his chest, clutching it.

Branch. Holding a knife to Mr. Dabir's throat.

No—I couldn't be seeing right.

I walked forward, breathless. "What's going on?"

I could see Branch's golden hair behind Mr. Dabir's head, and he shifted so his face was next to Mr. Dabir's.

"Laney, walk away."

I felt my whole world fall away in a single second. Bricks crumbling to the ground. Branch, who hated knives. Branch, who hated violence. Branch, who I almost kissed.

Branch, who had a knife on Mr. Dabir's neck.

"Branch, what are you doing?" I tried to stay calm. Tried to tell myself this wasn't what I thought it was.

"Get out of here, Laney!" Branch's voice pounded the air, and it was hard. In the light of the fire, I could see his face—red, angry.

I tried to swallow, tried to breathe. But I just stood there, a face in the hallway. A person who watched the world as it destroyed itself, piece by piece.

"Was it you?" I tried to speak, tried to get past the fist in my throat. "You were the one who took people? The traitor? That's what you were going to tell me?"

Branch shifted, and his eyes softened. "What? No. Laney—" Branch took a deep breath, clutched the knife more tightly. "Please. Just go. I don't want you to see this."

"Then why?" My voice came out louder now. "Branch…" I took a deep breath. "He knows where Nash is."

Mr. Dabir was standing completely still, his eyes a little wider. His face pale gray, like the Dome's walls.

Branch didn't say anything for a moment. His eyes were on me, his hand on the knife, and the reflection of flames on the blade looked like water. Orange water, rising and falling in a black ocean.

"Where's Nash?" Branch's voice was soft, calm.

"What?" Mr. Dabir sounded nervous.

"Where's Nash?" Branch pushed Mr. Dabir to the ground. "Tell us where Nash is, and then I'll kill you."

"What are you doing?" I stepped back against the wall without realizing it. Pushed my palms against it. Hard eyes, hard breaths. A voice like stone. This wasn't Branch. It wasn't him.

"Tell me!" Branch gripped the knife with his hand again, held it down at the tip of Mr. Dabir's chest, where his heart was. And I knew those eyes—hardened, unforgiving, hungry. Eyes that would kill.

"Branch!" I screamed the word in confusion and fear. Pure, cold fear. I was terrified. I was terrified of Branch.

Branch blinked. Seemed to take in his surroundings for the first time. He looked at Mr. Dabir, saw the man's face cringing for the hit, bracing for the feel of the knife plunging through his skin.

And the world seemed to stop.

Branch took the knife from Mr. Dabir's chest, pulled it away slowly. He held it for a moment by his side, his eyes on Mr. Dabir. Then he let go. The knife clattered to the ground, bounced on the blade before it stilled, and the hallway was silent again. I could hear my breath, could feel my heart pounding.

Then Branch looked up, at me. "I'm sorry."

He looked at Mr. Dabir again, at the man huddled on the ground. Branch held out his hand, the one that had held the knife, and looked at it. It was trembling. His eyes widened and he shook his head, back and forth.

"I'm sorry."

I stepped forward, my heart pounding. I looked at him, heart still beating in my chest, my head. "What's happening?"

Branch shook his head again, stepped away, backward, from Mr. Dabir. "I can't— I need to leave—"

Branch stopped. He looked at Mr. Dabir once more, horrified of himself and the man in front of him. Branch's face was white.

"You—you killed my brother."

Mr. Dabir froze, his hands still on the ground. I didn't move. Couldn't have heard right. Branch had a brother?

"Nonsense." Mr. Dabir finally spoke, his words sputtering from his lips, trying to make sense of it all. "That's impossible. Unless, of course, you mean…"

Branch didn't move. He stared at Mr. Dabir for a long moment. Mr. Dabir's eyes widened, his cheeks white with surprise.

"You're Lander's brother."

Branch didn't respond. He turned, walked away from the man on the ground. He passed the knife, still lying on the floor, cold, and walked into the darkness. He didn't look back.

65

ELSEWHERE

History: Entry 34

This isn't what I planned.

The black, the gray, is home. But the people are everything but.

They look at me differently now. See something in me they didn't see before.

There is still silence. But I can see it, plainly.

They're terrified of me.

66

HERE

I watched him walk away. Watched the darkness surround him like water.

I wanted to call out to him, wanted to tell him to turn around, to come back.

But I couldn't. I couldn't move my legs, couldn't form words on my tongue. Everything I knew about Branch was wrong, so wrong. But so right, all at the same time.

I should have seen it—the golden hair, like the petals of wildflowers. Golden eyes, soft, but bright, like the sun. And Lander's eyes—brilliant blue, like the ocean, with spots of yellow and green and gold. Same easy smile, same natural ability to love.

Branch was Lander's brother.

Lander had mentioned his brother once. I wondered where Branch had been all this time—his parents and brother went to see if the world was safe, Lander had said, before he went looking for them and ended up a prisoner in the Dome. Branch must have come back and saw that Lander was gone.

The eighty-eighth person.

I blinked.

Branch was the extra person. The person who made eighty-seven eighty-eight again after the first boy had died in the tree. He was the outsider who had come in. And that meant one thing: the traitor was from the Dome. He had always been with us.

Mr. Dabir was standing now, brushing dirt off his pants and smoothing his shirt. He cleared his throat. "Shall we?"

I wanted to go to Branch, should have gone to Branch. But Nash was still out there. And I didn't know how many chances Mr. Dabir would give us to get him back.

I narrowed my eyes. I didn't want to go anywhere else with this man. I was disgusted—at the way he acted like nothing had just happened, at the unbearable pain he had caused Branch.

"Nash is waiting." Mr. Dabir looked at me, let his words hover in the air.

"Go." I was in no mood to talk to him. I just wanted to get Nash and leave. Find Branch.

The dark-haired man nodded, picked up the torch, and continued down the hallway.

We walked in silence. I had never been this far before, had never seen this part of the Dome. The rooms were spread out now, few and far between.

Finally, Mr. Dabir stopped. We were at the end of the hallway, the cold walls coming to a close around a wide gray door. But the top of this door was clear, with glass fitted into the stone so I could see the inside. Chairs—black with gray legs. Dozens of them, placed around a long table. And a person, pacing next to it.

Mr. Dabir put his hand on the thick metal knob, turned it.

"Finally." The person inside the room spoke. "Are you ready to talk now? You keep disappear—"

Mr. Dabir opened the door wider, and the voice stopped. "Your friends are here."

Mr. Dabir stepped to the side, and I saw him. Brown hair, brown eyes, tanned skin.

"Nash." I started to move toward him, expected him to do the same. But he didn't. He stood there, and his face turned pale.

"Laney, you can't be here. You need to leave, now."

I stopped, confused. Hurt, and I didn't even know why.

"We came for you. To take you back. Are you okay?" I looked from Mr. Dabir to Nash. Both of them were silent. "What did he do to you?"

Mr. Dabir laughed, and I felt goose bumps on my arms.

"Don't be ridiculous, Laney. Nash came here on his own."

I looked at Nash, waited for him to say something, to protest. But he didn't.

"What is he talking about?"

Something about Nash's face had changed. His cheeks were tighter, his eyebrows creased in worry. I had never seen him so scared.

"Get out of here. Take everyone and leave." Nash's voice was desperate, and his eyes didn't move from mine. "Please."

"Uh uh uh." Mr. Dabir wagged his finger at Nash. "Your time is up. We had a deal."

I felt the ground rising up, felt my feet sinking into it.

"Let me tell you a story, Laney." Mr. Dabir closed the door behind him, pressed it with both hands. Then he walked forward, put his hand on my shoulder. Pushed me down into a chair.

"You said you wouldn't hurt her." Nash stepped forward, angry, but Mr. Dabir held up his hand. Waited for silence, and then looked at me.

"Once upon a time, there was a boy. He came back to the Dome from the big, wide world to get food, and he just so happened to stumble upon a handsome, powerful teacher." Mr. Dabir smiled, pointed to himself. "Now, naturally, the teacher wanted everything back that had been taken from him. So there, in the Dome, the teacher and the boy made a deal: If the people learned to live, love, and survive in the world in three weeks' time, that teacher would leave them alone forever. Not bother them, not try to kill them. But if the teacher could turn the people from love, could make them want to return to the Dome again, he would get to keep them all."

Mr. Dabir stopped. Let the words sink in. Then he looked at me, clapped his hands, delighted. "Quiz time! Who do you think won?"

I felt something thick rise in my throat. "Nash—"

"I thought we would win, Laney! I thought there wasn't even a contest. He was going to come after us, try to take everyone back by force. But if we won, he would be gone, forever. We would never have to worry about him again. We could live in peace."

"Please." Mr. Dabir laughed. "It was so easy. Take people, one by one, and get them to pretend to be crazy. The bear skin and pushing Alese so she hurt her leg were just the cherry on the cake."

Pretend. The word hit me like a wall of water.

"They were...pretending?"

"It was brilliant, really." Mr. Dabir was beaming. "I chose the people, took them myself. I told them if they went back to you the next morning, acted a little *off*, they could be the new teachers and leaders of the Dome. And they did a fabulous job, if I do say so myself. All it took was a little fear, and all of you went crazy. Complete chaos."

I looked at Nash, the words draining from my throat. "You let him do this?"

Nash shook his head, started to speak.

"The deal was this." Mr. Dabir's voice was sharp. "Nash let me do anything I wanted for three weeks, apart from killing anyone. Cause as much chaos as I wanted. All he had to do was sit back and watch. *And* try to save you all in the process, teach the people to want love more than this." He spread his arms wide. "Nash said again and again how nothing could break the people. How they would always choose love. How you would *win*. Well—" Mr. Dabir shrugged. "I knew better than that."

I didn't understand, couldn't understand. It was all a game. Everything, all of it, was a game. A bet, that Mr. Dabir and Nash had made.

"I wanted him gone, Laney." Nash watched me, pleaded for me to understand. "He would have done something much worse, would have started killing people—"

"So you made a deal with him?"

"I had to!" Nash took a deep breath, then let it out slowly. "I did it for you."

For me. I took a deep, shaky breath. After all of this, he was putting it on me. The sharp feeling of being used, of being left out of the truth, bit at my insides like teeth. I had *trusted* him.

"You should have told me! I could have helped you! We could have taken care of this together—"

"I didn't want you to get hurt!" Nash was shaking his head, looking at me like I was the only person in the room. "I had to protect you. I will *always* protect you, Laney."

His words hung in the air, but I let them fall to the floor. "You were right." My voice broke, and I swallowed. "You told me I shouldn't trust anyone in this world. You were right."

Nash opened his mouth, closed it. But in the silence of the room, I could see it: the pain in his eyes. Words may not be knives, but they can cut deep.

"Spare us the drama, Laney," Mr. Dabir spoke suddenly. "Nash made me promise I wouldn't hurt you if I won. And that promise, I will keep. Which is impressive, to say the least, considering everything you took from me."

I didn't say anything.

"Speaking of which." Mr. Dabir reached into his pocket. Took out a knife—stubby handle, pointed blade. Branch's knife. My knife. My blood turned cold. He had picked it up from the floor. I hadn't even noticed. "You gave Laney the notebook, correct?"

What? I turned to Mr. Dabir. He blinked when Nash looked up, surprised.

Mr. Dabir smiled. "Good. And her notebook was destroyed when Emily pushed her in?"

My mouth parted, and I could feel my face turn white.

Mr. Dabir nodded. "I'll take that as a yes. Oh, cunning Emily. I had another plan to get rid of that, but she took care of it for me."

Emily. I blinked. My head was spinning. Then Mr. Dabir pulled something from behind his back, under his shirt. I stopped.

My paper book.

Shiny red covers, filled with pages of white. But how——?

"What is this?" Nash spoke suddenly, his voice sharp. "I gave Laney the notebook so she could write in it. You didn't say it was a part of your plan."

"Okay, okay. I'll entertain you with one more story before you go." The smile on Mr. Dabir's face was so large it looked like his cheeks were touching his ears. "Once upon a time, there was a boy named Adrian. We sent him and seven others to the world above to find love six months before we sent you. The first group to see the world. Our first test."

There was another group? My head was pounding.

Mr. Dabir looked nostalgic, thinking back on the moment. Then his eyes snapped to mine again.

"But Adrian killed them all in just three weeks. The funny thing is, he kept a notebook throughout his time up there, as disturbed as it sounds. *History*, he called it. Entries that outlined every person he took, every kill he made. Apparently he played a little game with them all——chose them, one by one. We found this in his coat when he died in his cell." Mr. Dabir stopped pacing, turned to me excitedly. "Don't you see? Three weeks. Eight people. Taken, one by one. It's your story, Laney. I reenacted it."

I couldn't move——couldn't breathe. I just watched him, a man so disturbed he didn't even know anything was wrong with him. Adrian had killed the first group that went in search of love. And Mr. Dabir had taken his notebook, used it as a script for his game. A notebook identical to mine.

Nash took a step toward Mr. Dabir, his face red, outraged. "You lied to me. This was not part of our deal! If you do anything, I'll——"

"You'll *what*, Nash?" Mr. Dabir lifted the knife slowly. "Tell me."

Nash stopped. His eyes were on the knife, and he fell silent.

I was so disgusted, so overwhelmed with emotion, until one word pushed through my lips. "Why?"

The door opened suddenly, and I jumped, turned to it. Blakely stepped through.

"Is it time?" She looked at me, at Nash. At Mr. Dabir, who was holding a knife pointed at me.

Mr. Dabir smiled, and his eyes fell on me again. "This is why."

The dark-haired, dark-eyed man held out the notebook and placed it in Blakely's outstretched hand. He nodded.

A smile spread across Blakely's face. "Finally."

"Blakely." Mr. Dabir stopped her. "After you give the notebook to Brooke, go to the top of the stairs, by the door to the outside world. Pretend to be one of theirs—a woman Alese accidentally left in the canyon. Drowning in the storm."

Blakely nodded, then looked at me. "Oh, Laney. About the whole *Branch is mine* thing. I never really liked the guy. It was all part of the act for Mr. Dabir." She looked at me, smiled a smug smile. "Sorry about ruining your *almost* kiss!" She winked, and a laugh burst from her lips as she shut the door behind her. I felt the laugh echo in the room seconds after she was gone.

I looked at Nash, felt my cheeks flush pink. Confusion filled his eyes.

"You—you like Branch?" The sudden silence. His wide eyes searching mine.

"Nash, I— It's not—"

Nash held out his hand and I stopped. He took a few breaths, his eyes never leaving mine. His voice was soft. "I know you well enough to know when you're lying, Laney."

The air was silent. Heat spread across my cheeks, my back. And Nash stopped for a moment, gave me a chance to defend myself. But I didn't. I couldn't.

And then, in the long seconds that followed, something else filled his face. It was slow at first, like the prick of a needle. But then it rushed in, fast and without warning. It was an emotion I had never seen in him before, like someone looks after a knife has left a deep and dangerous wound in the flesh.

Betrayal.

I tried to swallow, tried to say something. But his distrust in me and now the secret I had kept from him collided against each other over and over again, until I felt raw.

He dropped his eyes, and I blinked. A feeling stabbed me—something deep and sharp and aching—and I tried to push it away.

But it felt like the world was crushing me from the inside out.

Mr. Dabir raised his eyebrows and looked between us, tried to hold back his delight. "Isn't love wonderful?"

Nash said nothing, looked away.

"Nash." Mr. Dabir turned to the boy with brown eyes. He stroked his chin slowly, thoughtfully. "Laney may have betrayed you, but I know you would never want her dead. Make sure Alese, Gavin, Dalia, and Theodore go up to help the drowning woman. All of them. Oh, and that new boy. Branch was his name? The boy who tried to kill me." He paused for a moment. "And when they're outside, looking frantically for a fake person, close the door. Otherwise, Laney is as gone as Lander was."

Nash didn't move for a moment. He looked up at me again, the pain still as visible as the gray walls. But then, his eyes locked on mine, and he took a breath. I watched with disbelief as the emotion—the hurt, the pain, the betrayal—slowly drained from his face, until it was gone completely.

I shook my head quickly, tried to take a breath. "Nash, no."

It was what we had done thirteen years ago, all of us, after the world was destroyed. Pushed our emotions so deep inside that we didn't have to feel anymore.

He blinked once, but his face was stone. He looked at Mr. Dabir slowly, and he nodded.

"Nash, you can't." The panic was rising in me now, as cold and as real as the knife on my neck. They would be locked out. The people would be left down here, abandoned to Mr. Dabir. He couldn't do this. He *wouldn't* do this. I looked at him, shook my head frantically.

Nash looked back at me. His eyes weren't full of regret anymore. It was like he had been stabbed with the knife, over and over again, and he had finally grabbed the blade. Stopped it.

"I'm sorry."

"Nash, no. Don't do this!"

Nash walked to the door, put his hand on the knob. Looked at me with eyes I didn't recognize, an emptiness that was deep and gray and strong.

"I loved you, Laney."

Loved. He said loved. I had never heard those words before, spoken just to me. I always thought they would be striking, powerful, breathtaking. Here, now. Not in the past. Not *loved*, as in before. As in *not anymore*. They made a hole in my heart.

"Nash. One more moment." Mr. Dabir's voice rose in the air, and Nash turned back to him, pulled open the door. Mr. Dabir tapped his fingers on the table, one by one.

"I hold honesty in the highest regard. Since you kept your word about our deal, there is a place for you too on leadership, if you should want it.

Nash paused for a moment. "I'm listening."

Mr. Dabir moved closer, pressed the knife against my neck. "First, she stays. The people need a reason to remember why they're down here." His eyes locked on mine, and he smiled. "And not up there."

Nash's eyes were on the knife, and he nodded.

"I'm glad we're in agreement." I could feel Mr. Dabir's breath against my skin when he spoke. "So, what's your answer, Nash? Do you want to head this Dome with us? To lead these people?"

"He would never join you." I struggled against Mr. Dabir's arms, tried to breathe against the edge of the knife.

The air was silent as Nash pulled open the door. "I'll do it."

The world shattered into a thousand pieces for the second time that night—pieces I didn't recognize. Pieces that terrified me. Pieces that were too broken to put back together.

Nash turned to me one more time, the boy I had first kissed, the boy who had helped me through the wildflowers, the boy who made me smile and laugh and feel like I was wanted. The boy I had known more than anyone up there in the world. And the boy I now knew nothing about.

And that boy—the stranger—shut the door behind him.

67

ELSEWHERE

History: Entry 35

My head is pounding, pounding.

Walls closing in, darkness suffocating me, over and over again. Reaching around my throat, my neck. I never thought silence could be so loud.

I've been locked in this indent for months, and it's been dark, so dark I forgot about this notebook. It's been in the folds of my coat, pressed to my skin.

There is a boy in here with me, in the indent next to mine. His name is Lander. I don't talk to him, but he talks to me. He tells me that everything is going to be okay. That love will win. He tells me to hold on, just a little bit longer.

Always just a little bit longer.

Something came with my food today. It was placed against the bread, under the napkin, by the man with dark hair—the man from my dreams. A knife, gray like the walls, but not dull.

Shining.

I killed seven people in the world above. And now, I will kill one more.

I hope they find this when I die.

68

HERE

I used to think silence was normal.

I used to think gray walls and tight buns and white skin were life as it was, and as it should be. I used to think time was kept by a bell and rules were decided only by a unanimous vote. I used to think people were only bad because they had tried and failed at being good.

I was walking down the hallway, my legs moving only because a hand rested on my back, pushed me forward. A thick strip of fabric was tied around my mouth, torn from the shirt I had seen on the ground in the indent, its arm frozen in a wave.

I walked down this hallway, and then the next. One foot after the other, echoing on the cold walls.

An army of one.

I didn't know what Mr. Dabir was going to do to me—didn't know what more he could do to me. But I knew this: I had taken everything from him. And now, he wanted it back.

When he pushed open the heavy door to the Dome's center, I heard a voice, rising from the middle of the room. Words, floating on the cold air. Brooke's voice.

"'—clawing at my skin like the way the spiked branches of the trees clawed the sky when we first came aboveground, first stepped through the Dome's door. It burns like touch. It's becoming me. And it's perfect.'"

She was reading something. I looked up. The book. It was the red paper book. Adrian's book.

"'—They don't know. They think they're safe, that this world holds everything they're looking for. They think everything has changed. And they're right, in a way. One thing has changed: me.'"

Everything was silent. The air was gray, so gray, and the fire was pulsing slowly, heartbeats in the Dome. I tried to swallow, but the fabric was pushing down on my tongue, my lips. Adrian had gone to the world above with seven other teenagers—hopefuls, just like us. And then it changed him. And no one found out until it was too late.

Dalia turned slowly, from her place at the front of the room. "Laney. Tell me it isn't true."

What? I looked at her, and she looked back, her eyes on mine. She saw the fabric tied across my lips, and she didn't say anything. A cold sweat rose on my back.

"It's not true." Branch. Relief fell over me like water. He was standing in the corner, in the darkness, the light of the fire winking in and out, on and off his face. "Take that off of her. You're lying."

"You heard him. Take it off now." Alese stepped forward in agreement.

Mr. Dabir did nothing. He blinked once, twice. Let out a sigh. "I'm sure at least *one* of you saw Laney with this book. Can anyone confirm?"

Mr. Dabir was trying to blame this on me? Say I was the traitor? They would never believe it. I couldn't breathe.

The room was silent, motionless. But Theodore took a half step back, sucked in his breath. It was a small act, something no one would have noticed if it had been a normal day in a normal world. But Mr. Dabir noticed.

"Theodore." Pause. "You saw Laney writing in this?"

Theodore didn't say anything. His red hair was chaos on his head, his face pale. "I...It can't be hers. She—she wasn't—" He stopped.

Emily took Theodore's hand, looked at me. "What did she use to write with, Theodore?" Her voice was understanding, soft. But it was a dagger in my chest.

Theodore hesitated, his words a jumble. "A—a black rock."

Mr. Dabir took a step forward, unzipped the pack on my back. Dug around for a moment, and removed his hand. When he opened it, my black rock was in his palm.

"You mean this?"

A few people sucked in their breaths. My heart was beating faster, slower, faster again.

"Theodore." Alese's voice was as soft as the fire, the cold, wet walls. "Is that hers?"

Theodore didn't say anything, his face full of pain. He blinked back tears, green eyes a little grayer. The world he knew shattered.

He hadn't said anything, hadn't said yes. But in so many ways, he had.

"It's true." Brooke's voice, in the darkness. "She's the one who took us. All of us." The others standing next to her, peach heads in the sea of black, nodded.

I felt the blood draining from my head.

Alese grew silent. Her head turned to me. I couldn't see her eyes in the darkness.

I shook my head frantically, tried to speak. They couldn't believe it. They couldn't.

"Now, now, Laney." Mr. Dabir patted my shoulder. "No need to try and scare them all—*again*."

Branch took a step back, and this time the light of the fire was just enough to see—his hair, golden, messy across his head. And his eyes, wide and white and horrified.

"So you were the traitor, all along." Arsen's voice. He was standing on the platform, his arm on Brooke's shoulder, and he looked half-betrayed, half-impressed. "You got us good, Laney. But not quite good enough." He took Brooke's hand in his own.

I felt my heart fall to my feet. I tried to walk forward, tried to get to my friends, to make them believe me, but Mr. Dabir held me back. He looked at the people in the chairs and the people scattered in the walkways, tight skin and pale faces. He held up one of his arms to the ceiling, the other arm on me.

"Oh, don't worry. She won't bother you again." He spoke loudly, strong, like the Mr. Dabir he once was. The Mr. Dabir who had once led the people down a hole to gray and darkness. The Mr. Dabir who had dug their graves and made them lie in them.

He turned me to him, slowly, his shoulders on mine, and winked.

I tried to scream, tried to turn their faces to mine. Tried to get them to hear me, to look at me, to believe me.

But a scream from upstairs, in the world, drowned out my own.

The world was a blur, a dream. I watched Alese spin toward the sound, watched her slowly realize she may have left someone in the canyon. Watched Dalia run to Alese, their mouths moving quickly, silent words in a silent Dome. Watched Theodore take Alese's hand, watched Emily try to stop him. Watched him shake off her arm. Watched Branch run from his place in the corner, his head down as he passed, his eyes away from mine. Watched Dalia and Theodore and Alese and Branch run past me, disappear through the door to the stairs, their faces white and worried and their eyes forward, focused, away from mine. Heard Nash's voice calling for more help, calling for Gavin, saw Gavin take a deep breath and run to the door, run through it. Watched a man smile, spread his hands, and welcome everyone back, welcome them to a world without flowers and trees and sky and love.

I used to think silence was normal.

I used to think gray walls and tight buns and white skin were life as it was, and as it should be. I used to think time was kept by a bell and rules were decided only by a unanimous vote. I used to think people were only bad because they had tried and failed at being good.

I heard the footsteps grow softer, higher, heard the screaming stop. I heard the door to the world closing, quickly, scraping against the stone floor, shutting out sun and air and people.

And it was only then, in the world where love was sucked out through the cracks, pushed through the spaces between stones, that I noticed there were flowers scattered on the ground. White, yellow, and green, colorful shadows on the gray floor. Hands empty, open. All eyes forward, frozen, blurred.

Focused on me.

Gray eyes on a girl with a knife against her neck, gray bodies on a carpet of flowers.

And silence.

I remember what it was like.

69

ELSEWHERE

Adrian's Notebook
History: Entry 1

I was chosen today.

The teachers chose me to go on a secret journey to the world above, that I might have the chance to find love all over again. That I might be the first to discover what disappeared seventy-four years ago.

I have heard a lot about love—that people fought for it, felt because of it. I only hope one thing is true: that it will save us all.

They say the world might change us, say that it's large and unknown and dangerous. Untouched, for twelve and a half years. But I know I won't change. I could never be someone with black eyes.

We leave tomorrow, and I'm nervous. I met the seven others going with me—one is a girl, and she made me feel something I never have before. Her name is Hope.

I'm taking this notebook with me, documenting my experience in this journey to find love. It was a gift from my mother, and I'm hoping it will only bring good luck.

So, here's to the world above, and everything we'll find. And here's to hoping we'll be fearless.